RECIPE FOR HATE

RECIPE
FOR
HATE

WARREN KINSELLA

DUNDURN
TORONTO

Cover image: © 123RF.com/Igor Stevanovic
Printer: Webcom

Library and Archives Canada Cataloguing in Publication

Kinsella, Warren, 1960-, author
    Recipe for hate / Warren Kinsella.

Issued in print and electronic formats.

ISBN 978-1-4597-3906-2 (softcover).--ISBN 978-1-4597-3907-9 (PDF).--ISBN 978-1-4597-3908-6 (EPUB)

    I. Title.

PS8621.I59R43 2017   jC813'.6   C2017-902799-9
                                               C2017-902800-6

1   2   3   4   5   21   20   19   18   17

We acknowledge the support of the **Canada Council for the Arts**, which last year invested $153 million to bring the arts to Canadians throughout the country, and the **Ontario Arts Council** for our publishing program. We also acknowledge the financial support of the **Government of Ontario**, through the **Ontario Book Publishing Tax Credit** and the **Ontario Media Development Corporation**, and the **Government of Canada**.

Nous remercions le **Conseil des arts du Canada** de son soutien. L'an dernier, le Conseil a investi 153 millions de dollars pour mettre de l'art dans la vie des Canadiennes et des Canadiens de tout le pays.

Care has been taken to trace the ownership of copyright material used in this book. The author and the publisher welcome any information enabling them to rectify any references or credits in subsequent editions.

— *J. Kirk Howard, President*

The publisher is not responsible for websites or their content unless they are owned by the publisher.

Printed and bound in Canada.

VISIT US AT

   dundurn.com | @dundurnpress | dundurnpress | dundurnpress

Dundurn
3 Church Street, Suite 500
Toronto, Ontario, Canada
M5E 1M2

For Lisa

Can't you feel it can't you see it?
The promise of prosperity
It's overwhelming you and me
It afflicts us like a disease
Ubiquitous, compelling too

We cling to you like krazy glue
And inject such a potent seed
It's best for all humanity

The spread of culture
The sword of progress
The vector of suffrage
A warm and septic breeze

The pomp and elation
The duty and vocation
The blood of the hybrid
It's just a recipe

Reliving our ancestry
The frightful lack of harmony
Our forefathers who led the way
Their victims are still here today
Now it's time to erase the story

Of our bogus fate
Our history as it's portrayed
It's just a recipe for hate.

Used with kind permission of Greg Graffin and Bad Religion.
Copyright © Warner/Chappell Music, Inc.

PROLOGUE

So, this is the story of everything that happened, more or less.

It was fucking cold that November night, and pretty dark out back, too. Someone had naturally broken the single light bulb above the rear entrance to Gary's, and no one else was around to see the knife go in. It slid into him like a whisper, and he'd have been dead in moments, the first punk rock murder of 1978–79. If he made a sound, no one was around to hear it.

No one else saw the flash of the knife, either, or who it was that held it. Definitely not Jimmy, who the cops said had been facing the painted-metal locked door, vainly knocking it to attract the attention of one of us inside the club.

He'd probably been yelling, too, and his voice was pretty hoarse from his band's performance, and from trying to get someone to unlock the fucking door. Behind him, the band's borrowed van was already full of their equipment. Two guitar amps, a bass rig, a battered old drum kit, and Eddie's construction work tools. He'd needed the key to move the van to the vacant lot at the side of Gary's, near Free Street, where there were some lights and less chance of someone stealing their equipment. But the key was inside the bar, where the city's punk scene was centered, and where it gathered every weekend night.

Jimmy was wearing the Hot Nasties' uniform: a black biker's jacket pinned with neon-colored badges promoting various British and New York punk bands; a pair of jeans coming through at the knees; his prized black brothel creepers; and a handmade T-shirt X gave him the year before. He would have been shivering because it was really cold now, around freezing.

When they found Jimmy, he was hanging from the redbrick wall behind Gary's. Blood from the wound in his neck had seeped out and covered his chest and legs, but you could still make out the words that X had written on Jimmy's T-shirt, in black, bold letters: "THEY LIED TO YOU."

CHAPTER 1

X entered Gary's from the front, off Brown Street, like always. Many of us preferred to come and go through the door to the alleyway, because we were nervous about the regulars. It was also a good way to avoid paying a cover, if there was one. But X preferred to use the front.

X, my best friend, was like that.

On the heavy, reinforced black doors, below the number 13, a prehistoric sign had been screwed into place at eye level: "NO COLORS, NO KNIVES." For a few years there, Gary's had been a biker bar — mainly Outlaws, but some other gangs, too. Before punk arrived on the Portland scene, the bikers had filled the basement tavern every night. They'd chug cheap, watered-down draft in the long, narrow part of the bar. And, where it opened up at the other end, near the stage, they'd hate-stare any country-and-western or cover band stupid enough to agree to play. If they were really pissed off, they'd throw beer glasses at the stage.

None of us ever argued about the bikers' claim to Gary's. It was their place, no question. But toward the end of the '70s, they were getting arrested a lot more than they used to. As Portland grew, and as it imported more yuppie douchebags from New York and Boston or wherever, tolerance for the Outlaws basically disappeared. A few blocks away, at City Hall, our idiot mayor had decreed that Gary's attracted the sort of customers who didn't fit into the "new Portland." So the police started cracking down and most of the bikers started to move on. The hookers and junkies, too.

Gary's owner was pretty unhappy at the thought of redecorating the place to attract a new crop of patrons, mainly because he was a cheap bastard. But he also knew that no self-preserving, upwardly mobile, Ivy League couple would ever come near Gary's: it was a temple of filth. It was the church of dirt. Which kind of made us love it even more.

Dirt and dust and grime were everywhere. There was the ancient carpet that stretched from the front doors to the cracked tile on the dance floor. No one could make out the pattern anymore because it was so fucking dirty. There were these mismatched metal chairs with torn strips of vinyl-covered padding on the seats. The tiny round tables were covered with stained, orange cloths. There were frames containing ghostly paintings of plants and cowboys on the walls, decades of dust and cigarette smoke stuck to the cracked glass. A few yellowish light bulbs hung from what was left of the fixtures overhead. And there was the air itself, always reeking of cigarette smoke and dust and sweat and piss.

It was awesome.

Earlier in 1978, Gary's owners had read in the local paper, the *Portland Press Herald*, that those of us in various local punk bands were putting on our own shows in veterans' halls and community centers around the city. We were attracting hundreds of kids by word of mouth alone, the article said. The arch-conservative paper hated us, of course, but Gary's owners decided to let us book bands a couple nights a week. Maybe they'd turn a profit on beer sales, they figured.

And they sure did. The bikers didn't like the change, at first. But, eventually, they were sort of amused by us — these skinny, acne-scarred kids with weird clothes and dyed hair. We punks were misfits, like the bikers were, but we were also completely different. In the early days of the Portland scene, the punks were mostly Maine College of Art students, gays and lesbians, cross-dressers, poets, nonconformists, anarchists, socialists, the socially awkward, the overweight, the alienated, the angry, the underage, and assorted other urban outcasts. The factions that made up the local subculture were diverse, but somehow we all got along back in those days.

So the bikers stayed up near the front doors, and we punks were stuck at the back, hanging out around the stage and the subterranean alleyway exit. We left each other alone, sticking to our side of Gary's demilitarized zone.

Gary's owner — who rarely, if ever, enforced drinking age limits — was happy because our friends liked to drink almost as much as the bikers. Soon enough, then, our bands were on stage every night of the week except Sundays, when every bar was still required by Maine law to be closed. The Portland punk scene got a hub. It started to grow.

Christopher X!

X, thou art Christopher.

He moved through the mass of hulking bikers, completely unfazed. Some of them looked up and glared. They had heard about X, and a lot of them didn't like him much. Unlike the other scrawny suburban kids, who seemed to cower whenever they were nearby, X was completely disinterested in them. To the other punks, the bikers were menacing, intimidating. But not to my buddy, X. And the bikers took notice.

Under one arm, X had a few copies of the *New Musical Express* — the super-hard-to-get British tabloid that had promoted the punk rock revolution first — along with a couple of notebooks. Under the other arm, he cradled some LPs, likely borrowed, by bands most people had never heard of. But it was *him* — his pale face, his blank expression, his total indifference to everything around him — that stood out. X was an outsider, even to the outsiders who made up the Portland scene. He was a misfit among the misfits.

X sat down with us, up near Gary's tiny stage, where the Hot Nasties had played earlier — and where the Punk Rock Virgins were still playing, but had just gone on a break.

X had called some of us that day, saying that he had some big news. He moved a couple glasses of draft out of the way and dumped the LPs, the notebooks, and the copies of the *New Musical Express* on the center of the table.

"Where's Jimmy?" he asked.

I pointed at Gary's rear door, toward the alleyway. "I think he's moving the van to the side, so nobody swipes everything again." I punched X in his leather-jacketed arm. I was a bit loaded. "Now buy me a beer, fag."

I could tell what he was thinking: *Fag? Really?*

X looked at me for a moment, an eyebrow up, then shook his head. He got up and went over to the bar to buy a couple of drafts for me and an RC Cola for himself. He returned to the table and pointed at the newer-looking copy of the *New Musical Express*. "Take a look," he said, expressionless. "The Nasties are in it."

Conversation stopped. We lunged at the magazines.

The Hot Nasties, as it turned out, had beaten everyone else in Portland at making a record, which was a pretty fucking big deal. They were one of the first punk bands in New England to do that. It had been Jimmy who'd pushed them into putting it together. The band recorded the four songs over three weekends at a garage converted into a mini-studio in Bayside. The two hippies who owned the place had never seen or heard anything like it before. They were totally disgusted.

The Nasties, however, were totally ecstatic with the results of the recording session. They came out of it with four original songs: "I Am a Confused Teenager," "The Secret of Immortality," "The October of Seven Oh," and "The Invasion of the Tribbles." Jimmy and Sam were big

Star Trek fans, and they stuck references to the old TV show in a lot of their songs — along with plenty of other references to junk culture, because we loved junk culture. Serial killers, *The Flintstones*, AMC Pacers.

The good stuff.

The Hot Nasties didn't have a recording contract; in 1978, no Portland punk bands did. So they put out the EP on their own made-up label, Martian Martian Records, taking the name from a Jonathan Richman song. The band members designed the sleeve. The cover had one of my photos of the Nasties, smiling outside Gary's one night, clutching some smashed-to-pieces guitars and drums from a particularly demented gig. We glued the sleeves together late one drunken night at Sam's parents' place in Parkside, and then X — pretending to be their manager — sent a couple copies off to the *New Musical Express*, which along with *Creem* magazine and *Melody Maker*, were all we generally read, pretty much.

Someone — incredibly, unbelievably — had noticed. Buried within the pages of the *NME*, there was a section called "New and Noteworthy." In there, in a single paragraph, titled "Portland Punk Pressing," a writer with the initials CSM had written: "If you can't locate Portland, Maine, on a map, fret not. We can't either. But if tuneful, snappy punk rock still matters in late '78, then the four lads in the Hot Nasties may well succeed in getting their portside hometown better known. The quartet is Sam Shiller, lead guitar; Luke Macdonald, rhythm guitar; Eddie Igglesden on skins; and bassist and lead screamer, Jimmy Cleary. Their debut EP, issued on their own label, crackles with Buzzcockian wit and snottiness, and is therefore worth a spin. Available through money order only, *The Invasion of the Tribbles* EP argues convincingly that punk — at least on the other side of the pond — ain't dead yet. A quid will get it winging its way to you. Check it out."

Holy shit. HOLY SHIT!

A thumbs-up from the *New Musical Express*: it was like getting a great review from God. We all stared at the review, speechless. Without warning, Luke jumped up on his chair and let out a Tarzan scream, beating his chest. He hollered: "I love you, X! I fucking love you! When we are famous rock stars, I will let you visit my mansion!"

We all laughed and read and reread the review. A few others started to wander over to see what was going on.

When X had told the Nasties that he'd sent their EP to the *NME*, none of them thought that it would ever get noticed. The magazine paid attention to the Clash and the Sex Pistols and other big British bands — not a band like the Hot Nasties, in Outer Buttfuck, New England, U.S.A. But X told me he thought the record was really good, like the Ramones. So he mailed it off with a cover letter that had somehow caught the attention of Charles fucking Shaar Murray at the fucking *New Musical Express*, for fuck sakes. Still hollering that he was going to be famous, Luke wrapped his arms around X, who was trying to resist smiling. X didn't ever smile.

None of us could believe it; it was like a dream. As they looked at the article over Luke's shoulder, the three members of the Virgins were similarly blown away. Gary's veteran waitress, Koby, not so much. "That's nice," she said. "Who wants another round?"

So we ordered a round to celebrate, and X asked again where Jimmy was. "He should have been back by now, actually," Sam said, pulling some keys out of his jacket. "Shit! I just remembered I forgot to give him these."

Sam and Luke got up and headed up the stairs to the rear door of Gary's. A burst of cold air swept in, so a regular named Marky pulled the door shut behind them.

Seconds later, *BANG! BANG! BANG!*

Someone started hitting the door so hard, it seemed like it was going to buckle.

BANG! BANG! BANG!

X looked at me and we both got up and jogged over and opened the door. On the other side, Sam had no color in his face; he was a ghost, tears streaming down his face. Behind him in the gloom, Luke was puking.

"X! No no no!" Sam hollered, frantic, his voice breaking. He stumbled inside, down Gary's back stairs. "It's Jimmy!"

CHAPTER 2

The headquarters for the Portland Police Department was really only a few blocks west of Gary's, on Middle Street, but the cops took what seemed like a fucking eternity to arrive. Trouble at or near Gary's — even murders there — were not ever high on the priority list for the city's police force.

So, by the time the cops arrived, every single biker except two had vanished. One guy was passed out on one of the filthy tables, snoring, and there was one other who worked at Gary's part-time, providing security. Most nights, this meant throwing drunks out onto Brown Street or whacking the violent ones in the alleyway with an old pool cue that had a metal rod running through it. His name was Mike. Nobody knew his last name, and nobody'd ever asked for it. Mike didn't ride with anyone in particular, and he was rumored to live in a cramped room two floors up in the same old brick building where Gary's was located. He was big, bearded, and brawny, but we all liked him because he didn't let any of the bikers push us around. You might say he was even a bit of a friend to the punks. He always wore jeans, a sleeveless jean jacket, and sometimes a T-shirt with FTW inscribed on it: FUCK THE WORLD.

Sounded right.

Mike squinted at the bar area. Most of the punks had taken off, too. He sighed. Business was about to take a big downturn; Gary's would be shut down for a while, maybe for good. He looked at the members of the Nasties and the Virgins, all still in the bar, along with me and a half-dozen other punks from other bands. Some of the girls were crying. Some were shaking, or had their arms around each other. We looked like what we were, I guess: a bunch of skinny suburban kids barely old enough to drink. He felt sorry for us, I think.

The bartender on duty and Koby were moving between the tables, clearing away overflowing ashtrays and abandoned glasses of draft. They also looked grim, knowing that tonight might be their last shift at Gary's for a while.

I looked at X as he stood, rigid as a mic stand, midway between the door to the alleyway and Mike the bouncer. He seemed to be in a daze. X was kind of a leader to the rest of us, but at that moment, his face was as white as the sheet I'm typing this on. I had never seen him like that before.

"How well did you know him?" Mike quietly asked X. "What was his name?"

X looked at Mike and started to speak, but no sound came out.

Mike pointed at a chair. "Sit down, kid," he said. "The cops'll be here soon enough. They'll have plenty of questions."

About five minutes later, we heard the first patrol car finally arrive, skidding to a halt outside the front door, sirens blaring. Two young-looking constables swaggered into the bar and down the stairs. Mike led them past us to the alleyway door. It wasn't long before one constable came racing back through the bar and out the front doors.

The other stayed outside with Mike, and I thought about the two of them staring up at Jimmy, nailed into the porous old redbrick wall of Gary's back alley wall, his black brothel creepers two feet off the ground.

"Holy God," we heard the cop saying. "Holy God, I've never seen anything like this before."

"Ditto," Mike growled, just as X and I appeared in the doorway.

"You can't come out here, guys," the cop said, trying to sound in control. He cleared his throat, nervous. "You shouldn't come out here, anyway. It's not a good thing to see."

X nodded, but stayed where he was. "He was our friend," he said, his voice flat.

"What's his name?" the cop asked.

"Jimmy," I said. "Jimmy Cleary.... Is anyone gonna call his parents?"

"We're waiting for the detectives. They're on their way."

By midnight, Gary's was swarming with a dozen police. I think it was the first time I was actually relieved to see the cops.

The uniformed ones were interviewing the bands and the bar staff. Some were out in the alleyway, trying to keep warm just outside the fluttering yellow caution tape and the Nasties' van. And some — the two lead detectives, in plainclothes — were sitting at tables with X and Mike the bouncer. Earlier, they'd spoken with me along with Sam Shiller and Luke Macdonald.

I watched and tried to remember what was going on, which was what I usually did.

I'm a journal-keeper. It keeps me sane. Sort of.

I looked down at the business card the detective had handed me. *Terry Murphy*, it said. *Detective, Portland Police Department*, plus a post office box and a phone number. His partner, Detective Savoie, was a table over, interviewing Mike and looking super pissed off.

Detective Murphy carefully watched as X turned over the business card in his hands, head down. Murphy spoke really quietly, almost in a whisper, like he had with me, but I could still hear him. He was going over the evening's events for the billionth time. "So, you and Kurt immediately went out there when you saw the reaction of the other two guys in the band, is that right, Chris?"

Chris? Uh-oh.

Everyone knew X didn't ever, ever like being called Chris; he actually didn't like being addressed by any name. "It's too intimate," he told me one time, a bit irritated, when I asked him about it. "The Koreans have it right. Don't use someone's given name." But that's another story.

This time, X didn't bother to correct Murphy. Instead, he just nodded. "Yeah, Kurt and I went out and we saw

Jimmy." He sounded weary. "We tried to get him down, but we couldn't. We checked if he was breathing, but he wasn't. His skin was cold when we touched it ..." He stopped, clearing his throat. Listening to him, I started to cry again. X didn't. He never cried, as far as I knew.

I tried to concentrate. I noticed that Murphy was quite a bit younger than his partner: square jaw, lots of muscles, longish hair, and a handlebar mustache. He had friendly eyes; I personally thought he was good-looking, too. Unlike his partner, Murphy wasn't wearing a tie, and his jacket was this semi-hip brown leather car coat thing, like from a TV detective show or something. Before making the decision to become a cop, he'd been a counterculture type, too, he'd told me earlier. When he was younger, he'd supported environmental causes, he said, and he had even gone to protests against pulp and paper mills along Maine's polluted Androscoggin, Kennebec, and Penobscot Rivers. "I opposed authority, just like you guys," he told me, trying to cheer me up, I guess. "I think my generation may have had better music, though."

To my surprise, Murphy actually knew something about the punk movement. In 1978, most adults didn't, or they didn't want to. But the detective said he had become interested in the punk scene, and he told us that it was good to see local teenagers doing something other than listening to Led Zeppelin all the time and getting stoned.

X looked up at Murphy, fatigue and worry on his face. "Jimmy's parents?"

Murphy shook his head. "They're still out, not sure where," he said. "But we've got some guys in a car waiting for them. They'll take the Clearys downtown when they get home."

X looked unsure, which was also something I wasn't used to. X was never unsure about anything. "Will they just tell them right there? When they get home?"

Murphy placed a big hand on X's shoulder. "We have to tell them as soon as we can, Chris. The guys who will do it have experience with these kinds of things. They'll be sensitive, but we have to tell them and get them downtown."

X looked alarmed. "Not to show them …"

"No, no," Murphy said. "We've taken pictures and done what we need to do. The medical examiner is taking care of Jimmy now. Then there'll be an autopsy and forensic tests. But we need his folks to identify him formally." He stopped and rubbed his eyes. "It's gonna be a long night."

"Can me and Kurt go there to be with them?" X asked. "We'd like to go and try and help them … or whatever." I nodded.

"That's not a good idea, guys. We need to work with the family at this point," Murphy said. "You should just go home and get some rest, if you can. We'll be in touch soon enough."

When Murphy stood, he towered over us, and I figured he was easily six foot five, maybe more. Despite a bone-crushing handshake, he had an easygoing way about him, one that you don't usually see in Portland cops. Since his arrival at Gary's, he was the only one of them who had shown any sympathy toward us. His partner, Savoie, meanwhile, could not have been more different: he was a total asshole, all terse and gruff. After a few more questions, Murphy told us we could get our friends together and head home.

"I'm very, very sorry about the loss of your friend," Murphy said. He regarded us with concern. "Are you going to be okay? We'd give you and your friends a ride home, but we've kind of got our hands full right now. The media are outside waiting for a statement."

"It's okay, Kurt has a car," X said. "What if the reporters try to talk to us?"

"We'd prefer it if you didn't say anything," Murphy said. "We need Jimmy's parents to hear it from us, not the media."

"That makes sense," X said. He looked down at the floor. After a bit, X stood and extended his hand. I did likewise. Murphy in turn gripped both our hands firmly. For a moment, I thought I spotted a flash of a tattoo below Murphy's sleeve, which certainly hinted at some kind of a less traditional pre-cop life.

"Thanks, Detective," I said.

"Good night, boys. We'll be in touch in the morning."

Heading toward the others, I decided I would break the no-tattoo vow and get Jimmy Cleary's name inked on my arm.

My own name, by the way, is Kurt Lank. My friends call me Kurt Blank, or Point Blank. This is our story, as I remember it, about what happened to all of us in Portland that winter.

CHAPTER 3

Jimmy's murder happened late Friday night, which I guess made it too late for most media to report on it. The one exception came as a quick mention on WBLM, the big Portland rock music station. Disc jockeys at LM, as it was called in city high schools, liked to mock us and the music we listened to. They liked big-hair, big-arena rock bullshit. "Portland police are saying that a teenager was slain in an alley near Brown Street late tonight, between Congress and Free Streets," the newsreader droned, just before excitedly reciting an ad about a mattress sale. "Police are withholding the youth's name until family members can be contacted. But the murder apparently happened at Gary's bar, where punk rock bands often perform." When he said the word *punk,* the newsreader sounded like he wanted to spit.

The two local papers in Portland were the tabloid *Daily Sun* and the broadsheet *Press Herald*. Both were pretty conservative, and the only stories they ever published about the genre were totally wrong, completely sensationalized, or both. The *Sun* headline the next morning wasn't very subtle: "BLOODY PUNK SLAYING ON HOOKERS ROW!" The story below it contained not much new information, but it did quote two "anonymous prostitutes" who said they were worried about what the murder would mean for them and their "clients." The story ran beside a grainy photograph of the Sex Pistols, above the cutline: "The Sex Pistols, punk rock's leading British band, favor songs about 'destroying' society."

The *Press Herald's* headline was on page one and above the fold. "TEEN'S DOWNTOWN SLAYING SHOCKS POLICE," it read. The story was written by the paper's police reporter, some guy named Ron McLeod. His story was only a few paragraphs long, but it contained a bit more detail than the *Sun's* version, and it actually hinted at the slightest degree of pity toward our friend. Among other things, it stated that the victim had been in his late teens and that he lived in South Portland. But it didn't name him.

X and I slouched at the kitchen table in his family's home on Highland Avenue, staring at the walls. We felt gutted. X's mother had heard us come in at about 3:30 a.m., even though we'd tried to be super quiet. She came downstairs and then collapsed, crying, on the living room couch when we told her about Jimmy.

It was now a few hours later, and the breakfast she had made for us was still untouched. Some light was creeping through the blinds. My head was throbbing.

This is insane. How can this be happening?

The early-morning editions of the two newspapers were on the table; the stories about the unnamed victim read and reread many times. The three of us had been listening to NPR, the sound down low, but there had been no mention of Jimmy's murder; stories about Maine, even murders, didn't ever attract the attention of big city media. Nobody gave a crap about news from Maine, actually, even people who lived in Maine. For what seemed like forever, there was total quiet. Finally, X's mom stirred. "I need to wake up your father and tell him," she said, red-eyed. "We'll let your sister and brother sleep a bit longer." She slipped out.

Apart from the buzzing of the fridge, there was more silence. I stared at the newspapers, then looked at my best friend. "Who would do this, X?" I asked. "This is the fucking worst, man."

"Yeah," X said. "But it wasn't random."

Before I could speak, X's father stepped into the kitchen, pale as a tombstone. He was wearing pajama bottoms and a Montreal Canadiens T-shirt. X's mother was behind him. She looked like she'd been crying again.

"Boys," he said, putting a hand on X's shoulder. "I am so, so sorry. I am so sad and shocked. I wish you had woken me when you came in."

"We didn't want to wake anyone up," X said. "There was nothing you could do, anyway. The cops told us to go home and wait to hear from them. But nobody's called."

"They must still be speaking to the Clearys, and dealing with the media," his dad said. You could still hear a hint of his Canadian accent. He scanned the newspaper articles. "I can't imagine what they must be going through. This is just beyond belief."

X's parents sat down at the table and started to ask us about what happened at Gary's. We told them what we could. When we gave them the details about how Jimmy had been found, they both actually lurched back in their seats. "Good God," his father said. "What did the police say?"

"Nothing," X said. "I heard a uniformed cop say he had never seen something like that before. He seemed shocked."

"Did they say anything about a suspect?" X's father asked.

"No," I said. "The one detective who spoke to us was pretty shocked, too. He seemed like an okay guy. For a cop."

The phone suddenly rang, and both X's parents jumped. His mother answered, listened for a few moments, then held out the receiver to X.

"It's Detective Murphy," she said. "He wants to see when you boys can come back downtown. He also says that *Rolling Stone* has called, and wants to talk to someone who knows something about the Portland underground music scene."

CHAPTER 4

X sat in the front, and his dad drove; I sat in the back. We were on the way downtown to police headquarters.

X looked like he was paralyzed or something. He didn't say a word all the way there. He just stared straight ahead.

X, what are you thinking?

I should have been used to this — the complete absence of emotion, the creepy quietness. But it still sort of pissed me off sometimes.

Right from Day One, X was completely different from anyone else I knew. His ears, for starters: that was one of the first things people noticed. In late-1970s Portland, no guys wore earrings, not even the punk guys. Nobody. But X did. And it led to a ton of fights, most of which started with him being called "a fucking fag" and then getting pushed. In one brawl, when a couple of drunken bikers and their drunken biker girlfriends stumbled into a punk community-hall gig we'd organized and called X a "fucking fag," he didn't blink,

as usual. But when one of the bikers called his younger sister, Bridget, a name, X's eyes went black and he
leaned into the biker's beard and hissed: "Apologize!"

Instead, the biker reached up and ripped out the
little gold hoop, which tore away a not-small chunk of
X's earlobe. Blood gushed everywhere. Even over the
noise of the band, I could hear Bridget screaming. As I
and everyone else present watched, astounded, X beat
the much-bigger biker's face into hamburger meat. In
his fist, he held a short length of lead pipe he sometimes carried in his pocket. The biker slumped to the
ground, and he didn't get up again. His friends just silently picked him up and hustled him out of there.

Word spread. All of the bikers knew about X after
that. They didn't like him, of course, but they also left him
alone. They'd never admit it, but a few of them seemed to
grudgingly respect this wiry, pale, leather-jacketed punk
rock kid. So they gave him a wide berth on nights we spent
at Gary's, the triangular notch in his right ear a sign that X
was totally different from the other punks there. Among
other things, nobody called his little sister names anymore.

X was different in other ways, too. Some of our friends
sported Mohawks, for example. A few had shaved their
heads, in the early days of the scene, favoring the skinhead look. Many had dyed their hair a variety of colors
not found in nature, me included. And all of us were
careful to have hair that wasn't too long, so we wouldn't
ever be confused with the hippies, who we mostly hated.

But not X. His hair was longish, and he clearly didn't
give a shit who disapproved. It went to his shoulders,

just about, and it was wavy and wild. Most of the North American punk bands, and all of the British ones, kept their hair short. X favored the Ramones look.

X also wore the sort of uniform the guys in the Nasties liked — a biker jacket in any weather, skinny jeans with the knees torn out, T-shirts, and Doc Martens or Converse Chucks. If it got really cold, like tonight, X would wear this crazy ancient knitted hunting sweater with ducks on it. He'd bought it for two bucks at a downtown thrift store, which is where us Portland punks bought most of our clothes. He didn't wear a hat, because real punks don't wear hats.

As the car moved toward downtown, over the Casco Bay Bridge, I looked at X's profile from my spot in the back seat. He had a slightly prominent jaw, like his dad, and a slightly off-center nose (cause: a fight). His face was broad, almost moonish, and there were two scars to be seen — one below his mouth and the other above an eyebrow (cause: two more fights). He was always clean-shaven.

His eyes, his mother and I had agreed one day, were probably his most memorable feature. Like Bowie, one eye did not dilate or contract properly. During yet another community center battle, when I was off fighting someone else, X was jumped by a couple of guys and one of them hit him in the eye, hard. Over his protests, and much later, we rushed him to emergency at the Mercy, but there was nothing they could do. The medical term for his condition, we were told, was anisocoria, meaning he had unequal pupils. X could see well enough in both eyes, but — like Bowie, whose music we thought

was mostly average, except around the *Low* period —
his eyes were mismatched. So people would stare at him
quite a lot. He would stare back. They would look away.

FUCK. Fuck fuck fuck.

My guts were churning, and my head still hurt.
Jimmy's murder had left me desolate, a total wreck.
But X remained silent. I looked at the notched ear, at
the set of the jaw. As far as I could tell, he hadn't even
cried yet.

X and I met back in junior high school, at Holy Cross,
which both of us regarded as an oppressive shit hole of
Catholic uniformity. We became friends because we both
regarded everything, and everyone, as seriously weird
and/or boring. I remember talking to X on the day he
found me burning some papers on the school grounds.

"What's that?" he'd asked.

"The school constitution," I said, as an unhappy gym
teacher started jogging in our direction. "I'm protesting
the fascist culture that exists here."

We had kind of known each other for a while at that
point, but we were more or less inseparable after the
constitution-burning incident, for which I was suspended for a couple of days. X seemed to be impressed
by that. Afterward, we put up posters to oppose war and
to commemorate the victims of the shootings at Kent
State. We circulated petitions about the environment

and Native American issues. For a joke, we even ran a fictional candidate in the Holy Cross student council elections. We called him Herbie Schwartz. Herbie won in a landslide.

Dave Heaney, who advised the student council, came to see us. "Joke's on you, fellas," he said. "If Herbie won, then one of you has to serve on council." So I did.

Dave Heaney liked us, and we liked him. Like X's parents, he always encouraged us to be suspicious of authority, even his. He seemed to like our refusal to be conventional teenagers. He liked how we read books, how we were aware of political issues, how we refused to be like our peers, how we asked questions that made people uncomfortable. At graduation, he told us his favorite "X-related" anecdote: the day X asked Father McLean, the pious, pompous old priest assigned to the school, if Jesus Christ might have been gay. "He was a lifelong bachelor, and he lived with other men for much of his life, after all," X had said with a straight face, just before being hustled off to the principal's office.

Dave Heaney was the one who advised us to go to Portland Alternative High School in Portland's east end. And so we did. Like at Holy Cross, we continued to stick together at PAHS, and we sort of became the nucleus of what we called the NCNA: the Non-Conformist News Agency. It wasn't really a news agency, or even a news-paper. It was, as X once noted, a weirdo club — it was "the island of misfit punks."

X wrote and edited most of the NCNA's organ; I sup-plied the photos and the art. It was our semi-regular bulletin of defiance, our "fuck you" transmission to the outside world.

A couple dozen other outcasts and outsiders moved into the NCNA's orbit, and we protected them from the jocks, who sometimes liked to beat up the punk kids. We, along with our new friends, published *The NCNA* as often as we could, about every two weeks. Usually it contained X's lengthy essays about culture and politics and music, and contributions from some of the others — poetry, album reviews, art.

Sometimes we even let in the occasional story about school.

So, that's the NCNA. Now, here's some stuff about me.

I was an army brat, *per* the stupid cliché. I was born in the same year as my best friend X, but in faraway Fort Buckner in Okinawa, Japan. My medical officer dad had been stationed at the base there with the 78th Signal Battalion.

The never-ending mediocrity of my life, and the awareness of my sexual orientation, led inevitably to punk in 1976. The first time I heard "Anarchy in the UK" by the Sex Pistols, I said to X: "This is a world where I can finally breathe." Like lots of others, I wasn't the same after that. For me, punk rock opened up this fucking huge range of creative possibilities — for my art, for my photography, for my music — and it did not give a shit, not one, if I was gay.

My dad was tall and lean; my stay-at-home mother was short and mean. From early on, all that I could remember was my mother shouting and screaming at him. She was a drunk, I sometimes suspected, but I never actually saw her drink much. She was, however, filled with an infinite rage about everything, particularly Dad. It was unrelenting; it was the thing that defined our collective existence, just about. Every morning, wherever we were based — Fort Buckner, Fort Huachuca in Arizona, Fort Lewis in Washington — I would dread the sound of her thudding down the stairs. Her face would be set like a hatchet, and she would immediately start shouting at Dad for any grievance, no matter how small. I fucking hated it, although probably not as much as he did.

She'd scream at him if he loaded the dishwasher, and then she'd unload it and do it over. She'd scream at him if he did the laundry. She'd lose her mind if he even hung a picture of one of his army buddies on the wall of his tiny den.

My father would sometimes react to her outbursts, but most of the time, he didn't. He would stay silent, head down. When there was a break in the shit storm, he would head out to work or to shovel snow or mow the lawn: anything to get out. Anything to get away from her. His disappearances would last hours. Eventually, days.

I could not understand, and still don't, why she was so angry all the time. We weren't poor or anything, we were all healthy, and we lived in reasonably nice places. I loved her, I guess, but I could be at the same time repulsed by her, too. I was also disappointed by my father, truth be told, because he never fought back.

One night, shortly after we moved to Portland, my dad and I watched a late-night showing of James Dean's *Rebel Without a Cause*. It was my favorite movie, and not just because Dean was a punk, or because he was achingly beautiful. In one big scene, Dean rages at his father, Jim Backus, for not being a man, and for always wimping out in front of Dean's mother. "You're tearing me apart!" Dean yells at his mother. "You say one thing, he says another, and everybody changes back again!" I turned a little and glanced at my father, who was staring intently at the screen. "I can't fight her, either," he said. "I just pray that it gets better, Kurt. It never does."

One night, I woke up to a huge racket coming from the kitchen. I ran downstairs. Dad was sitting on the floor, leaning against the dishwasher, weeping. My mother had balled up her fists, and she was delivering blow after blow to his head. Her face was contorted with rage.

When she saw me, she suddenly stopped the assault and her face weirdly changed. She smiled at me. "Oh, hello, dear," she said. "Is everything all right?"

My father left not long after that, slipping out of our lives one icy November night. We were in South Portland at the time, and my father moved into an apartment closer to the naval base in Kittery, almost an hour away. A high-priced and long-drawn-out legal battle ensued. Dad tried to get custody of me, but he didn't win. When he ran out of money, he gave up, and, crying again, apologized to me one morning as we sat in his car.

"It's okay, Dad," I said.

But it wasn't.

Mom and I stayed in the South Portland home. I never saw her again with another man. Silently, all the pictures of my dad — and all of his books, all of his stuff — disappeared, and she never uttered his name again, referring to him only as "that bastard, or "your bastard father."

All of this happened when I was at Holy Cross. I was beginning my first year there, and the separation fucked me right up. I was completely disconnected from my classmates and anything else at the school, like I was floating down a river of shit with my skin on fire.

It was around this time, too, that I became aware that I was supposed to be interested in girls, but wasn't. I secretly liked the looks of some of my male teachers and the swagger of some of the older male students. It dawned on me, eventually, that I might be gay. It didn't shock me, to tell you the truth, but it was a total pain in the ass at the time. It was another burden to carry around. I didn't need it or want it then.

In the middle of grade seven, I met X for the first time. This was just a few weeks before the constitution-burning incident. We both were among the biggest guys in our grade, but we had never really talked to each other much. I had watched him a lot, though. X, like me, didn't seem all that interested in any of our peers, or in the school curriculum. At the start, I admit, I was attracted to him. He was tall and slender and really good-looking, but he didn't seem to hang out with any-one. For a while, I wondered whether X was gay, too. He definitely was never around any girls at Holy Cross.

There were differences between us, though: I did pretty well in sports — hockey in the winter, lacrosse in the summer. X participated in no team sports. I was only an average student, with no big interest in any subject. X, however, seemed to outshine everyone else in every subject, and with no noticeable effort, either. X's hair was long; mine was short, like my dad's. X rarely smiled, but I — despite my shitty home life — usually did. X hardly ever spoke; I was a fucking expert in small talk.

In my experience, meaningless conversation helped to avoid conflict. It was a skill I acquired at a young age, a diversion that sometimes helped to ensure that my mother did not start shrieking at my dad, or me, for something or other. So, one day in February, at lunchtime, I spotted X reading a magazine on the gymnasium floor, where Holy Cross students had to eat lunch. It was *Creem,* which I also read when I could get my hands on a copy, which wasn't very often.

I couldn't make out the cover, but X was completely immersed in it. I decided to say something. "*Creem* magazine," I announced, ineptly, and I instantly regretted saying anything.

He looked up at me, expressionless, then looked back down at the magazine. "Yep," he said, "that's what it is."

Despite myself, I laughed.

Arrogant prick, aren't you? But I asked for it.

"Guess I kind of stated the obvious there, right?"

"Yes, you did," said X, eyebrow up. "You do that a lot?"

"I try not to," I said. "I just like *Creem*, I guess."

X looked at me. He didn't blink, which made me uncomfortable. "What kind of music do you like?"

"I don't like any of the crap on the radio, that's for sure," I said. "And I don't like anything that everybody else listens to, I guess." X said nothing for another long moment, which made me wish I was invisible or something. Finally he said, "Ever hear the MC5 or the Stooges?

"I've read about them," I said, "but I haven't actually heard any of their stuff."

"I've got some," X said. "I sent away for some albums. I'll make you a tape."

And he did. For me, that day was a pretty fucking important one. I met a boy who would soon become my best friend, my brother from another mother, and I was introduced to some of the music that would become the soundtrack to my life. And soon, Christopher X would become the most important person in my life, after my dad.

One day in the spring of that same year, I asked my new friend why he always called himself X.

"You wouldn't believe me if I told you," he said, which was true.

CHAPTER 5

The NCNA — whose format went back and forth between newspaper and magazine style, but was always called *The NCNA* — was distributed off PAHS's grounds so that the school administration couldn't stop students from reading it. Copies were handed out at Portland High and at local record shops, too.

X, Jimmy Cleary, me, and assorted members of the Nasties, Virgins, and Social Blemishes also handed mimeographed copies to students at bus stops, in parking lots, and along sidewalks that bordered the schools. The first page of the first edition featured a picture of *The NCNA* staff, sitting in PAHS's school auditorium staring at the cameraman (who happened to be me). None of them were smiling. The cutline below the photograph read: "The future, *maaaan*."

The first edition featured a lengthy essay on punk rock written by X. It was titled "Punks of the World, Unite!" The subtitle: "PAHS students, throw away your Led Zep records: you have nothing to lose but conformity."

He wrote:

> What is it that all punks share, whatever their race, religion, gender, or partisan affiliation? ANGER. All punks are angry at something — at the music industry, for producing so much garbage; at governments, for helping bad situations get worse; at their parents, for being parents; at conservative politicians, for being born; at corporations, for putting profit before people; at anyone in a position of power, for being powerful; at other young people, for being racist or sexist or conformist. Being punk means being pissed off. Punks have pushed young people to embrace the transforming power of anger.

Me and Jimmy and X were laying out *The NCNA* on a lighted desk in the shop area in the basement of PAHS, where we were unlikely to be disturbed, or caught by a member of the administration. After reading the first bit of X's polemic, we looked up at him. "So," I said, "do you think anyone will actually understand this?"

X shrugged. Jimmy and I laughed and kept reading. The next part was something lots of Portland punks would come back to that winter.

> Punk is the search for real. If you're a teenager — and everyone is, at one time or another — you end up believing that everything is phony, and fake, and fraudulent. Parents. Teachers. Governments.

Other kids. Everything, when stripped down to its core, is without any truth. It's all lies.

When you are young, you react to this news with disappointment, or anger, or both. You break things, you take drugs, you punch someone out, you make something.

PUNK IS WHAT WE MAKE. Punk is about trying to scratch out some meaning in a big old world that seems pretty meaningless, most days. It's about being angry at being lied to, and smashing your fist against the doors the liars cower behind, even if you know you're the one who is probably going to get hurt. Punk is about raging against all the powers that be, to try and make things better, if only for just an instant.

It's also about being yourself, and finding something that is real, and holding onto it like your life depends on it.

Which, when you get right down to it, it does.

Portland's punk scene was like most punk scenes outside New York and London, in the early days, I guess. It had a lot of young musicians, artists, poets, writers, drama types, and assorted societal outcasts in it. In those days, the scene attracted this weird mix of urban subcultures, from skinheads and mods to faux–Teddy Boys to Rastafarians. And, of course, all the young punks.

No band had a real manager, no band had actual roadies, and no band even bothered to make a phone call to a big record company. None of us could generate media interest in what we were doing — until, that is, one of us was crucified outside a punk bar one night in downtown Portland. At that point, reporters started to fall over themselves to write hysterical bullshit accounts of what punk rock was. But ninety-nine percent of the media didn't have a clue what we were.

Within every city's scene, there were lots of different theories about what had given rise to it all in the first place. Hatred for what rock music had become. A return to rock 'n' roll's primitive roots. A form of political or artistic expression. But the thing that unified the different subcultures that made up the scene in those early days was — as X had written in *The NCNA* — anger. Anger was energy, as X put it to Dave Heaney one day in Social Studies class.

Heaney was intrigued. He suggested to X that he explain why anger and fury can be a positive force. So X did, in an essay. Much later on at PAHS, it formed the basis of a big rant in another issue of *The NCNA* titled "Anarchy, Anger, and Punk."

He wrote:

> With their records, their art, their words, their clothes, and their thinking, punks have electrified youth culture, shaken up rock 'n' roll, and made it okay to be angry. Angry about our parents, our teachers, our life, angry about everything. Punk

rock is a rejection of everything rock 'n' roll has become in the 1970s — namely, an arena-sized, coke-addicted, disconnected-from-reality corporate game played by millionaires. Punk changes all of that. Punks are loud, loutish, pissed off. They are of the streets, and for the streets. Punks are what every teenager should be: they are angry. They are insolent. They frighten their parents, teachers, and the elderly. And they are ready to murder the popular culture.

They want to kill it all. Kill it, kill it, kill it. DEAD.

CHAPTER 6

Me, X, and X's father sat in chairs ringed around Detective Murphy's gray metal desk at Portland police headquarters. It was still super early, and, apart from Murphy and Savoie, no other cops seemed to be around.

Savoie, grizzled and red-faced, read out the last few sentences of X's essay and glared up at him. "They want to murder. They want to kill it all," Savoie repeated. "Kill it, kill it, dead." He paused for dramatic effect. "Kill who? When? Why?"

Before X could answer, his dad jumped in, sounding a lot like the lawyer he was. "Wait a second, Detective," he said, leaning forward and holding up his hand. "What does Christopher's article about music in a high school publication have to do with Jimmy's death? As you know, that bar is in a pretty seedy area, with plenty of dangerous people around. Are you looking at any of them?"

"And where'd you get that anyway?" I asked. "We only distributed that to PAHS and PHS students."

Savoie was at least a decade older than his partner and looked like a human version of a greasy, wrinkled brown paper bag. He had obviously been up all night.

He ignored my question and addressed X's dad. "We think Jimmy Cleary's death may have had something to do with this punk rock crap," he said, holding up the months-old edition of *The NCNA*. "We don't see the boys as suspects, or any of the other kids, either. But, whoever did this wasn't working alone — they killed him and had him nailed to that wall in what must have been minutes. It's pretty damn unlikely one person could do that."

"So why does my essay matter?" X asked.

"Because," Savoie said, "normal people don't understand this punk thing that you guys belong to. And maybe it's what set the killers off."

Is he serious? Someone killed Jimmy because they objected to his taste in music?

Detective Murphy, who was looking uncomfortable with Savoie's questions, jumped in, big hands gesturing all over the place. "We don't know if that motivated the killer or killers, of course," he said. "That's just a question we have. But it was a terrible, awful way for your friend to die, boys, and we are working overtime to solve this, fast." Murphy, like in some stupid TV show, was apparently playing Good Cop. Savoie, meanwhile, was the other part of the cliché.

X and I said nothing, but X's dad was obviously unimpressed. "Why do you think the music is connected to this, Detective Savoie? Isn't it possible there is some other motive? I can tell you, Detective, my wife and I have been listening to these kids and their music for a couple years now — and, if anything, it's more peaceful than the hippie movement. They may talk tough, but they're good kids."

Savoie looked at X and me — his piggish bloodshot eyes taking in our size, our expressions, our biker jackets — and his squinty eyes lingered a bit on X's notched ear lobe. "Fine," he said sarcastically. "They may be peace-loving hippies. But the person or persons who killed Jimmy Cleary sure aren't. And I think his involvement in this stuff played a role."

Nobody said anything for a bit. Eventually, Detective Murphy stood, looking weary, and handed X a pink phone message slip. "This is the *Rolling Stone* writer who wants to talk to you," he said. "We didn't have anything we could tell him."

"Okay," X said, as we all stood to go. "What should we tell him?"

Detective Murphy shrugged. "We'd prefer you not talk about what you saw last night," he said, quietly. "But about the music, tell him whatever you want. You guys clearly understand that better than we do."

No shit.

CHAPTER 7

The members of the Nasties, Blemishes, and Virgins flopped in our shared practice space in the basement at Sound Swap, a used record store on Free Street, a few blocks from Gary's. The owner, Pierre, was an older guy, but he came out to some of the punk shows and liked us. So he offered us the space for free.

Upstairs, racks and racks of LPs and posters for old rock 'n' roll shows lined the walls. At the back was a counter for the cash register, the entrance to the alley-way, and a tiny washroom. The basement space, mean-while, had an actual dirt floor. That wasn't so good for our amps, so we'd scavenged some old rugs from dumpsters and laid those down over the dirt. On the walls, we tacked up posters for some of our past gigs. On the rare occasion when a New York or Boston punk band came into town, they'd get top billing, of course, because those shows were a pretty big deal. Most of the posters were for the more unforgettable community hall performances of the Punk Rock Virgins, the Hot Nasties, and my band, the Social Blemishes. We generally felt a gig was "unforgettable" if the cops raided it.

Since mid-1977 or so, the Virgins, Nasties, and Blemishes had been the only bona fide punk outfits in town; many of the others in Portland were either new wave poseurs or metal bands who cut their hair to attract some media attention. Since the start, we had been at the center of the *real* punk thing in Portland. Other groups were pretty competitive, and a lot of them were jealous of each other. Those of us in the PAHS and PHS bands were different, I think. We defended each other, we hung out together, and we even swapped members if we needed to. At gigs, we usually traveled in a pack that some other bands in town called, sometimes mockingly, the X Gang.

X Gang: they meant it as an insult, but whatever. I liked it. It fit.

The basement walls at Sound Swap were lined with a crappy old drum kit, two antique guitar amps, a bass amp, and three microphones that were wired to an ancient PA system X and I had scored at a garage sale. Occasionally, the PA would deliver an electric shock to whoever got their lips too close to one of the ungrounded mics. You'd actually see a blue arc coming off the tip of the microphone, and you'd feel the resulting voltage bouncing around inside your head. We called that the blue spark.

We used the practice space after hours, when the store was closed and no one was around. Gary hid a key for us in a rusty tin can by the alley door. The building had a pawnshop on one side and a small engine repair on the other. No one ever complained about the racket emanating from the basement. It wasn't the kind of neighborhood where anyone complained about noise.

When we all met up there a couple of nights after Jimmy's death, some of us started crying again. For most, it was the first time we had experienced a death of someone who wasn't a grandparent. The mood was bleak as shit. Already, some parents — like my mother — were telling us to quit the punk scene, right away.

"It's too violent," my mother had hollered at me that morning as I ate my corn flakes. "And now that boy is dead."

No fucking kidding, Mom. He was my friend.

Sam Shiller strummed his battered Fender Telecaster copy, the amp off. X was silent, as usual. The Virgins were whispering amongst themselves. It was pretty depressing.

"Is there any more beer?" I asked, peering into an empty case of Bud.

Patti Upchuck pulled a Sam Adams out of a backpack and handed it to me. "It's not cold," she said. "Sorry."

Patti Upchuck's Virgins were Portland's only all-female punk band. They were a trio, and one of the most popular bands in town, with some amazing super-fast punk-pop tunes about the uselessness of hanging out at the Maine Mall or watching TV or whatever. They were all pretty, so, to compensate, they dyed their hair black or various shades of pink and green, purposely applied too much eye makeup, and always wore ill-fitting army jackets. All three members of the Virgins attended PAHS — lead singer and guitarist Patti Kowalchuk, her bassist sister Beth (Betty), and drummer Leah Yeomanson, who was an off-reserve member of the Mi'Kmaq First Nation and who wore a biker jacket with "American Indian Movement" inscribed across the back.

On stage, the Kowalchuk sisters called themselves Patti and Betty Upchuck. Offstage, Patti had an un-requited affection for X. She never did anything about it, though.

Me and X often hung out with the Upchuck sisters, at school in Room 531 and at shows, but he had never "dated" either of them. Nobody really dated in the local punk scene. It wasn't really done — it was too normal.

The Social Blemishes, my crew, were more of a punk rock collective than an actual band. Like some of the lesser-known arty groups in London and New York and other places —Wire, X-Ray Spex, Ohio's Pere Ubu — we liked performance art over musical structure. The band's membership changed about every two weeks, with the only regulars being me, as lead singer, and the drummer, a big football player from PHS named Dan O'Heran, who went by the name Danny Hate.

The Blems were well known for shows where I'd in-vite Maine College of Art students on stage to paint a mural while we played a twenty-minute, three-chord dirge — or the various gigs where my friend Leeanimal would strip off a leopard-skin halter top and pogo. At one community hall show in North East Portland that had been broken up by the police, one of the cops threatened to arrest me for obscenity. At the time, I was wearing a shirt that had been hand-painted for me by Leeanimal. It featured an oversized penis; below it, the words THIS IS A MAN'S BRAIN. It was my favorite gig shirt.

The Hot Nasties, meanwhile, had been the first real punk band in town, and they had built up a loyal audience that showed up at almost every show, no matter how poorly publicized. The band sounded like the Beach Boys with distorted guitars, I liked to say, and they did. Their hummable songs, all written by Jimmy and Sam, had been about how it generally sucks to be a teenager. They were tight, and they had the right look: skinny, pale, hungry looking. They were destined for great things, and we all knew it.

Their EP was the first punk recording in Maine, and it had gotten some media interest — even in the pages of the *Sun* and the *Herald*. The *Herald* didn't bash them nearly as much as we had expected. "Ham-fisted pop in a leather jacket," the reviewer had sniffed.

"Better than what the *Sun* had to say," X said. ("The lead singer can't sing, the guitarist can't play guitar, and the drummer can't keep a beat. Other than that, they have a promising future ahead of them pumping gas.")

All of that seemed like a long time ago. Now, with Jimmy gone and Gary's shut down while the police continued their investigation, the remaining Nasties were uncertain about whether to go on. On the same night they had found themselves getting a positive review in the *New Musical Express*, their lead singer and driving force had been murdered. They were a wreck, all of them.

All of us, pretty much, were exhausted from being up the past two nights and from answering questions from police and our parents.

Sam Shiller said he'd spoken by phone, earlier in the day, to that freelance writer who said he was with *Rolling Stone* — the one who X and I hadn't bothered to call back. The reporter had finished the interview by telling Sam their EP would quickly sell out.

"Why?" Sam had asked.

"Because death sells in rock 'n' roll" was the reply.

"Fuck you, bastard. He was my best friend," Sam had screamed before slamming down the phone.

"Good for you, man," I said. "Good for you."

The others nodded their heads in agreement. There'd be no further chats with the *Rolling Stone* douchebag. More silence followed.

I cleared my throat. "Anyone else being told *no more punk* by their parents?"

Just about everyone present nodded or held their hand up.

X, sitting on an amp, shrugged. "Mine wouldn't bother," he said. "They know I won't listen."

I laughed.

"Mine are fucking freaking," Sam said, still picking at his guitar.

"Mine, too," said Danny. "They say they're gonna ground me for the rest of my life."

Leah, who had been crying off and on since arriving, finally spoke. "I just can't fuckin' believe this," she said. "Who could possibly want to hurt Jimmy? He's the biggest sweetheart. He's such a great guy."

"Was ..." Danny whispered. Then, a few second later, "Uh ... sorry."

X looked at Danny, whose freckled face had gone crimson. "It's okay, man. You're right. He's gone. No use pretending otherwise."

"And nobody knows *anything*?" said Patti. "Nobody *saw anything*?"

"I do," Betty said, "... or, at least I know someone who says they saw something ..."

Everyone turned to look at her.

CHAPTER 8

Betty Upchuck brought home the lost and the lonely, Patti liked to say, so their Sandy Road home was often a safe haven for lost dogs, lost cats, and — at least once that I know of — a lost kid. Motorists who had gotten trapped in the maze of South Portland's streets were also welcome at the Kowalchuk home. Betty and Patti's mother would then work the phones and connect the lost dog, kid, or tourist with the right destination.

In high school, Betty kept on providing shelter, but mostly for punk kids who needed it. If they'd run away from home — if they'd been knocked around by a parent for a bad mark or for leaving a joint around or whatever — Betty would offer refuge for a day or two until the heat had dissipated. I called her Sister Betty.

Punk rock kids, at PAHS or PHS or wherever, were in need of sanctuary a lot. At the start of the scene, nobody above the age of twenty understood punk rock, and not many adults appreciated the look. Most everyone under the age of twenty — the lemmings, as I called them — didn't like punk. Thus the need for a safe place. Sister Betty's place.

There was often a kid or two crashing on the smelly old couch in the Upchuck sisters' unfinished basement. Occasionally, one of them was Mark Upton.

Marky Upton was a first-year PAHS student, with glasses, acne, and a frame so tiny he looked like a strong wind off Casco Bay would blow him away. He was incredibly insecure and shy. Marky didn't just read poetry, he actually wrote it, and he was not bad either, sometimes contributing to *The NCNA* under a pseudonym.

Marky adored me and X, the Upchucks said, and so he could usually be found at the Social Blemishes' rare, chaotic gigs, smiling up at me from the front row. Marky was gay, too, I knew, but he hadn't done anything about it yet. He was an only child and lived with his single mother in a townhouse complex down on Congress. His life was heaving with anxiety and confusion and fear until punk came along and saved him.

That's how it was for most of us.

Saved by punk! Praise Lord Ramone!

Although he was totally underage, Marky had been at Gary's on the night Jimmy was murdered. Sitting by the rear door, waiting for the Virgins to start playing again, he had been the one who had closed the alleyway door after Sam Shiller and Luke Macdonald went out looking for Jimmy.

Marky was always willing to watch the door at our gigs; it gave him an official role, sort of. He'd take

tickets or cover charges or whatever, and truthfully report the results to us. We'd make sure to sneak him a
beer, which he'd hold onto all night, under the folds of
his oversized army jacket.

He was doing that now, listening closely as me and
X and the Upchuck sisters sat around him, debating.
Sitting there, perched on the couch in the Upchuck
sisters' basement with his can of beer, he also looked
nervous.

"Well, I had some poppers with me," he said, looking at X, who obviously disapproved of snorting alkyl
nitrate, but who said nothing. "So I went out in the
alley while the Virgins were playing to do some. I
propped the door open a bit."

"Was Jimmy out there yet?" X asked.

"No, but the van was there," Marky said. "The doors
were closed and nobody was in it. I looked in the windows but didn't see anybody."

"What time was that?"

"I don't know," Marky said. "Maybe just past nine or
so. I didn't check. I was just looking to see if anyone was
around. No one was, but ..." He trailed off.

"But what, Marky?"

"Well, I don't know if it was anything important. But
farther down the alley there was this car parked. It was
right up against the building on the other side of the
parking lot, maybe a bit closer to the Congress Street
side. The lights were off, but then I saw this little red
light inside the car," he said. "It looked like somebody
was smoking in there. I couldn't see them, though."

X asked him if he knew what kind of car it was. Marky shook his head. "I don't know anything about cars, sorry," he said. "It looked like a regular American car, I guess. Nothing fancy or foreign about it. It was dark — black or brown, I think. Not new."

"What happened next?"

"Well, I figured I wasn't alone anymore, so I went back inside and went to watch the band," he said. "And that was it."

We asked Marky a few more questions, but it was obvious he didn't know anything else super-significant. Seeing a car parked in the alleyway, however, right before Jimmy was killed, a car with someone in it? That was probably important.

As Marky looked on, sipping his Bud Light, the rest of us argued about what to do. I wanted to call Detective Murphy right away; X wanted to call his father first, in case Marky needed a lawyer. Sister Betty wanted Marky to stay at the Kowalchuk home and sleep on the couch.

"I can't," Marky said. "My mom's out. I told her I'd look after the dogs. Walk them and stuff."

X looked uncertain. "Okay," he said. "Kurt and I will take you back to your place, all right? I'll talk to my dad tonight and we'll figure out what to do tomorrow."

"Sure, X, sure," Marky said, clearly thrilled to be the focus of his attention. "Sounds good."

Twenty minutes later, X and I watched as Marky waved at us and disappeared inside his mother's dark townhouse.

"You believe him?" I asked, pulling away and pointing my battered AMC Gremlin toward South Portland. "I think he'd say anything to get your attention, man."

"I know," X said, rubbing his eyes, looking exhausted, "but I don't think he'd lie about something like this. That wouldn't be cool."

"Agree," I said, speeding over the Casco Bay Bridge. "You call your dad?"

"Yeah," X said, looking at the bay as we passed, heading toward our nighttime ritual of Coke Slurpees at our favorite 7-Eleven. "I called from the Kowalchuks before we left. Bridget said he and my mom were still out. So I'll talk to him later."

CHAPTER 9

When Marky's mother found him, she fainted and dropped to the floor. When she came to, much later, and again saw the body of her only son, she fainted again. It would be a while before the police were called.

Marky Upton lay on the living room carpet, white and tiny, like a piece of broken china. He had been placed between the couch and the coffee table. His pants and underwear had been pulled down to his bony knees, and there was a clump of what looked like half-frozen bacon balanced on his testicles. His arms were sort of sticking out from his little body, pointing at the townhouse walls.

On his left side, between two ribs, was the gaping wound that had killed him. It was much bigger than a regular knife wound, we were told later. On Marky's head, the killer or killers had hooked a jumble of rusty wire into his hair. The wire had scratched the skin across his birdlike skull, and some blood could be seen there, too. His eyes were open, wide.

The police found his mother's two Shih Tzus jammed in the microwave oven in the kitchen, cooked to death.

There was no note left behind, no clues scrawled on the walls in blood, no nothing. The townhouse was in exactly the condition Marky and his mom had left it. Nothing had been moved or taken. We were later told the front door was still locked when Marky's mother returned from her movie.

Problems.

Marky Upton's murder, coming about forty-eight hours after Jimmy's, created a lot of problems for a lot of people. For the detectives Murphy and Savoie, it apparently made the Chief of Police super pissed. As a result, Savoie was in a spitting fury that we hadn't called them the second we heard what Marky had to say. "Why the hell didn't you call us right away?" he yelled at us. This time X's dad didn't intervene.

Problems, problems. The problem is us.

"You're all lucky we don't charge you with obstructing justice," Savoie said, glaring at X and me with his eyes bulging. "Who the hell do you think you are? The punk rock Hardy Boys?"

Even Detective Murphy, who had been mostly on our side, held back a laugh on that one.

For X, me, and the Upchuck sisters, Marky's murder caused a ton of fucking problems, too. X's father was angry — angrier than I'd ever seen him — that we hadn't tried harder to contact him about what the kid had witnessed.

"Here's what's happening next," Savoie said, jabbing a tobacco-stained index finger in the air. "You are going to stay out of our investigation! You are going to keep your mouths shut! And you are going to tell us the minute … the *minute* you remember or hear about something that may be useful to us. Do you understand?"

We nodded our heads, silent. But X just stared at him, his face pretty vacant.

"Good," Savoie said. "Now everyone go to wherever you live, and stay there until you hear from us."

X looked at Savoie, expressionless. "Stay there? Does that mean we're under house arrest or something?"

"No, it doesn't mean that!" Savoie barked. Unlike his partner, Savoie was obviously no big fan of my friend X. In fact, he looked like he wanted to punch him in the face. "But it does mean that the next time we see you, it had better be under better circumstances, got it?"

X said nothing for a few moments, then: "Got it. Check. See you when we see you." And we got up and left.

That went well.

CHAPTER 10

The next time we all saw each other was a week later. The coroner had released Marky's and Jimmy's bodies to their families, who decided to hold a joint funeral Mass at Portland's big old Cathedral of the Immaculate Conception, where X and I had both taken our First Communion. The cathedral had been around since the 1800s or something, and was across from a park that overlooked the bay. In all its years, I'll bet it had never seen a funeral like this one.

An hour before it started, the redbrick church on Spring Street was packed with teachers and administrators from PAHS and PHS, and tons of students. Some who were there had regularly tormented Jimmy and Marky when they were alive. X and I glared at them.

The holy water should have been boiling.

Fucking hypocrites.

Many of the lemmings were putting on a good show of grieving, however, which made me want to puke. In the last two pews were a big group of media people — print, radio, and TV — along with some hippie guy claiming to be writing for both *Rolling Stone* and the *NME*. All of them kept looking at us and making notes or whatever. The *Press Herald* guy, Ron McLeod, stood apart from the rest of them, near the confessionals, taking it all in.

Those of us in the X Gang, meanwhile, were gathered at the rear of the church, close to its big wooden doors. All of us — X, me, the Nasties, Blemishes, and Virgins — were wearing black, head to toe. We said little. For most of us, it had been the first time we'd seen each other since the night at Sound Swap. The big stained-glass window over the main doors threw this rainbow of colors over everything.

Not far away, Detectives Murphy and Savoie watched as mourners filed in and started looking for a place to sit on one of the crowded pews. Savoie had his arms crossed, and he looked as pissed off as he had been when we had last seen him. X caught Savoie glaring at him, and he glared right back.

"Think it's a good idea to get in a staring contest with a guy who wants to throw us in jail, brother?" I said, my voice low.

"Couldn't care less," X said. "That old bastard seems more interested in blaming punks than finding a killer."

I looked over at Savoie. "True enough."

At that moment, Mrs. Upton materialized, wearing all black. Two short men were at her elbows, there to make sure she didn't collapse, I guess. She looked frail beyond belief, a wisp, and she looked medicated, too. Before anyone knew what was happening, she suddenly let out a screech, pulled away from the two men, and dashed toward us. Everyone in the cathedral turned around as she pointed a shaking finger right at X's face.

"You killed him!" she shrieked, totally wild-eyed. "You killed my son!"

CHAPTER 11

Ah, Portland, you festering crap hole by the sea.

Two things are worth mentioning about Portland, Maine, U.S.A., I guess: its origins and its orderliness. Both of these things did not make it very hospitable toward something like punk rock, or people like X and me.

First, its origins: Portland was founded by Native Americans, of course, but later on, pink-skinned residents (typically) liked to tell themselves that they were the ones who "discovered" the place. In or about 1623, allegedly, a British naval officer was given a few thousand acres to start up a settlement on Casco Bay. The officer built a stone house, left behind a company of ten men to guard it, then returned to England to write a book about his experiences. The company of men was never heard from again. So said our PAHS history teacher.

For the next two hundred years or so, Portland was a fishing and trading village, and underwent a bunch of name changes. It also burned down at least three times, but — unfortunately, I say — was rebuilt each time. Thus the phoenix on the city's crest, and its motto: "I will rise again." Portland did, becoming a real town, with citizens and a municipal government and all that crap, when Maine became an official state, in 1820.

I hate, hate this place.

Having been founded and dominated by military forces for its first two hundred years or so, Portland has always been a law-and-order sort of town. Portland residents are always voting for right-wing get-tough-on-crime political douchebags, too, even though we actually don't have much crime. They generally tend to be more pro-police than the citizens of other American cities. It's part of their biology. Like herpes.

Have I mentioned I hate Portland?

Second, orderliness: If you look at it on a map, Portland looks like mud splattered all over a boot-shaped peninsula in Casco Bay. It looks messy from four miles up. But Portland was always preoccupied with order and was compartmentalized right from the start. If a couple guys who grew up in Portland met each other for the first time on the other side of the planet and exchanged their street addresses, the chances are excellent both would say, "I know exactly where you live."

East Bayside had a mix of Irish, Scandinavians, and industry, and was at the toe of the boot; at the heel was the West End. Portland's downtown, meanwhile, was home to Victorian residences and fancy-looking parks like the West End. It had wealthy parts and poor parts, like every city. Above it all, gulls constantly squawked and screeched and the downtown area always seemed to stink of fish. Fog was a constant, too, making everything look like a graveyard.

Running along the top of the boot, like an untangled lace, was Interstate 295, a fifty-three-mile auxiliary road that connects to Interstate I-95 in the north and south of the state. I-95 starts in Kittery, where my dad worked and lived, and ends in New Brunswick, up in Canada.

In Portland, there were neighborhoods where people had money — like the West End, where Sam Shiller and Luke Macdonald lived. But South Portland was pretty uniformly well off, too. For X and the rest of us, this created a bit of a philosophical problem. It was difficult to holler about the rich (as the Clash did), or favor anarchy (as the Pistols did), while living in the suburban splendor that was South Portland. It was really difficult to do it while getting to gigs in your mom's borrowed Volvo wagon (as the Upchucks did).

X tried to deal with all of these contradictions — Portland's militaristic origins, its orderly present, the relative wealth of our neighborhood — with what I referred to as "The X Philosophy of the World." It had three elements, but one of them was about the existential dilemma of being a punk in a place like South Portland.

The X Philosophy of the World decreed that human beings are flawed, so human institutions are flawed, too. "People are stupid, and they come together to do stupid things," X said, shrugging, when I asked him how a punk like him could still periodically attend Mass, as he did. "The Church does stupid things, but so does every other institution, group, government, union, or corporation. They are only as good or as bad as the people who make them up."

I didn't agree with him, but whatever. Trying to change X's mind was impossible, pretty much.

So, anyway, with X's theory, his home on Highland Avenue — in upwardly mobile South Portland, Maine — was no better or worse than any other place. Said he: "Living there gives us stuff to write about. It's like being under Republican rule. It gives us something to be pissed off about."

Maybe. Possibly. Anyway, the murders of Jimmy Cleary and Marky Upton gave the law-abiding citizens of orderly Portland, Maine, something to be pissed off about.

Unfortunately, us.

The murders whipped the media, and by extension, Portland's establishment, into a total fucking feeding frenzy. They went insane.

When Marky's mother screamed at X at the Cathedral of the Immaculate Conception, it basically marked the beginning of open season on Portland punks. In an instant, popular opinion had shifted, from sympathy for some oddball youth subculture thing to open anger, hostility, and hatred for us. The *Daily Sun* tabloid devoted front page after front page to crazy headlines about the made-up punk rock menace. One unforgettable example, published without a shred of proof, contained quotes from some anonymous "former punk rocker." It's headline read: "PUNK KIDS LINKED TO SATANIC CULTS."

What the fuck?

Other media pulled the same sort of crap. None of the reporters and editors appeared to notice, or care, that it was punks that had been the actual victims. It didn't matter to them. At both PAHS and PHS, more gloom descended, and members of the X Gang, Room 531, and the NCNA were targeted with lots of bullshit new rules, including ones that prohibited wearing or displaying anything to do with the punk movement. To ensure there was no confusion about the administration's new rules, the door to Room 531 was filled with discarded chairs and locked up to keep us from congregating there. The administration wanted the punk subculture to wither and die. Us, too, we suspected.

PAHS was an "alternative" school, and claimed in its glossy promotional pamphlets to be "a learning environment where students are encouraged to be creative, independent, and most of all — individuals." But following Jimmy and Marky's funeral, PAHS started a campaign to drive the punk rock menace out of its halls. In no time at all, those of us in the X Gang — as well as the NCNA and the 531 Club — were being pulled into meeting after meeting in the administration's first-floor boardroom. There, we were handed mimeographed rules describing strict new dress codes, codes of conduct, and even something called "education contracts."

At one of these totally fucked-up meetings, one of the school's vice-principals shot hate-stares at us, arms crossed, while X held the document like it was a soiled diaper. "An education contract?" he said, staring at the vice-principal. "Really?"

"Recent events have dictated some policy changes," the vice-principal said, arms still crossed. "Some of these sub-cultures, or whatever they are, have gotten out of hand."

X looked at him like he was a slug. "Wouldn't it be easier to just have us wear identifying badges?"

"What do you mean?" the vice-principal said, his features darkening.

"You know, like yellow Stars of David, or pink tri-angles," X said. "Preserves law and order, doesn't it?"

After that, X and I — along with the Upchuck sisters and a few others — were forced to attend "dialogues" with the Portland Board of Education's chief psychologist, Dr. Eugene Fogel. The encounters were to take place in the PAHS music room every Thursday afternoon for four successive weeks.

When we arrived for the first session, Dr. Fogel had placed the chairs in a circle, with his at the top. He was this little guy, and he stood there, his arms wide like a scarecrow. "Welcome," he said, beaming at us beneath a beard and John Lennon–style eyeglasses. "Let's get to know each other, shall we?"

Once seated, and after we grunted out our names, Dr. Fogel looked around, smiling some more. "Anyone know why we're here?"

"If you don't know," I said, "we sure don't."

Dr. Fogel raised his hands in mock protest. "Okay, okay, I deserved that," he said, beaming again. "But let's try again, shall we? Anyone want to take a stab at why we are getting together like this?"

"*Stab*," Patti said. "Really? *Stab?*"

Dr. Fogel looked flummoxed, and his smile faded a bit. Before he could speak again, X leaned forward. "We're here because the police, and this school, don't know what the hell to do, as usual." His voice was low, menacing. "So they want us to go through this bullshit exercise instead, in the hope that it'll help. It won't."

Dr. Fogel's smile looked more like a death's-head grimace, now. "You must be the one they call X," he said, sounding uneasy. "Why do they call you that?"

"Why does anyone call you a doctor?" X said. He then stood up. "This is a joke. I'm gone." And without another word, he walked out. After a few awkward moments, the Upchucks and I and the rest did likewise.

Dr. Fogel did not return.

While the administration's efforts to stifle us failed, other people sure didn't stop trying. Once off PAHS and PHS property, lots of punks were targeted with something else: fists and boots. Other students — mainly the jocks — took advantage of the anti-punk hysteria and lashed out. Beatings became routine and went mostly unpunished.

X and I were larger and therefore usually able to win fights, so the jocks generally kept away when we were around. But we couldn't be everywhere. Lots of kids, bruised and bleeding, started to wonder if all the trouble was worth it. Their parents angrily answered the question for them: No, it wasn't worth it. It was *dangerous*. "I don't want you to be the next victim," parent after parent said. "You are to stay away from this punk rock garbage until the killer is caught." So, more and more, they did.

A few days after the funerals, me and X stood shivering at the blue bus shelter nearest to PAHS, on Congress Street, where someone had scrawled "PUNK KILLS" on the window. "This sucks," I said. "What should we do?"

"Punk show," X said.

CHAPTER 12

In the beginning, holding a punk show had been simple. Ask bands to play, rent a PA system, put up some posters around town, and get someone to watch the door. Whether in Portland or London, the early punk shows were pretty easy to organize. Later, things got harder.

When the Sex Pistols started out, for example, nobody knew enough about them to object. So finding venues for Johnny Rotten and Co. wasn't impossible, and the Pistols played at places like London's 100 Club, the Marquee, or the Nashville. After the December 1976 Bill Grundy episode — in which members of the Pistols and their entourage appeared on a TV program called *Today* and hilariously called Grundy a "dirty sod" and "a dirty fucker" — gigs became a lot harder to arrange. "THE FILTH AND THE FURY," the *Daily Mirror* called it. After that, and after few more media-manufactured controversies, the Pistols were forced to tour as the SPOTS — that is, Sex Pistols On Tour Secretly.

Same thing sort of happened in Portland in 1977, although on a much smaller scale, of course. Back then, nobody knew what punk rock was, so booking a community hall — or a veterans' hall, or a Freemasons' hall, or a union hall — wasn't too hard. There was no stigma or whatever to overcome. By 1978, however, finding a venue had become harder. Word had spread, and the word wasn't good. Made-up media stories about the Sex Pistols throwing up in airport lounges, or the Clash getting arrested for acts of mischief, *blah blah blah*. And the photographs they printed with the stories usually didn't help: they made the punks look like homicidal maniacs.

Locally, things were not helped by some of the gigs that had been put together by us local punks. At one, an anti-police Riverton Community Center gig, someone kicked a hole in the drywall in the men's bathroom that was big enough to walk through. For fun, some idiots also smashed a couple toilets to pieces, sending water everywhere. X and I had to pay for the damages out of the draw at the door, and — when that wasn't enough — out of our own pockets.

Ah, the glories of rock 'n' roll.

Another notorious gig, at a veterans' hall just outside downtown, also added to punk's bad reputation locally. While there wasn't as much damage as there had been at Riverton, there was a police raid instead: the place was busted by hordes of cops for no fucking reason whatsoever. They charged in with police dogs, which sent nervous punks scurrying for the exits. Things were knocked over and broken. Another mess. More damages to pay for.

At that gig, one Portland cop hustled straight up to X's younger sister, Bridget, who was the most un-punk-looking kid there, and demanded that she spit out the gum that she was chewing — into his hand. Bridget, shocked, did. We then watched speechless as the cop brought the gum up to his nose and sniffed it repeatedly like a dog. He was looking for the odor of drugs, apparently. "Wow," I whispered to X, "good thing these morons don't carry guns or anything."

The police raids and the damaged rental halls caused us lots of hassles. By mid-1978, renting out venues had become basically out of the question. Gary's had started booking bands again, but it wasn't enough: only one or two could play there a night, and there was an occasionally enforced age limit. Younger punks couldn't get in very easily.

Where to go, and what to do?

Sam, Jimmy, Danny Hate, and I had come up with a solution. Because we all had (mostly) short hair — and because we all had access to thrift-store ties and jackets that (mostly) fit — we could pass ourselves off as young businessmen or even Christian missionaries. So we had fake business cards printed up at a place downtown. The cards advertised us as representatives of something called M and M Entertainment. Sam or Jimmy told booking managers that they needed a space for a "youth dance," and the stunt would almost always work.

The gigs were never licensed, of course. Only government-approved charities could get those, and punk rock was not in any way government approved. So punks were encouraged to bring their own booze, but in plastic containers to avoid broken glass all over the floor.

In 1977, then, gigs were pretty easy to set up; by early 1978, a bit harder; by late 1978, around the time of the murders of Jimmy Cleary and Marky Upton, finding a hall was virtually fucking impossible. With Gary's closed for the next few weeks, and with no one wanting anything to do with the scary punk rock menace, and with the media's punk rock panic spooking lots of people, the scene basically had nowhere to go.

So X, me, the Blems, the Virgins, and the three remaining members of the Nasties again got together in the basement of Sound Swap. We sat on the amps and rickety chairs and drank cheap beer that had been donated by Sister Betty. All of us agreed that a gig was needed if punk rock was to stay alive in Portland. But where? And how?

"I heard Gary's may be reopening soon," Danny Hate said. "Someone told me the cops gave them the go-ahead, so I guess they got their liquor license back."

"That's good," said Patti, "but we need to do something right now."

"Agreed," said Sister Betty. "But easier said than done."

X started noisily finishing off a Coke Slurpee, which — along with RC Cola or water — was pretty much all he ever drank. "We're going to do a gig," he said, looking in his cup as he stirred the contents. "And we're going to raise money for a reward — to catch the bastards who killed Jimmy and Marky."

CHAPTER 13

I've been typing this thing for most of the fucking night. So, I figure it's time I tell you a bit about my friend X.

X was born in the old Mercy Hospital in 1961, on a February day when a brutal nor'easter was howling down Spring Street. Story goes, his father, Thomas, suggested to his mother, Bridget, that the unforgiving coastal wind — arriving at the same time as their first kid — was some sort of good omen. "Try squeezing out a basketball and say that," his mother had apparently said. "Typical male."

His father laughed.

X was a big baby, nearly ten pounds. He was different in other ways, too: he didn't cry much, he slept for hours at a stretch, and he was nameless. For the entirety of his stay at the Mercy, three days, his parents could not agree on what to name him. The nurses, therefore, started calling him Baby X. It stuck.

But that wasn't why he called himself X, he told me. Not even *close*.

"Then it's about the twenty-fourth letter in the alphabet," I once said to him, reading off a list of guesses I'd put together in the PAHS library. "In math, it means unknown. Or a hidden treasure on a pirate's map. Or the number ten in the Roman system. Or Malcolm X. Or it means multiply. Or it's how you vote. Or negate something. Or some secret society. Or it's the symbol for the sun god Osiris. Or the witch symbol. Or porn. Or it's a placeholder. Or it's the X chromosome in genetics. Or it means strong. Or it's the cross. Or, the double cross for betrayal. Or it's a Christogram, representing Christ, like in Xmas!"

X sort of grinned, but he said nothing.

Bastard.

His mother was a nurse at Bayside's Maine Medical Center, on the other side of downtown, and his father had just been called to the Maine bar. They were penniless when they got married. So X's arrival — while good news — made life pretty complicated. For the first few years, the family didn't have much in the way of material possessions and all that.

At the start, X was so quiet his parents worried he might be deaf. They took him to a specialist at the Mercy, who was amused by their concern. "He's not deaf, he's quiet," said the doctor. "Be grateful."

His parents had met at a wedding. Bridget's cousin was getting hitched to Thomas's older brother, and Thomas was in the wedding party. At the reception, Thomas had also been asked by his brother to be the master of ceremonies. Bridget had laughed, uncontrollably, at Thomas's jokes — she was the only one who found them amusing —

and so he asked her out. She was beautiful and tall, he was handsome and tall, and they were both considered a bit odd by their respective families. He moved from Toronto, where he had only just been called to the Ontario bar, to be with her. That's true love — moving from a real city, like Toronto, to a shit hole like Portland.

"What were some of his jokes?" we asked his mom one night at the kitchen table.

"I only remember one," she said, snorting at the memory. "What's the difference between a lawyer and a jellyfish?"

"He asked that? So what's the answer?"

"One's a spineless, poisonous blob. The other's a form of sea life," she said, howling. "None of the other lawyers at the wedding thought it was funny."

Adults are weird, I thought to myself.

Anyway, Bridget married the Toronto lawyer at the Cathedral of the Immaculate Conception in 1958. He became an American after that.

Portland was conservative and religious; Bridget and Thomas were neither. Portland was suspicious of big government; Bridget and Thomas were both happily employed by government, she as a nurse, and he as a junior attorney with the U.S. Attorney's Department, District of Maine. Portland, like the rest of the state, was overwhelmingly white, Anglo-Saxon and Protestant; Bridget and Thomas, meanwhile, while also white, were super-liberal Catholics who cheered on Martin Luther King and the civil rights movement, always voted Democrat, and kept a small shrine to the Kennedys in the kitchen of their rental house.

Years later, their eldest son would carry on the family's progressive tradition, organizing anti-police concerts at the Riverton Community Center, not far from their first home. His sister, also named Bridget, came along in 1963; his brother, Michael, in 1965. The family needed more room, so they moved to Bayside in 1969, around the time that the city was expanding in all directions. By the mid-'70s, they were in South Portland, the suburban hell hole we would rip in lyrics written in our various bands. The "bland, satanic monoculture" of the place, as I put it in one tune, provided us with tons of material.

Anyway, that's X's family.

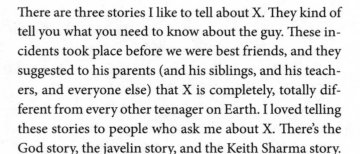

There are three stories I like to tell about X. They kind of tell you what you need to know about the guy. These incidents took place before we were best friends, and they suggested to his parents (and his siblings, and his teachers, and everyone else) that X is completely, totally different from every other teenager on Earth. I loved telling these stories to people who ask me about X. There's the God story, the javelin story, and the Keith Sharma story.

So, here's the God story.

In grade five, X and the kids in his class were assigned the task of writing a brief essay about their "relationship to God." The rest of his classmates all wrote up sunny first-person accounts about Heaven, in which God and Jesus were depicted as fatherly

Caucasian men. X (of course) did not. Without smiling, he painstakingly typed up his essay on his parents' Selectric and presented the thesis that God was a total sadist. "I believe in Him, but we should wonder if He believes in us," he wrote. "There is no other way to explain why He stands by and does nothing when we are killed by Nature or by each other. He must hate us. It is also possible that He is dead. I have nothing against Him, but I see no proof for Him, either."

The essay led to a lengthy summit between his parents, his Religious Studies teacher, the principal, the vice-principal, and even a child psychologist. X, from the school's perspective, was a problem to be fixed. Either that or he was possessed by Satan. "This is written at a level that is impossible for a child in grade five," said the teacher. "It is also blasphemy," said the vice-principal. All of them suspected that one of X's parents had written the essay. One said so.

"We did not!" said Thomas angrily. "And we can assure you that he reads and writes at a very advanced level. He has been writing a daily journal since he was in grade three. He reads what we read."

"What is he reading now?" the vice-principal asked, horrified.

"*A Portrait of the Artist as a Young Man*, I think," Bridget said.

"That is not suitable literature for a ten-year-old. It was on the *Index Librorum Prohibitorum* list for many years, in fact." The principal was pleased by his use of Latin.

"That's why he wanted to read it. And we'll make the determination as to what is appropriate, thanks," Thomas said. "Is this meeting over?"

Next up: the javelin story.

It happened in grade seven, in his first year at Holy Cross, the year we met. Dave Heaney was the only teacher there that he liked, and he urged him to go for the track team. So, X reluctantly showed up one day for the tryouts wearing cut-off jeans and a Karl Marx T-shirt. He was taller and leaner than a lot of the other students, and probably stronger and faster, too. We watched him as he totally dominated in every event in his age group that day — sprint, high jump, long jump, all of it. At the end of the tryout, the coach was basically begging X to join the team. We listened, sort of in shock, as X refused.

"But why?" the coach asked. "You're a natural!"

X shrugged. "Thank you, but I don't want to. You don't have javelin."

"None of the junior high teams do javelin," the coach said, exasperated. "What's so important about javelin?"

X pointed in the direction of the other students, as they continued running and jumping. "Animals can run faster than us, and jump higher than us," he said, impassive. "I want to do something an animal can't do." And with that, he walked back to his locker. When some of the rest of us discussed what he had said, we also lost enthusiasm for track, because none of us liked the idea of being beaten by an animal either.

Okay. Now, the Keith Sharma story.

This one also happened during seventh grade — just before X and I became buddies over the burning-the-school-constitution incident. Coming out of Holy Cross at the end of class one sunny afternoon in March, on a day when I was at home with the flu, X saw three grade eight boys beating the shit out of another grade eight student named Keith Sharma. They were at the far end of the schoolyard and surrounded by maybe twenty other students, all cheering. Keith was a Pakistani kid and one of only a handful of non-white students at our school. We all knew that Keith was frequently mocked, but none of us had ever seen something as bad as this. Throwing down his book bag, stripping off his belt, X ran up to the crowd of students, where some were actually chanting: "Kill the Paki! Kill the Paki!"

Without a word, without stopping, X plunged into the center, his belt wrapped around the knuckles of his left hand. He started punching the three grade eight guys who had Keith down on the ground. He slammed his fist into the backs of their heads, hard, and when they turned, he cascaded blows on their faces with everything he had. They pulled back, bleeding, shocked at this maniac grade seven, just as some of their friends grabbed at X's arms and hair.

Pinned down, X looked over at Keith, who — while also covered in mud and blood — was staring at X, shocked. "Run!" X barked at him, and Keith did. Fists started to rain down on X until Dave Heaney and another teacher ran up to stop the fight.

The next day in his office, beneath a huge, ugly crucifix they had up on the wall, the principal told X's parents and Heaney — while a bruised and silent X listened, expressionless — that the three boys who had beaten Keith had been suspended for three days. X would be suspended for three days, too, he said.

"Really?" X's dad said. "Those three little bastards beat that boy in a racial attack, and you don't expel them? Really?"

The principal waved his hands. "Language, language. And, yes, what they said and did was wrong," he said, in soothing tones. "But what your son did was wrong, as well."

"He deserves an award for what he did," Mr. Heaney nearly shouted. The principal glared at him.

X's father edged forward on his seat, furious. "I'm telling you right now, if you do not expel those three little monsters, I will contact my best friend, who is the editor-in-chief of the *Press Herald*, and I will ensure they write a story about how Holy Cross is indifferent to the presence of violent racists, and punishes those who oppose violence and racism. That's a promise."

After the three grade eights were expelled and X was at home serving his one-day suspension, he quietly said to his father, "Dad, I didn't know you were best friends with the editor of the *Press Herald*."

"I'm not," Thomas said, not looking up from the paper. "But in cases of extreme injustice, you are entitled to sometimes embellish the evidence."

X actually gave a rare smile. "I'll keep that in mind," he said. And he did.

CHAPTER 14

Next I guess I should tell you about our gang. The X Gang.

X and I met Jimmy Cleary near the end of our third year at Portland Alternative High School. It had been an insanely cold day in April, cold as fuck, and so Jimmy was actually wearing these blue long johns under Ramones skinny jeans with the knees totally gone. We could see the long johns through the kneeholes. It impressed us.

Over a white T-shirt, Jimmy also had on an over-sized men's white dress shirt, on which he had carefully inscribed "HATE AND WAR," in block letters on the pocket. This, we knew, was a song on the still-impossible-to-get first Clash LP, and the punk movement's unofficial slogan or whatever. Hippies claimed to be seeking "love and peace." Punks, meanwhile, saw hippies as a bunch of hypocritical liars. We figured that no matter how much you wanted peace and love across the universe, hate and war was all that was currently available, down here on Earth.

Jimmy Cleary, the newish kid, walked past us in the hallway outside the Social Sciences study area. His hair was short on the sides, a bit wavy on top, and on his feet were a pair of too-big army boots. He was pale and rail-thin, with a bit of acne on his Irish mug, but I thought he was actually kind of good-looking. I was surprised we hadn't really noticed him before.

We were near my open locker door, and I had taped a picture of the Clash on it, one I'd cut out of the *NME*.

"Hey," I said to him. Not friendly, not aggressive, just that. *Hey.*

"Hey," Jimmy said, slowing, wary.

I tapped the picture of the Clash and pointed at Joe Strummer. "That's the fucking Messiah, right there, man," I said.

"Hallelujah," said Jimmy, seeing Strummer and smiling. "Yes, he is."

We all became really good friends after that. Jimmy had moved to Portland from Boston with his parents and two brothers a few months earlier. His father was a doctor at the Mercy, his mother an artist. Like X and me, he considered himself a prisoner of conscience in the teenage gulag that is South Portland. "Welcome to the soulless suburban wasteland," I told him, which made him laugh, and which he later used in a Nasties lyric. Like me and X, Jimmy had been attracted to the stories and rumors about the early punk scene in New York City and London. He'd gone to Portland High for a short while, but transferred to PAHS when the beatings by punk-hating jocks became a bit too frequent.

At PAHS, jingoistic jock culture was also celebrated, but not as much as in other high schools. The only students considered to have real value — by most of the teachers and the administration, at least — were the jocks. The only ticket out of Portland, they thought, was professional sports, which, of course, was insane. The chance that any of these Led Zep douchebags would ever make the NFL or whatever was somewhere between slim and zero. They were, and always would be, lemmings.

At PAHS, the likes of me, X, Jimmy Cleary, and the NCNA gang had very few places to hide out. Most days, a dozen or so of us would occupy the windowless Room 531 and talk about music and poetry and art and politics, and never do any actual schoolwork. Room 531 had four walls, three tables, and eight chairs. Door at one end, blackboard at the other. That was it. But we loved it there.

Room 531: home punk home.

PAHS, meanwhile, sort of was and sort of wasn't home. While those of us in the NCNA were totally aware that we didn't fit in at any other high school, we were under no illusions about PAHS's bullshit claims to being a progressive place of higher learning that valued the individual, *blah blah blah.*

It wasn't progressive and it wasn't all that interested in the individual. "And the learning isn't all that higher, either," I said to Jimmy. From the outside, PAHS resembled a gray concrete factory, like just about every other suburban high school. With the difference that, at PAHS, you could move through courses (or fail in them) at your own pace.

The school's exterior had the architectural appeal of a medium-security prison, X liked to say, because it did. The walls were concrete slabs, and the few windows were long but narrow, too narrow to squeeze through. (Luke Macdonald had once tried, and gotten stuck, earning him a month of detentions.) Inside, there was a gym, an auditorium, and a cafeteria. The thing you noticed right away was that there were no classrooms to speak of, just rooms in which seminars were held, and which were filled with lots of trapezoid-shaped tables and uncomfortable metal chairs. Like prison.

Every morning at 8:30, we were expected to appear at our homeroom, where attendance would be taken by the teacher who was supposedly keeping track of our progress (or lack of it). The national anthem would be played and the Pledge of Allegiance would be mumbled. After this stupid morning ritual, we would then head to our various corners of PAHS. If we had a seminar to attend, we'd go to that. Otherwise, we'd hang out with our friends, almost always in the same areas, working on course modules called "units." The jocks had a spot, the geeks theirs, the drama and music students theirs.

The vast majority of the other students looked like clones, with their flared jeans, sweatshirts or T-shirts, jean jackets, and long, teased hair. The ones who could, grew mustaches. The girls wore platform shoes, and some of the guys did, too. From our vantage point in Room 531, the other students at PAHS were mindless, clueless conformists. They all listened to the same (bad) music, and they all took the same (bad) drugs, and they all thought and looked and dressed the same (bad, bad, bad).

They were, however, the majority, and those of us in the NCNA/X Gang were the minority. We, as a result, generally kept to ourselves. To the high school's ruling classes, we were "fags," "geeks," and "losers." Most of the student population despised the NCNA and the punks. That was okay, because we despised them right back.

"They're just lemmings," I explained to Jimmy the newcomer, as X listened. "They're lemmings, with their ridiculous Farrah Fawcett and John Travolta hair, and their recycled hippie clothing, and their single puny brain. It's a single brain they all share, so that they all do, and say, and believe, the same things, always. In five years, the girls will be popping out more lemmings, and the boys will be employed in some environment-killing industry, figuring out ways to make life less livable for the rest of us."

Jimmy laughed. "Is he always like this?" he asked X.

"Get used to it," said X. "He's just getting warmed up."

CHAPTER 15

Mike lit a cigar. "It feels like someone's trying to put you out of business," he said. "It's what the cops do to us."

X nodded and I shifted from one foot to the other. I was uneasy. We were in the last place I ever thought we'd be: Mike's crappy room above Gary's.

I looked around. There was a sweat-stained bed with a sleeping bag on it in one corner, a bedside table with a tower of true crime paperbacks balanced on it, and a small fridge and two-element burner in the far corner. On the streaked, shiny walls, there were these phantom rectangles where pictures had hung long ago. And, above the bed, Mike had tacked up an old *Easy Rider* poster, with a grim-looking Dennis Hopper and Peter Fonda motoring down a highway toward their fate. I hated that stupid hippie movie.

Opposite the door was one large, cracked window that looked out onto Brown Street. Across the road was a windowless brick wall that ran almost the entire length of the block. If Mike craned his neck, he could see Free Street to the left and Congress to the right. This was Mike's home, I guess, and X had come to ask for help.

The biker/bouncer examined the lit end of his cigar. "Cops in this town aren't so good at solving crimes, but they're really good at making your life a living hell," he said, sprawled out in his creaking easy chair. He grunted. "That's what they're doing to you guys. That's what they do to anyone who rides."

X was sitting on Mike's only other chair, borrowed from Gary's bar. He said nothing, so I spoke for the first time. "Doesn't make sense," I said to Mike. "It's our friends who were killed. We didn't kill them. But the cops are acting like we did."

Mike shrugged. "Maybe they think you did."

X waited a moment before returning to the reason for our visit. "So can you help?"

Mike squinted at X and then me. "For twenty percent of the door. You get the place, and you pay for our beer, and we'll do it. Okay?"

"Okay."

CHAPTER 16

Every big town, just about, has a punk house. Usually, a punk house is an abandoned place where bands play at parties or practice or whatever. Sometimes, when they can't afford a hotel, touring bands will stay there. Not as often, punk houses are places where punk zines are produced, or where independent, DIY record labels are based. Most of time, however, punk houses are just someone's rundown old home where the kids start squatting because they basically don't have anywhere else to go.

Portland's punk house, for as long as anyone could remember, was Coyle Street. Coyle Street was an actual two-story home, built by a shipbuilder's family during the First World War or something like that. It was located at 176 Coyle, just west of Deering Avenue, in Deering Center, in a stand of trees and overgrowth and right beside the railroad tracks. At one time, it was probably a pretty dignified affair, with yellow wood siding and ornate white trim. There was a nice balcony out front, and a big picture window looking out toward the street. The railway tracks ran north-south, from downtown.

It must have been pretty nice. But by the start of the '70s, Coyle Street was empty and rundown; by the end of the '70s, local punks were using it for parties or as a place to crash.

In 1978, no one lived at Coyle Street full-time. Punk kids would stay there for a day or two — three or four at the most — then move on. It wasn't heated and it had no electricity, so places like Sister Betty's basement were a lot better.

But Coyle Street was a big part of the local scene because it was kind of viewed as more faithful to the punk philosophy than a bar like Gary's. Gary's, as filthy and disgusting as it was, was still a money-making business — and it was the bikers' home first, not ours. Coyle Street was ours. It was also a bit like the punk movement itself: it welcomed the outcasts and the misfits, it was a creative and pretty safe place, and it was free. For a lot of us, Coyle Street became our safe Portland home.

But the Portland cops knew all about Coyle Street, too, and they didn't want us to treat it like it was our home. Every so often, officers would sweep down on the place, claiming to be following up on a noise complaint. The truth, of course, was that they raided Coyle Street because they hated our guts. So they'd drive some punks out onto the railway tracks, or arrest some of them, and tell them not to come back. City workers would come and hammer up some sheets of plywood over the doors, but those would be gone almost as soon as the police had left, used for firewood or added to the skate ramp out back, near the ramshackle two-car garage.

X's decision to hold the punk benefit show at Coyle Street was going to be tricky. We couldn't advertise it like we did with our other gigs — postering construction sites downtown, putting ads in high school and college papers, or making public service announcements on the University of Southern Maine's radio station, WMPG. If the cops found out about our plans too much in advance, they'd use force to shut us down. The media insanity that came in the wake of the murders of Jimmy and Marky had dropped off a little bit, but the general hostility sure hadn't. Portland's establishment — the police, the politicians, the educators — still wanted us to totally disappear. To X, to no one's surprise, it became super important that we didn't. The Coyle Street gig would need to attract enough punks to raise enough money for a reward — and to show everyone that the Portland scene was not dead. It would also need to be completely violence free, for reasons that were super obvious.

X and I debated all this as I piloted my battered Gremlin east toward Sam's house near the Promenade, where he and Luke and Eddie were waiting for us.

"Fuck, X, the cops will be on us like a fat kid on a Smartie," I said, when he continued to insist that the best venue was Coyle Street. "Can't we hold it outside city limits or something?"

"Sure," X said. "But I called around. Nobody will rent to us. And no bus companies will even return my call. So, even if we'd gotten a place, we'd have no way to get anyone there or back again. Coyle Street is the only option."

"So the Blemishes play, the Virgins play," I said. "Who else?"

"I called Moe Berg up in Toronto. He said the Modern Minds will come down for it."

"The Modern Minds? Wow, that's fucking awesome," I said, starting to warm to the idea. "So they'd headline?"

X shook his head. "No," he said. "We've got to send a message to show we're not going to just die, like they want us to. So the Nasties have to headline."

"What?" I said, looking sideways at him. "Without Jimmy? How can they play without Jimmy? They won't do it, man."

"That's why we're going to see Sam and Luke and Eddie," X said as South Portland slid by. "We're going to do this show for Jimmy and Marky."

CHAPTER 17

One week before the Coyle Street gig, the phone rang at X's house. It was a super cold Saturday morning; his whole family was at his brother's hockey game. No one was there except X and me.

X hated small talk, even with me, so he rarely used the phone. When it rang, he'd usually just ignore it. But that day, we were expecting a call from Mike about the gig, so he answered.

"Is this Christopher, uh, X?" a male voice asked.

"Who is this?" X motioned me closer.

"It's Ron McLeod from the *Portland Press Herald*. I'd really like to meet with you, if possible … you know, off the record. Do you have time?"

"Why?" X asked, concerned that a reporter had heard about the Coyle Street show, which would effectively kill it. "What do you want?"

"I've just got a few questions … as I said, off the record. Don't worry, I won't quote you anywhere. Plus, I've got some information that may interest you."

X said nothing for a long time.

"Are you still there?"

"Yeah, I'm here," said X. "I know what off the record means. But why should I trust you?"

"I can't speak for other media, and you obviously don't have to trust me if you don't want to," McLeod said, "but hopefully you realize I don't make things up like they do at the *Sun*."

"All of you make things up," X said.

He was silent again for a full half-minute. McLeod waited patiently.

"If we meet, I want to bring my friend Kurt. No witness, no meeting."

"Absolutely. No problem," said McLeod. "I actually wanted to speak to him, too."

Me?

That afternoon, X and I took the bus into town and met with McLeod in the cafeteria at the *Portland Press Herald* building, an old five-story, gray stone structure perched at the corner of Congress and Exchange Streets. A security guard escorted us upstairs, warily eyeing our black leather jackets, skinny jeans, earrings, and hair. McLeod was waiting for us when we got out of the elevator. He was short and balding, with a reddish mustache; behind his wire-rimmed glasses, his eyes seemed to be continually watching, evaluating. We had run into him before, briefly, at the funeral for

Jimmy Cleary and Mark Upton. He gingerly shook our hands and led us to the cafeteria.

On the table in front of him, he placed three note-pads, a couple copies of the *Herald*, a tape recorder, and a manila file folder.

X pointed at the tape recorder. "I thought you said this was off the record."

McLeod nodded. "It is," he said. "I don't need to quote you, anyway. I've got contacts with the police who are keeping me up to speed."

"Oh yeah?" I said. "So what are your sources saying?"

"A fair bit, I guess," McLeod said, flipping through one of the notebooks, "but I can't use a lot of it at the moment, because I can't get independent confirmation."

"So, what do you need us for?" X asked. "If you've got the cops talking to you, you don't need us."

"Because I don't think the cops know what to make of the murder of your friends," McLeod said. "I know it, in fact. They're under a lot of political pressure to solve this, but they don't seem to know where to start." He paused. "The punk scene isn't one they know par-ticularly well."

"Detective Murphy seems to be pretty clued in," I said.

"He's smart, a good guy," McLeod said. "But his part-ner's actually got more experience —"

"Experience at what?" I asked, cutting him off. "Being a total asshole?"

"Right," McLeod said, changing the subject. "Just a couple questions, okay? Were either of your friends religious?"

"Cops already asked us that," X said. "Most of us went to a Catholic junior high, for what that's worth. Why?"

McLeod opened the manila file in front of him, but held it in such a way that neither of us could see what he was reading. "Jimmy was found in a crucifixion position. That is obviously significant."

"Obviously. So?"

"So ... the cops haven't disclosed everything they know yet," McLeod watched us closely to gauge our reaction, "... particularly about Mark Upton."

We kept quiet, so McLeod continued. "The wound in Mark, it was in his side." He paused again, waiting for a response, but again, we said nothing. "Also, there was a bunch of barbed wire on his head. Like a crown."

"Christ!" I exclaimed.

X looked surprised, too, but he just sat glaring at McLeod. "What else?" he asked.

McLeod squinted at his folder. "There was some meat found defrosting on his, um, genitals," he said. "Pork apparently."

I felt like I was going to be sick. X looked down at the floor.

"I'm very sorry, boys," McLeod said. "But apart from the obvious references to Christ's wounds, I needed to see if any of that meant anything to you. Was, um, Mark Upton Jewish?"

We said we didn't know. Lots of Jewish kids went to PAHS, I told him.

"Well, do your bands have any songs with religious

references?" McLeod asked. "I've heard punks aren't generally too big on organized religion."

"That's true," I said, "but definitely not Jimmy's band, the Hot Nasties. They wrote songs about girls and being a teenager and stuff like that."

McLeod looked at us, expressionless. "Well, guys," he said, looking at his watch. "I don't know what to tell you. But I think you have done something to piss off someone who *is* big on religion."

CHAPTER 18

The Coyle Street gig was one of those ones that everyone in attendance would remember for a long time. It was like Lester Bangs's immortal words about what rock 'n' roll — or, in this case, punk rock — could attain if the circumstances were just right. Bangs had written this, in 1977, after seeing the Clash play:

> Nothing can cancel the reality of that night in the revivifying flames when for once if only then in your life you were blasted outside of yourself and the monotony that defines most life anywhere at any time, when you supped on lightning and nothing else in the realms of the living or the dead mattered at all.

It was afterward, and a medicated X was reading from his well-thumbed copy of Bangs's *Psychotic Reactions and Carburetor Dung*. He looked a bit stoned, something I had never really seen before. "That was the

Coyle Street gig," he said, staring off in space. "Supped on lightning, and nothing else mattered at all."

I looked at him, feeling a little uncomfortable. I mean, X was what a couple of years later would be referred to as "straight edge." In all the time I had known him, I had never, ever before seen him drunk or on drugs.

Me? I took plenty. But him? Never.

"It was quite a night, X," I agreed, still a bit weirded-out by his behavior. "It was definitely something else. Now, just take it easy, okay?"

After the bikers took less than their cut, the Coyle Street gig raised over a thousand bucks toward a reward for the capture of the killer (or killers) of Jimmy and Marky. Like X had hoped, it showed everyone that punk in Portland, while down, was definitely not out. It came off without a cop raid, or in fact any kind of trouble. Until the very end, that is.

The gig was more of a festival than an actual show, I think. The Virgins played, the Social Blemishes played, and others played, too — Toronto's Modern Minds, Bangor's Mild Chaps, Animal Kingdom plus the Sturgeons, the only all-black punk outfit in all of Maine. At the end, the remaining Nasties appeared for the final number, a rendition of the Nasties' traditional show closer, "The Invasion of the Tribbles." Things got emotional at that point.

For days, and as I had predicted, the Nasties had not wanted to play. Even after X and I asked them, Sam, Eddie, and Luke said it was too soon — and not right — to do any shows as the Nasties. "He was our best friend,"

Sam said. "He was the fucking heart and soul of this band. How can we go forward without him?"

So they did, but they also didn't. Sam, Luke, and Eddie, all looking pretty uncomfortable, showed up at Coyle Street surrounded by about a dozen hardcore members of the Nasties' fan club. They, like everyone else there, were dressed in all black.

X had asked everyone who came to the Coyle Street gig to wear black. To show that we were in mourning for Jimmy and Marky, partly, but it would also make it harder for the police or nosy neighbors to see the punks as we crept off the railway tracks and onto Coyle Street. The cracked windows had been carefully covered with boards, to keep light from seeping out, and then some old mattresses were brought in to line the exterior walls, to eliminate the possibility of a noise complaint. A makeshift stage was set up, on top of milk crates. On the walls, black flags.

To offset the December cold, X and I had rented some cheap portable heaters, powered by two big generators out behind Coyle Street's garage, where they were less likely to be heard. The PA and the amps were powered by the generators, too. As a fallback, me and Danny Hate had connected a series of long extension cords and quietly plugged them in to untended electrical outlets found on the neighbors' properties. No one noticed.

Without any advertising, I had worried that few would come. But by word of mouth alone — no posters, no ads, no PSAs on WMPG — more than three hundred punks showed up, some coming from as far as Boston and Montreal, to show support. The Modern

Minds, led by their resident genius, Moe, brought more than thirty Ontario punks with them alone.

As Sam, Luke, and Eddie stepped through Coyle Street's big front doors, X and me and the Upchuck sisters hustled over to greet them. "Thanks for coming, brothers," I said, shaking their hands, as Patti and Sister Betty hugged the three remaining Nasties. "We're going to have a good night."

And we did. The Mild Chaps took to the makeshift stage first, and all the young punks moved closer, clapping and whistling. The band's lead singer, a funny guy known as Conan, shook his wild head of red curls and hollered into the microphone. "Welcome to Coyle Street, motherfuckers! Tonight we make history!" He looked up to the manor's cracked ceiling and shook his fist. "Tonight is for Jimmy and Marky — we love you, boys!" And the band launched into their first number, a noisy punk rock version of the Monkees' "I'm A Believer."

At a Portland punk show, in the early days, some did the pogo, like British punks, jumping up and down like salmon swimming upstream to spawn. But, mostly, the local punks preferred slam dancing — which, like the name suggests, involved slamming into each other in a swirling, sweaty pit at the foot of the stage. Halfway through the Mild Chaps' set, it had gotten hot enough that the guys stripped off their black shirts and hoodies and danced shirtless. By night's end, some of the girls had even stripped down to just their bras, or nothing at all.

As the night went on, the bands played with total intensity and commitment — playing better than any of them had ever played before, I think. The walls of Coyle Street were shiny with sweat and condensation, as if they were alive. The floors heaved, too, almost at the breaking point, as dancing, slamming punks disappeared into their music, their friends, their moment.

Beside me on the stairs, X was surveying the scene, and I caught him with a bit of a smile on his face as he watched punks careening off the walls, off the mattresses — or off the tops of amps and onto the uplifted hands of their friends.

"Man oh man," he said quietly. "I love this world."

The draw at the door, with punks contributing whatever they could afford, was way better than we expected. Later on, during the Modern Minds set, Moe asked that some baseball caps be passed around. The hats were full of grimy, crumpled singles in no time.

Mike the bouncer showed up late with two of his unaffiliated biker friends, but they weren't really needed for security during the bands' performances. The punks wanted to avoid trouble, and everyone there wanted to avoid anyone getting hurt. It was that kind of a night: it was awesome. So Mike and his pals loitered by the door, keeping an eye out for the cops and knocking back a couple cases of Bud that X had brought for them. Once or twice, I saw Mike tapping a booted toe to some of the Virgins' set.

Around midnight, all of the bands crowded around the stage. There weren't enough amps to plug into, but it didn't matter. As the Modern Minds, the Virgins, the Mild Chaps, the Sturgeons, Animal Kingdom, and the Social Blemishes crowded around me and my battered

Fender, I turned to the crowd. I was soaked with sweat and felt happier than I had been in a long time.

"The generators are almost out of gas, and everyone's broken too many fucking strings, so we'd better make this one count," I hollered, my voice hoarse. And, at that point, Sam, Luke, and Eddie stepped forward, and the assembled punks erupted in a single roar of what could only be described as joy. I handed Sam my guitar, Eddie pulled up two milk crates beside Danny Hate's drum kit, and Luke joined me at the microphone.

"This one is for Jimmy and Marky! We love you, boys!" Luke yelled, and started the count-in to the three chords of "The Invasion of the Tribbles." At that point, Coyle Street went wild. The room was a sea of writhing, slamming, dancing punks, screaming the song's "oh yeah" chant louder than any of the guitars. I glanced up at X, still on the staircase, at one point. It looked like maybe, just maybe, he might actually get emotional.

As I watched, he turned and headed downstairs and over to the front door, past Mike and his friends. Mike, completely wasted, slapped him on the shoulder. The door opened, then quickly closed behind him.

That's when it happened.

CHAPTER 19

"You die tonight."

After he heard those words, and after the bat came down, X didn't remember much of anything. He would be left with a concussion, bruises over most of his body, cracked ribs, and two-dozen stitches to his scalp. The bat didn't kill him, but the three neo-Nazis did their best.

After X fell to the ground, the skins started kicking him with their steel-toed Docs, cracking the three ribs in the process. The bat fell repeatedly on his back and legs, producing what X called a wet cracking sound each time. He tried to shield his head with his arms and heard one of the skins yelling "Die, Jew" every time he delivered a kick.

With the final song over inside, a group of female punks stepped out of Coyle Street to share a joint and saw what was happening. They started screaming at the skinheads to stop. Their screams almost immediately brought Mike the bouncer and his two friends flying out the door. Right behind them, about thirty of us came pouring out of the house. Later on, I filled X in about what happened next.

"The skins were outnumbered, so the one with the bat and one of the others took off toward their car, which was a street over, down the train tracks. The third guy decided to stay and deliver a few more kicks to your back," I said. "That was a big mistake." Within seconds, Mike and his friends had tackled the skinhead and thrown him to the ground. "They were just wailing on him," I said. "It was awesome. Then, about ten minutes later, there were cops, ambulance guys, and about a million super-pissed-off punks everywhere. We figure a neighbor must have had heard the girls screaming and called the cops."

The area around Coyle Street was total chaos. The pumped-up punks wanted to exact revenge on the skin-head, now handcuffed and bleeding in the back seat of a police cruiser. "The cops told us they wanted to avoid a riot and get you both out of there. They promised us that you'd be taken care of, and that the skin would be head-ing to jail. So we moved back, and the ambulance took off for the Mercy. Patti was with you the whole time. Detective Murphy, too, later on."

"I don't remember them being there," X said.

"Yeah, they were," I said. "Patti was with you all night, with your folks. She was a mess."

X closed his eyes. "My head is throbbing," he said. The drugs were wearing off. "So who was the skinhead?"

"He won't tell the cops his name. Says he's John Smith, believe it or not, and says he lives at 88 Main Street."

"Does that mean something?"

"Yeah, it does, apparently. Danny Hate's cousin is into the whole skin/punk scene in California. Apparently some of the skins there are getting into the racist thing big-time. He says the eighth letter of the alphabet is H, and so 88 is HH."

"Heil Hitler," X said, slowly shaking his bandaged head. "These guys are the real deal, eh? Nazi skins in Portland."

"Looks like it," I said. "And that ain't all."

"What else?"

"Guess who's been leaning on him to get him to talk?"

"Murphy and Savoie?"

"Yep," I said. "They think it could be these guys who killed Jimmy and Marky."

X tried to sit up, but couldn't. He tried to shrug, but winced instead. "Fuck," he said. "I can't even shrug without needing those stupid fucking painkillers."

"What did they give you?" I asked, knowing X's aversion to any and all drugs. Also, swearing.

"They gave me stuff at the Mercy. Dunno what," X said. "My folks are making me take Tylenol 3s, but not for long. Not my thing."

"Dude," I said, "I know you are all against drugs and booze and all that, but seriously: those bastards almost killed you. You're entitled to some pain relief."

X shrugged again, and winced.

We heard the doorbell ring downstairs.

"What time is it?" X asked.

"Dunno. Eleven or so."

"It's the cops," X said. "My folks said they were coming. Want to talk to me."

We could hear the murmur of male voices. A minute later, X's father stepped into the room. "They're here," he said. "You still okay to talk to them?"

"Sure," X said. "I don't remember much, but I'll talk to them."

I stood up to leave. "Should I go? I already talked to them a couple days ago."

"I don't see why you can't stay, Kurt," X's dad said. "We'll see what they say."

When he came in, Savoie looked rumpled and haggard and stunk of cigarette smoke. He seemed to be wearing the same clothing he always did: unpressed pants, unpressed shirt, and a jacket that looked like it had come from a landfill. Murphy, for his part, seemed to occupy half the room with his mass. He was a big, brawny boy. He also seemed upset and was shifting from one foot to the other.

"Hey, Chris," Murphy said, all forced jocularity. "How you doing, buddy? You had us all pretty worried, there." Even Savoie nodded at that.

"Fine, thanks. Getting better," X responded. "At least I get to miss some school."

The detectives laughed, a bit too loudly, and looked for places to sit down. They settled on a desk chair and a borrowed Darius guitar amp. Both extracted notebooks. "Okay if we take some notes?" Murphy asked, looking up at X's father, who stood in the doorway. He nodded.

Savoie spoke first. "So, um, Chris, we understand from your folks you don't remember much," he said, sounding much friendlier than the last time they had spoken. "Is that right?"

"That's right," X said. "The bands were almost done, so I went outside to get some fresh air. I'd gone maybe forty, fifty feet toward the rail crossing when they let me have it."

"What happened next?"

"The big one, the one with the bat, called me a faggot and brought it down on the top of my head," he said. "They beat on me a bit. And then it all went black, I guess. Don't really remember anything else until I woke up in the hospital."

Savoie nodded, peering down at his notebook. "That's fine, that's fine," he said. "We have plenty of your friends who have given witness statements." He snorted. "First time any of them have cooperated with the police, I think."

Asshole.

Murphy frowned.

Then he spoke next. "Look, Chris," he said. "The guy we caught isn't saying much, so we wanted to see if you somehow knew him or his friends. All we have at this point is his name and his record."

"Who is he?"

Murphy extracted a small black-and-white mug shot photo from inside his leather jacket and handed it to X, who took a look, then showed it to me. The skinhead glared out of the photo, an SS lightning bolt tattoo clearly visible on one side of his neck. "His name is Peter Wojcik. No fixed address. Lots of arrests for assaults and break and enter. Born in Nebraska, drifted around the West a lot. Sometimes calls himself Nathan Forrest."

X stirred. "Nathan Forrest? Why?"

Savoie looked down at his notes again. "Nathan Bedford Forrest was the founder of the Ku Klux Klan, apparently," he said, sounding uncomfortable. "We don't know if this guy's a member of the Klan or not. He won't say anything, other than he's John Smith, and he gives a fake address. Seems to think this whole thing is funny."

"He won't find it too funny when we charge him with attempting to murder you … and the murders of your friends," Murphy said, clearly agitated. "He may be a minor, but he's looking at serious time as an adult."

Savoie looked down, saying nothing.

"What about the other two?" X's father asked. "Any leads on them?"

"Wojcik isn't talking. One of them, we have no idea who he is," Murphy said. "But the big one, the one who swung the bat, is probably a guy named Martin Bauer. Lives in Portland. He's known to police. Has a record for the same kind of stuff — assaults, B and Es, vandalism."

"Where is he?"

"We're still looking," Savoie said. "He lives in the East End with his mother, but no one's seen him for days."

Murphy looked at X intently. "Chris, do skinheads ever attend any of your gigs?"

"Sure, at the start, in '77 or so, skinheads used to come to the shows," X said. "In those days, they weren't all neo-Nazis. A lot of them were into bluebeat and ska."

Savoie looked bewildered. "What's bluebeat and ka?"

"*Ska.* It's kind of like Jamaican reggae, but a bit faster," I explained. "Better to dance to. Lots of punks are into ska and reggae and bluebeat. Before they went to the dark side, lots of skins were, too."

"The dark side?" Murphy asked. "Racism, you mean? When did that start to happen?"

I spoke up. "We've all noticed it. In the past year, maybe the past nine months or so, we've noticed that a lot of the skins had gone all white supremacist — insignias, white bootlaces, fascist salutes, the whole deal. Some are racists that just started dressing like skinheads. Some of the racist groups are actively recruiting skins as muscle. Maybe even the Klan. But I couldn't tell you what the groups are."

Savoie and Murphy scanned their notes. "Ever hear of something called Hammerskins?" Savoie asked.

"Think so," I said. "From some stupid Pink Floyd songs, right?"

"Right," Savoie said, looking again at his notes. "Two crossed hammers, shoot the Jews and all that." He paused. "Great entertainment, there. Anyway, these guys apparently call themselves Hammerskins."

"You ever see this Bauer creep or Wojcik at any of your shows?" Murphy asked.

We shook our heads.

Murphy gave a little pat to X's foot. He looked at Savoie, who shook his head: interview was over, apparently. "All right, thanks, guys. We just wanted to see if you knew something about these creeps — and also how you were doing, of course."

"Thanks," X said. "I'll be fine. Just find out who killed Jimmy and Marky."

"We think we already have," Murphy said, with conviction. As they got up to leave, Detective Savoie didn't look so sure.

CHAPTER 20

Down at the concrete bunker that was the Portland police headquarters on Middle Street, an officer who identified himself only as Constable Brown laid out the mug shots, which he called "packs," in front of X. I sat off to the side, watching. I couldn't see the photos, and I had been told to say nothing in case they needed me as a witness or something.

"I am doing this sequentially," Brown said, as if he had said the same thing a million times before. "I do not know who the suspect is, or even if he is in the photographs I am showing you."

Beside him on the desk, an old cassette tape recorder was whirring away, ready to record whatever X would say. Outside in the hallway, Detectives Murphy and Savoie were waiting with his father.

X was better, much better, than he had been just a week earlier. His broken ribs still caused him a lot of pain whenever he sneezed or yawned, and the headaches were more or less constant. But he was off the painkillers, and the bandages had been removed from his head. He would be back at PAHS, and back to sort-of-normal, soon enough.

X studied the photographs carefully. He told me later that all the photos showed young white men with shaved heads or close-cropped military-style hair. All looked like they were capable of assault, or worse.

X slid one away, then pulled it back. "This one," he said. "This one looks …"

Constable Brown said nothing. The tape recorder hissed, waiting.

"This guy," X said, holding up the photograph and showing it to Brown. I could see it, too, but said nothing. "I think this is him. It was dark, so I'm not totally certain. But I'm pretty sure this is him."

Impassive, Brown said nothing. He took the mug shot, looked at the back, and said into the tape recorder microphone, "The witness has selected number six."

That was it. As he put away the other photographs, he told X that he would be typing up a "verbatim account" of the lineup.

"Okay," X said. "I guess nobody can tell me if I picked the right guy."

Brown said nothing. He collected the cassette tape and the photographs, and stepped out of the interview room.

A minute letter, a beaming Detective Murphy entered, followed closely by X's father. "Well done, Chris," Murphy said, sounding relieved. He put a big hand on X's shoulder. "Thank you. You did great."

"Is it Bauer?" X asked.

Murphy settled into one of the metal chairs on the other side of the tiny desk, and waved for X's father to do the same. "I probably shouldn't say," Murphy said, throwing an elaborate wink at X, then at me. "But I can tell you that we picked up Bauer earlier this morning. His friend, too."

"Where were they?" X's father asked.

"At the border," Murphy said. "We got a tip. The two of them were on a Greyhound trying to cross into Canada near Newport. We think they were heading to Toronto."

"Have they said anything?"

"Nothing," Murphy said, "but they're being transported back here so we can question them. Now that we have all three, the DA will feel better about moving ahead with prosecution, even though they're minors."

"What does that mean, 'even though they're minors'?" I asked.

"Well, basically, criminal offences for young people are the same as they are for adults," Murphy said. "Except Maine law says we have to treat them as 'misdirected youth.'" He made quote marks in the air as he said this. "So there's a separate court system, a Youth Court, but because these crimes are so serious, and because they all have records, we think we have a good shot at pushing for adult sentencing." He paused, looking from Thomas to X to me. "And I think the charges will ultimately include attempted murder."

I was about to ask why Murphy felt the case against the three was so open-and-shut, but before I could, the door to the interview room flew open. It was Detective

Savoie. He looked at Murphy. "Murph, we gotta go," he said. "We've got another situation."

"Another kid?" Murphy asked, and Savoie nodded.

"He's not dead, yet, but he's non-responsive," Savoie said. "They pulled him out of Casco Bay. Nearly drowned. ID in his wallet says his name is Daniel something."

"Is it O'Heran ... Dan O'Heran?" X quietly asked, his voice sounding raspy, staring at them.

Savoie, Murphy, and his father all stared at us. Savoie spoke: "Yeah, I think that's his name. You know him?"

Danny! I'm going to puke. *FUCK FUCK FUCK.*

"Yeah," X said, rubbing his head. "He's one of our friends."

CHAPTER 21

Danny had been found near a pier in Casco Bay, not far from the tourist whale-watching boats that had been boarded up for the winter. By the time the detectives, me, X, and his father arrived, there were already three police cruisers parked by a boarded-up fried-clams place, the closest spot to the pier. Danny was found by a couple out walking their dogs. At first they'd thought he was dead.

The three of us remained in the back of Savoie's battered Oldsmobile. No one said a word. After the two detectives had conferred with the uniformed cops, Murphy returned to the car and opened the door. "He's in the ambulance on the way to Mercy. But we've got some Polaroids of the scene," he said. "You sure you still want to see them, boys?"

His jaw set, X slid out of the car. "Yes," he said. "I can do it. I want to help if I can." I got out behind him.

The uniformed officers looked up as we approached. X's dad walked between us, his hands on our shoulders. Near the pier, there were little markers on the sand, indicating where Danny's body had been. As we approached a line of yellow caution tape, one of the cops extended a handful of Polaroids.

We looked at them. Right away, we saw that it was Danny. His skin was unnaturally white, so his freckles stood out more than usual. Frost clung to his eyelashes. He looked like he was dead.

My God my God my God.

"It's him," X said.

"It's Danny," I said. "Is he dead?"

They shook their heads, but looked grim. We stood there looking at the photos a bit longer, while the gulls clattered above us, and then Murphy and Savoie ushered us back to the idling Olds. We all got in, and the detectives turned in their seats to look at us. X was staring out the window in the direction of the pier. "He was breathing," Murphy said. "But we think he was lying in the shallows for a while. We're all praying he'll pull through. Are you guys okay?"

"I'm fine," X said, his uneven eyes still on the pier. "This wasn't an accident."

Savoie and Murphy looked at each other. Sounding uncharacteristically human, Savoie said, "It could have been a suicide attempt, son."

"Suicide?" I said, pissed off. "That's total bullshit and you guys know it!"

X looked like he wanted to punch Savoie.

"Okay, okay, Kurt," Murphy said, in soothing tones, "Nobody knows what happened yet. We'll know more once the doctors have seen him, okay?"

"Right," Savoie said, rubbing his lined forehead with a nicotine-stained hand. "EMS says it looks like an accident and nothing more. But, given the fact that he was one of your friends, and part of this punk thing, we obviously have to seriously consider that it might be something else." He sighed.

"Nobody knows what happened yet," Murphy said, in soothing tones. "We'll know more once the doctors have seen him."

X turned and glared out at Casco Bay, which was black and surging, a living thing.

"How long had he been there?" I asked.

Savoie shrugged. "Hard to say, exactly. If he recovers, he'll tell us. I don't know."

These guys are making it up as they go along.

"You've had this Wojcik guy in custody since the Coyle Street gig, right?" X said. "And you say Bauer and the other guy were picked up at the Canadian border just this morning?"

"That's right," Murphy said. "We don't know yet if they left town early this morning or late last night. We'll know soon enough."

X turned to look at the detectives, unblinking, and said, "Then there's no way they could have done this. The border's hours away."

Murphy was about to speak, but a scowling Savoie interrupted. "Leave all that stuff to us, okay? Let's just get you and your dad home. We'll call you when we have something to pass along, okay?"

"That sounds like a good idea," Thomas said. "Let's go home, boys."

X didn't say a word all the way back to South Portland. I kept quiet, too, super pissed off that anyone could even think that Danny attempting suicide was even a possibility.

When we arrived at X's place, we found the Upchuck sisters and Sam Shiller waiting for us in the living room. Betty'd been crying, Sam couldn't speak, and Patti looked like she wanted to hug X, but didn't. X, meanwhile, was angrier than I think I'd ever seen him. After his dad went upstairs, he finally broke his silence.

"They got to Danny," he said quietly, looking at us all intently. "He may not make it. And the idiot cops are going to claim he tried to kill himself, just watch. So, enough is enough. We need to deal with this ourselves. Okay?"

We all nodded. But I, for one, didn't know what he meant.

Yet.

I'd find out.

CHAPTER 22

It was night at the old Greyhound station at the intersection of Congress and Valley Streets.

The bus station was an unmitigated dump. Single-story, built in the '50s, the floors were grimy, the walls were grimy, and the air reeked of grimy diesel coming from the buses idling outside in the three bays. Across the street were a shitty strip mall and a few rundown clapboard homes. The area was pretty crappy, but we actually liked it. That fall, before Jimmy Cleary was killed, the X Gang relied on the Greyhounds to follow the Ramones around New England. It had basically been like a religious pilgrimage for us, to see Da Brudders. So we knew the station pretty well — riding buses, as we did, around Connecticut, Rhode Island, New York, Massachusetts, and wherever. We'd see a show, and then we'd crash in a youth hostel. It was an amazing time, but now it seemed like a long time ago.

X and Patti and I sat on an unoccupied stretch of bench in the dimly lit station. The attempted murder of

Danny Hate — because that's what it clearly was, not a fucking suicide attempt or an accident — had hit me the hardest. He was in my band, ya know? I couldn't eat, couldn't rest, I couldn't do anything. But I also didn't want to be alone, so when X said he and Patti were heading downtown, I told them I wanted to come.

Quietly, X and Patti examined a copy of Greyhound's New England schedule. I was exhausted, so I just watched them, unsure what X was up to.

They don't actually think they can solve this all on their own, do they?

"Okay," Patti said. "Newport, Vermont, is pretty far north of here. Takes about three and a half hours to get there, at least. That's with no stops."

"There's a bus just before seven at night, and one just before noon," she continued, tracing a black fingernail along a column of departure times. "So, I don't understand how …"

"So," X said, "Bauer and his friend had to have left town last night, or even yesterday morning."

"And Sam and Luke were with Danny at Matthew's two nights ago," she said. "That's the last anyone saw him. So, Bauer and the other skinhead could have gotten him that night …"

"No way," X said. "No way. Danny's a big guy, but his parents are very religious and super-protective. They wouldn't have gone two nights without calling around to see where he was. No way he was gone that long."

"Yeah," Patti said. "I tried calling them, to offer support or whatever, and they hung up on me."

I stirred, my head pounding. "What are you getting at, guys?"

Neither of them said anything for a bit. "Someone tried to kill Danny yesterday, Kurt," Patti said, "when it would have been pretty difficult for that big skinhead, Bauer, to do it."

"Impossible for him to do it," X said. "He and his buddy were already on that bus on their way to the border. Or they were already crashing near there, getting ready to cross the border. But there's no way, none, they could've done it. No way. And there's no way Danny could've been lying in the water for that long without being spotted." X shot a glance at me. "There's no way Danny could have been there that long and still be alive."

"Couldn't some other skinheads have done it?" I asked. "Maybe there are more of those pricks in Portland than we know."

"It's possible," X said. "But having a shaved head, a bomber jacket, and a pair of Docs would make you pretty easy to spot, even by a Portland cop." He paused. "But the cops sure seem pretty eager to charge these three guys for the murders and be done with it."

"One youth subculture goes after the other," Patti said. "End of story. Neat and tidy."

"Right," X said. The two of them said nothing for a while, looking around the station, as I waited.

I felt like I was going to puke.

Even if they were right, who was going to listen to them? Who cared what some teenage punks thought?

While Patti was facing the bus station's double doors, I saw X steal a look in her direction. I'm not into girls, but I can tell you this: she had the face and body of a model. Her dyed-black hair had been backcombed, though, and she kept it aloft with what Sister Betty called "punk rock hair gel" — moistened bar soap. Her make-up was like the girls in the Slits or Siouxsie Sioux or Soo Catwoman — an abundance of black liner around the eyes and a slash of deep red lipstick across her mouth. Under her oversized PUNK ROCK VIRGINS army surplus jacket, she was wearing a studded leather belt, ripped skinny jeans, and an Eagles T-shirt, over which she'd written, in black marker, "I HATE." On her feet, she wore knee-high Docs. She looked totally amazing.

X suggested we head to Matthew's to get something to eat, and offer a toast for the speedy return of Danny O'Heran. "Maybe someone there saw something un-usual, when he was there with Sam and Luke," he said, pocketing the Greyhound schedule.

I drove, and we headed east to Matthew's on Free Street. On its blue canvas awning, Matthew's billed itself as "Portland's Oldest Bar and Restaurant, est. 1872." It was really just an old man's bar, a dive, much like Gary's, but in better shape and with an arguably better clien-tele. It was across from a vacant parking lot and near the abandoned Chamber of Commerce building.

Most Saturdays, especially in the summer, the X Gang would gather there around lunchtime to eat chicken and chips and down a cheap draft or three (or, in X's case, RC Cola). The bands who played there were country and western, not punk, but no bikers were there to give us a hard time. If any bikers or rockers were around, they would usually be at the Big Easy, farther down by the water.

The chicken and chips at Matthew's were much loved in the Portland punk scene. The Polish-born Blitt brothers, who had owned the place for decades, bought big baking potatoes and fresh chicken from some Mennonites who lived an hour or so out of town. The Blitts would batter the chicken and chips, then pressure-cook them in their basement bar. For $2.25, we'd get a heaping paper plate of food and a safe place to hang out. Most of the time, Matthew's was frequented by old vets, old Native American men, and old country-and-western fans. Nobody bothered with us as we devoured our food at the long table near the back stairs.

I was starving. As we got settled in, a grizzled veteran sitting at the next table, Roy, introduced himself. He started chattering amiably with Patti. As X and I got up to order the food, he said to her, "You're a beauty. That boy should ask you to marry him!"

Patti and I laughed.

X and I returned with the grub, the sodas, and a few drafts — two of which X donated to a grateful Roy. After we ate, Patti slumped back her chair. "I needed that," she said. "I haven't been eating much lately."

"Me neither," X said.

I continued to pick at mine, saying little.

"Have you guys heard anything about Danny?" she asked.

"Nothing," I said. "Spoke to one of his brothers. No visitors, still in coma. Induced. They moved him to the Maine Medical Center."

Patti gazed at X, hesitating, as if she wanted to say something and couldn't, probably because I was there. I took that as my cue to go to the can.

Hi, I'm Kurt, the fifth wheel.

Now, here's the thing: nobody, with the possible exception of me, ever asked X personal questions. To the 531 bunch, to the NCNA, even to the X Gang, he remained this totally mysterious presence. Because X usually spoke so little, and because he never really revealed what he thought — except in his essays in the pages of *The NCNA*, all of which Patti could practically recite by memory —X was always an enigma wrapped in mystery. Even to most of his friends (except me, I guess).

I think Patti had adored him, and possibly loved him, since the first time she spotted him at an early Blemishes show. He was escorting his little sister, Bridget, around the all-ages gig we'd helped organize at the Southern Maine Community College. X was doting on Bridget, listening to her, and sticking with her wherever she went. I remember Patti stood near X and Bridget and me, at one point, and I also remember she could not stop looking at him.

X caught her looking, and she flushed. "Excuse me," he finally said to her. "I don't want to impose, but I was wondering if you would mind taking my little sister into the washroom."

"Yes," she said, quickly.

"Yes, you'd mind?" he said, as me, X, and Bridget looked at her.

"No, no, no," Patti said, waving her hands. "No, I wouldn't mind. Yes, I'll take her."

That was the sum-total of their first conversation. A few days later, they met, more formally, in the Language Studies area at PAHS. In no time, X was urging Patti to form the Virgins and play some gigs. "The scene is too male," he'd said. "We need some pissed-off feminist punk bands." She, for her part, helped us with publishing and distributing *The NCNA*, setting up gigs, or whatever else we asked her to do.

So, they had been friends for almost two years. In all that time, I know for a fact that he had never touched her, much less made a move to kiss her. During the Ramones tour in the fall, we couldn't find space in the hostel in Amherst. So X had rented a no-frills hotel room for Patti and Sister Betty, and he and I crashed on the floor near the door. The next morning, while X showered and I watched *The Flintstones,* Betty looked at her sister. "Holy crap, you are totally in love with him," she whispered, but I heard her over the sounds of Fred and Barney.

"Holy crap, I totally am," Patti had whispered back.

Breeders. Lovable, but so, so ridiculous.

Anyway, I kept killing some time in Matthew's shitter. Much later on, Patti would reluctantly tell me how that historic conversation went.

"Hey," Patti had said, going for broke. "Can I ask you a personal question?"

His picked-over chicken leg hovered in the air, momentarily, but X didn't look up. "Depends," he said, "what the question is."

Flustered, Patti sipped at her draft, trying to summon up the courage to speak. "It's ridiculous," she said. "Never mind."

X finished with the chicken leg, sat back in his chair, wiped his mouth on a paper napkin, and looked at her. "No, please," he said. "Ask away."

Patti was feeling profoundly uncomfortable. "It will make me sound stupid," she said. "It will make me sound like a dumb female."

"I doubt that," X said, and Patti thought she could see a faint smile on his face.

"All right, then," she said, busily rearranging the glasses on the table. "Why haven't you ... why haven't you ever made a move on me?"

Long pause.

"Like this?" he said, and he abruptly stood up, leaned over the table, and kissed her on the cheek, then on the lips.

X then sat back, watching her. She looked like she couldn't speak. Like she was in shock.

Roy, who was still sitting at the next table, gave them an enthusiastic thumbs-up. "Way to go, son," he hollered. "She's a keeper!"

CHAPTER 23

The Upchuck sisters, née Kowalchuk — all four of them — were a pretty rare example of East-West reverse migration. Meaning, they all started out in sunny and warm California and ended up in cold-as-fuck Maine. Usually, Maine residents move somewhere else, looking for work or better weather. Very few Californians, as far as I know, ever move in the opposite direction. So, the Kowalchuks were pretty unusual, in more ways than one.

Pretty crazy, actually.

All four of the Kowalchuk sisters were great beauties. The eldest two had left home to get married or attend Boston U. Patti and Betty were the youngest and a lot less conventional than their older siblings. From an early age — in Menlo Park and then in South Portland — Patti and Betty stood out from the crowd.

Patti and Sister Betty always told me everything, by the way. Half of the stuff I know comes from them, in fact.

Betty was Sister Betty, as I had called her — bringing home strays, fundraising for charities, volunteering for food hamper deliveries for seniors. Betty was the one who loved to dance and laugh and go to parties. Patti, mostly, did not. She was quiet and sometimes a bit of a loner, like X.

Everyone knew that Patti was tall and beautiful — but not as many people knew that she hated being tall and beautiful. She was the smartest of the sisters but, whenever possible, she hid her IQ. Until punk rock happened, and until she and Betty and Leah formed the Punk Rock Virgins — and until she met X and me, I guess — she had considered her life to be a downward spiral.

The summer before she started at PAHS, she was sexually assaulted. I was the only one she ever told, she said. She confided in me one night at the tail end of a drunken basement party at Luke Macdonald's place.

She had been working three nights a week at Taco Bell at the Maine Mall. It was a hot Friday evening in July, and she had agreed to work until closing. Not far from the tollbooths leading to the turnpike, at the edge of the darkened parking lot and some trees, Patti waited alone for the bus. Two clean-shaven young guys who she had served earlier in the evening drove up in front of her as she sat on a bench, where she was reading some Vonnegut. They tried to engage her in small talk; when she didn't respond, they got out and grabbed her and pulled her into their van. While one stood outside, the other one raped her. When he finished, they switched places.

Afterward, they ordered her to put her Taco Bell uniform back on and clean herself up, and then pushed her out of the van. They drove north, toward the airport, and she could hear them laughing as they went. She was just sixteen.

Patti didn't scream for help, or call the police or her parents, or even Betty. Instead, she continued waiting for the bus, gasping for breath, and went home. She hid the blood on her uniform with her backpack.

Patti slipped in through the garage, went upstairs, and took a shower that lasted until the hot water ran out. She then went to bed and stared at the ceiling, weeping without making a sound. She never told anyone what had happened to her. Not until she told me, at least.

For the next few weeks, she spent all of the money she earned at her part-time job on drugs and home pregnancy tests. By late August or so, she knew that she was not pregnant. But, by then, Patti had a pretty impressive drug problem.

She bought weed from a coworker, but it didn't do what she needed it to do. So she started regularly popping mushrooms, or dropping acid, or — when she didn't have money — sniffing some glue she found in the garage. Twice, she told me, she tried crystal meth, snorting it.

She stopped washing her hair as often. She started smoking. She chose to wear lots of makeup, enough to get her mother to ask her why she was "covering up a beautiful face with paint." But covering up was what Patti wanted to do. She wanted to atomize, she told me, and fall between the blades of grass on the front lawn.

At PAHS, in her first year, her drug use dropped off a bit — mainly due to a lack of income — but she made no effort to know anyone. In the first half of that year, when she was thinking about running away, a British cousin sent her a bootleg tape of the Slits performing on the Clash's 1977 White Riot tour. She played it over and over; it electrified her. She went looking for stories about the Slits in imported copies of the *NME* and *Melody Maker*.

The Slits were all beautiful women, but they deliberately covered their faces with makeup. They all were hip as hell, but they wore baggy, mismatched clothes that made them look like androgynous circus freaks. They were theoretically part of the male-dominated music business, but they wrote and performed songs about being girls, and the idiocy of men. Patti adored them, and wanted to be like them, however possible. With her saved Taco Bell holiday pay, she bought an old Fender Stratocaster copy and a tiny cube amp at a pawnshop downtown. She started writing songs, some only a minute in length, about being a girl. Inspired by what her sister was doing, Betty found an old bass guitar at a garage sale, and soon they were playing together in a corner of the basement of her family's home. For the first time in a long time, she started to feel better.

It was around mid-year, as punk rock (in general) and the Slits (in particular) were making her feel alive again, that she encountered X at the Southern Maine Community College all-ages show, and met him again a few days later, when X and I were sitting in PAHS's

Language Studies area. She was only there to pick up a unit in a course in which she had fallen behind.

After she was sexually assaulted in the mall parking lot, Patti ignored any guy who exhibited interest in her. One time, she experimented with a girl she met at the mall's lone cinema, at a late-night showing of *The Rocky Horror Picture Show*. They kissed and groped each other as the movie played. But Patti told me that she had no interest in taking it any further.

X and I were both seated at one of the stupid trapezoidal tables, not speaking, reading. Patti later told me she thought we were tall and tough looking and, with leather jackets draped over the backs of our chairs, had this amazing wordless fuck-you thing happening. That day, I was wearing a sleeveless shirt with ska-type black and white checks on it, she said. "X, meanwhile, was long-haired, and so fucking gorgeous, and he was wearing a white T-shirt on which he had expertly recreated the Clash logo, in these brilliant blue letters. You guys looked so amazing, that day."

It's true. And I usually look amazing, truth be told.

She was walking past, casting surreptitious glances at X and his shirt, when he suddenly looked up. "Hi again," he said. I looked up, too.

"Hi," she said, looking awkward, hesitating. She pointed a finger at X's shirt. "The Clash. Nice!"

X's uneven laser-beam eyes were on her now, and Patti looked like she wished she hadn't said anything. She waited for him to speak. Finally, he did, as I looked on, grinning.

"You a fan?" X asked.

X Test.

"Of the Clash?" Patti said, knowing that X could only be referring to the Clash, but realizing that he might think she was a fan of something else. Like, say, him. "Of course. I like them."

By this point, I had turned over my book, crossed my arms, and was totally enjoying the exchange.

"Got any of their stuff?" X asked her. *Another test.*

"Yes," she said, then shrugged. "But I like the Slits better."

Wow.

I was surprised that she knew about a still-pretty-obscure British punk band. She now had our full attention. We looked at her. "You know the Slits?" I asked her. "Really?"

"Yeah," she said. "I've been listening to them for a while."

We looked at her some more, and then we both stood up. X extended a hand.

"I'm X," he said. "This is Kurt Blank."

CHAPTER 24

The bail hearings for the two skinheads, which most of us attended, took place three days after Bauer and his buddy Dragomir Babic were brought back to Portland by some border services officers. Babic preferred the street name Hess — as in Rudolf Hess, Hitler's deputy führer. Like Wojcik before them, the two skins refused to say anything to anyone, including the idiot defense counsel who had been assigned to them. At their hearing, the two stood when the bail commissioner entered the courtroom, and then gave him a bloody Nazi salute.

Seriously.

This caused a big stir, naturally, and persuaded their idiot attorneys to put off the bail hearings for another three days.

The charge was assault causing bodily harm, for the attack on X. Missing, however, was the charge of attempted murder, as Detective Murphy had promised. Also left unsaid was any news of charges for the murder of Jimmy Cleary and Mark Upton, or the attempt to murder Danny O'Heran. The Portland punk scene, which turned out in full force at the bail hearings, was massively pissed off. A couple punks voiced their anger and were escorted out of the crowded courtroom by Portland police, who were also there in great numbers. The two dissenters flipped the cops the finger as they were hustled out.

Not present in the courtroom was the victim — X — or the main witnesses to his assault — Mike the biker and his two unaffiliated biker friends. All were expected to testify at the trial. Despite the lack of murder charges, Detectives Murphy and Savoie, and their police chief, did their best to make sure that every frigging reporter in Maine was there for the bail hearing. They told the media, anonymously, that "more charges were pending" — which most of us took to mean murder charges.

So, of course, just about every reporter in the state had obediently filed into the second-floor courtroom at the old, gray stone Portland district courthouse on Newbury Street. Something like four TV crews waited in the cold outside, and killed time by shooting footage of the exterior and the big stone columns out front. Inside, their colleagues checked their hair and waited for something to happen.

In a waiting room in the courthouse basement, X sat with his father, me, the Upchucks, and his sister, Bridget. His dad explained the process to us as we waited. "There are really only three grounds for detaining someone," he said. "To ensure the attendance of Bauer and his friends in court. To protect the public. Or to help maintain confidence in the justice system." He paused. "I'd argue, in this case, Bauer meets all three criteria. There's no way he's going to be granted bail, even if he hasn't been charged with any of the murders."

"Do they have to prove their case at a bail hearing?" I asked.

"It's not a trial. The DA only needs to show they have a case on the balance of probabilities, not beyond a reasonable doubt. For that reason alone, I don't see Bauer going anywhere anytime soon. There are too many witness statements from your friends, and he's got a record of violence. Besides, he may consent to staying in jail."

"Why would he do that?" X asked.

"If he knows he's unlikely to win, he'll probably get credit for time served. I also suspect he fears that some of your friends may come looking for him, if he gets out. It's probably safer for him to stay incarcerated."

"I'd say that's definitely true," I said.

X gave a little snort. His dad looked uneasy.

The door to the waiting room opened and Detective Murphy stuck his head in. "They're bringing Bauer up," he said, quietly. "Thomas, you're free to come up, as well as the girls, but obviously not you, Chris, as I explained ..."

X's dad, Bridget, Patti, and Sister Betty followed Murphy out. I decided to stay with X. We slumped back in the uncomfortable wooden chairs. "How's your head, brother?" I asked.

"Getting better," he said. "Could live without all this crap, however."

"I hear you. So, any idea why they haven't charged these guys with the murders yet?"

X put his Converse-clad feet up on a chair and shrugged. "I don't think these bastards could have tried to kill Danny. Jimmy and Mark maybe, but not Danny. They weren't even in town. So, if they didn't go after Danny, maybe it creates reasonable doubt that they killed the others." He paused, thinking. "There's got to be another reason, though. The cops and the DA just aren't saying."

I shook my head, disgusted. "Okay," he said. "Then why not at least fucking charge them with attempting to murder you?"

X shrugged again. "Hate to disappoint you, man, but I don't think they were. I mean, even the stupidest bone-head would know not to commit a murder twenty feet from where hundreds of pumped-up punks were party-ing. There's no way."

A few minutes clocked by. We waited in silence. Sooner than expected, the door pushed open again. It was X's father, followed by Bridget and the Upchuck sisters, all looking confused. They sat on the available chairs. "What are the fourteen words?" X's dad asked us.

"The what?" X asked, sitting up. "Why?"

"Because Bauer came in, and all he said was that he was going to say 'the fourteen words,'" his dad said. "I wrote them down."

He read off a scrap of paper: "'We must secure the existence of our people and a future for white children.' And then he sat down, and he didn't say anything else."

X's dad took us to a door on the south side of the court-house, away from where the media were hanging out. "Here you go," he said. "Head out this door, and then you can jump on the bus and get back home. I'll go out the front with Bridget and the Kowalchuk girls, and then I have to get back to work."

"Thanks for coming, Dad," X said. "We really appreciate it."

He patted us on our backs and headed in the direction of the interview room. We pushed open the court-house door and stepped out into the cold. Stomping his feet, waiting for us, was the *Press Herald*'s Ron McLeod. "Hey, guys," he said. "When I saw your dad in court, I figured he'd know the back exits." He gave a self-satisfied grin. "Can I buy you lunch? Coffee? Tea?"

X and I looked at each other, considering. As he had promised, McLeod actually hadn't used anything we discussed during our earlier meeting. And unlike any of the other stupid reporters, McLeod actually hadn't written anything that was too sensational. We didn't exactly trust him, but we didn't *dis*trust him yet, either. "All right," X said. "Where?"

McLeod took us to a Dunkin' Donuts a couple blocks west, on Congress. The old coffee shop provided a place for lawyers to meet clients who were uncomfortable talking in the courthouse. It was a pretty good hideout for stoned teenagers who were skipping school, as well, and a respite for homeless people who had nowhere else to go when it got cold. After McLeod had paid for our drinks — vile coffee for him and me, herbal tea for X — we sat at a table far from everyone else, at a window over-looking the street. McLeod pulled out his notebook from his puffy, down-filled LL Bean jacket, then focused most of his attention on his doughnut, which was covered in sprinkles. "So," McLeod said. "I would expect you're full of questions."

"You could say that," I said, putting down my coffee. "Why haven't they charged any of them with something more serious than assault? Why haven't they charged them with murder, or at least attempted murder?"

McLeod kept eating his doughnut. He didn't even look up. "Because they didn't kill anyone," he said matter-of-factly.

X nodded, agreeing.

"How the hell do you know that?" I said, annoyed. "Why put on this big media circus, and then not bother to charge anyone with anything that's important?" Then I remembered the assault and the stitches in X's head. "Sorry, brother," I said.

"No probs," X said, carefully extracting the micro-scopic tea bag from his cup.

"That's a very good question, actually," McLeod said, peering up at me above his wire-rimmed glasses. "Why oversell the bail hearings, and then deliver so little? The cops' answer might be to hint that more charges are com-ing, which is what they've been doing all along. But I don't see how they can ever charge these three with murder.

And I hear the DA doesn't think they'd get convictions if they tried."

"What does Savoie think?" I asked. "What does Murphy think?"

McLeod waggled a finger in the air, as if he was giving a lecture to two bright students. "Again, a good question," he said. "Savoie and Murphy aren't of one mind on this case, from what I hear. There's quite a difference of opinion down at police headquarters, in fact." He looked at X through his thick glasses. "Savoie is the doubter. But Murphy apparently wants to hang the skinheads for what they did to you, with or without a trial. Or so he tells anyone who will listen."

We waited, saying nothing. After a bit, McLeod delicately inquired about X's well-being and asked about the mood within Portland's punk scene. But, apart from those questions, he didn't ask us anything else. We could tell he knew more than he was letting on, though.

He cleared his throat. "I'm, uh, sorry," he said, when he had eaten the last of his doughnut. He peered at some scribbling in his notebook.

Great. Now what?

"About what?" X asked.

"I forgot to mention something. I, uh, managed to find out the results of Daniel O'Heran's tests," McLeod said, getting a bit quieter. "Cops told me he has acute respiratory impairment, which is what you get from drowning." He paused. "Unlike Jimmy Cleary or Mark Upton, there was nothing unusual about his circumstances, or so I'm told."

"You mean, apart from the fact that anyone would want to go swimming, fully clothed, in the Atlantic in the middle of winter?" I said. "Besides that?"

"Yes," McLeod said. "That's correct. He wasn't in any way impaired — no alcohol or drugs were found in his system — so it is highly unlikely he just decided to take such a big risk." He paused again. "And the bruises."

"What bruises?" X asked.

"There weren't really any," McLeod said. "It doesn't *seem* like anybody wrestled your friend to the water's edge and pushed him in. And that is why the attempted suicide theory persists. But, like you say, if he wasn't trying to hurt himself, someone must have put him in the water."

He paused. "And, I'm sorry, boys, but apparently some believe he may be left with permanent brain damage ..." He paused again. "In any event, most of the cops, Murphy and Savoie in particular, really want to classify what happened to Danny as a suicide attempt. Which, among other things —"

X cut him off. "Which eliminates the need to address the alibi the skinheads clearly have in Danny's case."

"Right," McLeod said and looked right at X, impressed. "That's exactly right."

I was about to ask another question, but stopped. Detective Murphy was suddenly standing behind McLeod, and Savoie was wheezing up to us behind him. Some of the winos in the place looked on warily.

"You shouldn't be talking to them, McLeod," Murphy said, his features dark. "These boys are witnesses, and they don't need to be manipulated by the media. You know better."

McLeod started to protest, but Murphy held up a beefy hand inches from the *Press Herald* reporter's face. "You know the rules," he barked. "And I don't give a crap about the First Amendment. So, if you don't want to get charged with contempt, you should piss off. Immediately."

McLeod grabbed his notebook and scuttled out without another word. Savoie, still huffing and puffing, glared down at us. "You guys really need to leave the solving the crime stuff to us," he said, irritated.

"We'd like to do that," X said, tossing his Styrofoam cup in a trash can, "but our friends keep getting hurt while we wait for you to do something."

CHAPTER 25

To no one's surprise, that Christmas was a bleak, grinding piece of crap. Despite the fact that Bauer, Wojcik, and Babic remained behind bars, and despite the fact that no other punks had been killed, the murders of Jimmy Cleary and Mark Upton remained unsolved — and the attempted murder of my band's drummer remained a big question mark. Danny was still in hospital in a coma, his ultra-religious parents keeping watch at his bedside. No other visitors allowed, and his siblings had been told not to talk to any of us anymore.

The skinheads were collectively charged with assault causing bodily harm, and some drug and theft offences. The Portland police had apparently discovered stolen stereo equipment when they searched Bauer's East End apartment, and lots of speed when they searched the Bayside flat Wojcik and Babic shared. But no murder charges. No statements, either, from the skinheads. They refused to say anything to anyone, including to their addled court-appointed lawyers. The trio remained in the Cumberland County Jail for the holidays, and they were probably happy about it.

The Virgins and the rest of us jammed occasionally in the basement at Sound Swap. Once or twice, Sam, Eddie, and Luke would join in, and we'd play half-hour-long versions of Patti Smith's take on "Gloria" and the Modern Lovers' "Roadrunner," which had been two- and three-chord favorites of Jimmy's. But no gigs were planned or even discussed. A deep, dark pall had descended on the Portland scene after what happened to Danny, and no one seemed to be interested in doing much of anything.

Patti Upchuck, meanwhile, confided in me that she was consumed by guilt. Like many other Portland punks, the deaths of our friends had left her grieving and scared. Her new relationship with X, however, had exactly the opposite effect. She told me it made her feel happier and more self-confident than she had been in a long time.

I was still a bit shocked by their relationship, too. It was something X just did not do, like *ever*. None of us had ever seen him express affection toward any girl. This had led to rampant speculation at PAHS that X was gay, but Patti had never believed it. X wasn't gay, as I of course knew very well, but he hadn't ever seemed interested in any girls, either.

Patti knew I was gay, but no one else really did except X and my dad. In Portland in the '70s, being gay was a super-fucking dangerous way to go through high school, even for a guy as big as I am. Later, Patti would learn — as I had — that X's parents briefly thought their son was gay, too. He had been writing pro-gay editorials in *The NCNA*, he had been listening for months to the Tom Robinson Band's British hit "Sing If You're Glad to be Gay," and the two of us visited the proudly gay Blackstones bar more than once. He also wore earrings, and many of his other friends at PAHS were gay, closeted or otherwise. As a result, X's sexuality was kind of ambiguous — which, to most high school students, kind of meant that he must be gay. Some days, X even seemed to promote the notion that he was.

X did not ask Patti to keep their relationship quiet, but she felt compelled to, except with me and her sister, of course. X was, as we all knew, the most intensely private person she had ever met. She was determined to respect that.

Well, with one exception: Patti told me everything, pretty much.

There was another reason for being careful, however: the guilt. Like anyone raised a Catholic, she figured that misery was all we could reasonably expect in life, and that happiness was a trick. It felt wrong to feel happy — about someone, about anything — while a maniac was stalking and murdering your friends.

So they kept quiet. X because that was what he usually did, and Patti because she did not want to do anything to upset X or anyone else.

So, Patti spent as much time with us as she had before they got together. And, as before, X continued to hang with me in the Language Studies area, because our hangout in Room 531 was still locked up by the school administration. Most days, Patti sat with the 531 crew, *NCNA* staff, and the X Gang at lunchtime. I noticed that she always took care not to sit too close to X, though. She preferred that, she told me: she could observe him better when he wasn't sitting right beside her.

Away from PAHS, we killed time together going to record stores like Electric Buddha and Enterprise, searching for punk rock gems amidst the cock-rock dreck. Saturdays, we'd gather with the rest of the X Gang for chicken and chips at Matthew's. And, in the evenings, we'd sometime go to the movies, usually at the Nickelodeon in the Old Port, which screened the more obscure stuff we liked.

X, as I knew too well, didn't drive or even have a driver's license. Most of the time, he relied on Portland Transit or me to get him around town. But once they started seeing each other, Patti started borrowing her father's car in the evenings and she would drive to Highland Avenue to pick him up and they'd just cruise around. He'd wait for her at the corner by his house, leaning against a pole in his biker's jacket and his ancient hunting sweater.

On one such drive, a couple of days before Christmas, they had exchanged gifts. She and her family were heading to Boston to spend a week with relatives, so she wanted to give him his present before they left town. She drove all the way down to Kennebunk, parked at an isolated place called Mother's Beach, and they watched the waves crash onto the rocks below the homes of the rich summer residents. She told me she told him to close his eyes.

"I haven't been told to close my eyes since I was a kid," he said, going along with her request. "Are you giving me a Lego set?"

"Better than that, I hope," she said, lifting a blanket off the item in the back seat and moving it into the front. She told him to open his eyes.

"Oh, wow," he said. "Wow."

It was a red Fender Telecaster, used, with a grain finish.

"Do you like it?" she asked.

"I love it," he said, taking the guitar. "Thanks, Patti." He strummed it with a fingernail and then reached across to hug her. "This is too much. It's way too generous."

"No, it isn't," she said. She told me she wanted to tell him she loved him, but — like previous occasions — she didn't. "Now you just need a band."

He moved the guitar into the back seat and addressed her. "Okay," he said. "I got you something. And Betty and Kurt, too, I guess."

"Betty and Kurt, too? What?"

He reached into the pocket of his jacket and extracted a gift-wrapped box. She opened it. Inside, there was an envelope as well as a silver ring — two small hands grasping a heart bearing a crown. "What is it?" she asked.

"It's a Claddagh ring," he said. "To the Irish, it means loyalty, friendship, and love."

"I love it, X," she said, sliding it onto various fingers until she found a spot where it would fit. She kissed him. "Thank you. I love it."

"Now open the envelope," he said.

"What is it?" she asked. "Tickets?"

"Yeah, tickets," he said. "But tickets for all of us to go to Boston next month to see the Clash play at the Harvard Square."

CHAPTER 26

It was the dead zone between Christmas and New Year's Day. Patti and Betty and their family were still in Boston. The rest of the Portland punks had gone into hibernation, with no gigs or get-togethers taking place anywhere. Gary's had finally let on that they were reopening, but that punk acts wouldn't be on the marquee just yet.

So, a couple days after Christmas, X and I were walking to Bull Moose Music in the city's Old Port, which usually had better (but pricier) import punk singles and albums from the U.K. He'd gotten some dough for Christmas and he said he was looking for the Ruts' first release, "In a Rut," and Wire's newest single, the artsy "Outdoor Miner." I told him I'd come with him.

As we were walking along, two young punks approached us near Pearl Street. They were both short and wore matching army surplus jackets and jeans. The lapels of the jackets were ornamented with badges for bands like Eater, a British punk outfit whose members were about the same age as the two young punks — fourteen or fifteen maybe.

"Uh, X? You're X, right?" one of them said.

Looking at them up close, I figured they were twins.

"Yeah, that's me," X said, stopping. "Why?"

"I'm Peter, and this is my brother John," the boy said, looking a bit nervous. "Do you guys have a minute to talk?"

"Sure," X said. "We've got lots of time this week. Let's go somewhere, though. It's pretty cold out."

The brothers led X and me to a tiny diner near the Plaza Nickelodeon, at Spring and Union. They were obviously excited that *the* X had agreed to talk to them. While John got hot chocolates at the counter, Peter told us that he and his brother went to King Junior High. They were likely the only kids in the entire place who were into punk. "We're used to getting hassled all the time at school, but now we're getting it from our parents, too." He paused as his brother put the drinks on the table. "Our dad's a cop."

"Probably the only Asian cop on the Portland force, too," John added, sitting down. "That's pretty pathetic in a city like Portland."

"Agreed. Is he a detective?" X asked.

"Yeah," Peter said.

"So," X said, warming his hands on his hot chocolate, "what's this got to do with us?"

"Well, like I said, we've been getting hassled a lot," Peter said. "There's always been a lot of that, but it's gotten really bad since …" He trailed off. Both brothers looked uncomfortable.

"Since the murders," X said, finishing the thought. "Yeah. It's been bad for everybody."

"Our parents, and the teachers, they're all super pissed," John said. "They keep asking us why we're into the scene. Why take the risk, and all that. They want us out. All our friends' parents want their kids out."

"Especially our dad," Peter said. "He's really freaking out. He's worried something'll happen to us."

"Well," X said, shrugging, "To them, it's just these weird-looking bands. Maybe you need to explain to them it's more than that."

"How?" Peter asked.

X ran a hand over the gash on his head, the stitches still visible. "Well, I just wrote a thing for the paper me and Kurt put out, *The NCNA*," he said. "Your dad isn't the only one asking. I've even been hearing it from guys who've been in the scene for a couple years, too. It's fair, given everything that's happened."

"Do you have a copy?" John asked.

"I do, but I just wrote it," X said, pulling out some sheets from his jacket. "I haven't even typed it up yet. The gist of it is my argument against what the Pistols say in 'God Save the Queen.' You know how Rotten sings 'there's no future, no future,' over and over?"

The twins nodded in unison.

"Well, I say that punk is *all about the future*. Getting one. Keeping it."

The boys waited, sipping their hot chocolates.

X looked at them, considering, then handed over the papers. "Go ahead, read it," he said.

The essay was in X's distinctive handwriting, which was half printing, half longhand. He'd let me read it earlier, so I knew just what it said. It was good. We watched as the brothers read it.

Peter looked up, smiling. "This is great," he said. John was behind his brother, reading over his shoulder.

"Wow," Peter said, returning the essay, "that's amazing, X. That's it."

After a bit more talk, X and I told the Chows we had to get going.

As we were getting ready to go, John turned to X. "Our dad hasn't been working on the cases involving your friends … but he's pretty upset about it. Just before Christmas, he said that there was a good reason why the skinheads hadn't been charged with the murders or anything serious …"

"Oh yeah? What did he say?"

"He said that nothing's happened because some of the cops in Portland are on their side."

CHAPTER 27

I got a copy of the police report later on. The report said it was about five minutes to go until midnight — and just about five minutes to go until his sixty-sixth birthday — and Ken Haslam was sitting on the couch in his television room on Ocean Street in South Portland, smoking a cigarette and watching a report on the prospects for the Red Sox that season. His wife had gone to bed.

When the doorbell rang, Haslam was surprised because he and his wife didn't get too many guests late at night. He wasn't concerned, though. They lived in one of those super-peaceful, law-abiding Portland bedroom communities, not far from the local cop shop. Two weeks earlier, around midnight, some drunk had left a Christmas party and stumbled down Ocean before knocking on their door to ask for directions. So this night, Haslam was unconcerned as he mounted the short flight of stairs that led to the main floor and opened the front door.

Standing on the bottom step was a young man with a shaved head. Haslam later told police that he was wearing a black T-shirt with a picture of some sort of sword bisecting an "N" on it, a pair of polished military-style boots, and a navy-blue nylon bomber jacket. Behind the man, in the shadows, stood a larger man, but Haslam could make out little of his features or what he was wearing.

"How can I help you?" Haslam said, addressing the man with the shaved head.

"Are you Mr. Haslam?" the man asked.

"Yes," Haslam said, bewildered.

"Are you the same Mr. Haslam who worked for Moscow Radio?"

Haslam squinted at the young man, and then back at the bigger one, still standing in the near darkness. "No, son," he said. "I never worked for Moscow Radio."

"Well," the man said, undeterred, "were you ever involved with a story about a man in Canada, in Manitoba, who ended up hanging himself?"

"Well, kind of …" Haslam said, hesitating. "I never worked for Moscow Radio, son, but I was involved in a story a little bit like that when I worked in Canada. My wife's from there." He paused. "But why do you ask? Who are you?"

"That man was my grandfather," the young man said. "And you shouldn't have done that."

"Son, you can think what you like, but we did the right thing."

Haslam recalled that he was uneasy at that point and started to edge back into the house.

"You shouldn't have done that," the young man repeated. He suddenly lunged forward, kicking at Haslam before he could close the door, and pulled him outside. One of his boots struck Haslam in the shin, and the old guy fell awkwardly, sprawling on the front steps. He bent forward, trying to protect himself as the young man started kicking him.

Haslam yelled out to his wife to call the police. It was at that point he caught a flash of movement out of the corner of his eye. To his left, the bigger guy had come closer. Haslam saw that he was holding something in his hands.

The blow was to Haslam's face: his eye popped like a grape. As he gasped for breath, he yelled out to his wife again. "They've got my eye! Dorothy! Call the ambulance!"

His wife, frantic, was already on the phone in the bedroom, speaking to an operator.

Haslam could hear the young man's boots echoing as he ran down driveway. Just before he heard the car doors slam shut, one of the men yelled out "White power!"

When his wife came outside, she found her husband kneeling on the front lawn, gasping for breath and clutching at his eye. The two men were gone. She heard the sound of sirens wailing in the distance.

CHAPTER 28

Ron McLeod told us he knew what had brought the men to Ken Haslam's door in the middle of the night. Many years before, Haslam had been a pretty popular young disc jockey at a radio station in the Canadian Prairies. He was the station's late-night man, and he had already been working in the radio business for more than a decade. He started out in Nebraska, when he was still a teenager. From there, he crisscrossed the Canadian Prairies and the U.S. Midwest, meeting his wife at a dance at a Manitoba Bible college. The two of them moved around a lot, and then ended up at a station in Winnipeg. With 50,000 watts of power, it was one of the biggest radio stations in the middle of the continent. On a good night, it could be heard as far away as Montana. The station hired Haslam to be host of a dusk-to-dawn show.

One Saturday night in late 1960 or so, the chief engineer phoned Haslam with a possible news tip. While fiddling with a short-wave radio at home, the engineer said, he had picked up a segment of Moscow Radio, a regular

English-language propaganda program broadcast by the Soviet government. The program, the engineer told Haslam, was about Nazi war criminals living in Canada. And it said a man living in the Winnipeg suburb of St. James was a war criminal.

Haslam searched through the Winnipeg phone book and quickly found the man's name: Alexander Laak. "It was a hell of a scoop," Haslam told McLeod from his bed at Mercy Hospital. "But we knew we had to get the guy on tape first." Using directory assistance, Haslam had reached Moscow Radio. After discussing Laak with an English-speaking man there, Haslam was told he would be sent the tape containing information about Alexander Laak. Within a week or so, as promised, the tape arrived in the mail. Haslam's station checked the story. Laak was the owner of a bricklaying business he ran out of his home. Like a lot of Nazis, apparently, Laak immigrated to Canada after the war, where he lived more or less right out in the open with his family. Haslam concluded that Obersturmführer Alexander Laak had overseen the mass murder of thousands of German and Czech Jews at a railway station near the Jägala death camp. Later reports linked Laak to the murders of hundreds of thousands of Jews and Roma people at Jägala, too.

Haslam broadcast his big story about Laak, and Laak denied it all. "Shortly after we broadcast the story, Laak's wife found him hanging in the garage of their home," Haslam told McLeod. "There was an investigation of his death and the police ruled it was suicide, and it was. That was the end of it, I thought."

It wasn't. In the spring of 1978, months before Jimmy Cleary's murder and nearly a year before he was attacked, Haslam was watching the news. Apparently the Canadian government had been talking about setting up some sort of an investigation into war criminals living in Canada, and the U.S. media wrote all about it. Ken Haslam saw one of the stories. A Canadian security official said in the story that they had "no knowledge" of any Nazi war criminals living in Canada. When he heard that whopper, Haslam was angry.

"It was a bloody lie," Haslam told McLeod. "How can the Canadian authorities say they didn't know about it when they questioned me about one of these people in 1961?"

Haslam called the city desk at the *Winnipeg Free Press*. He related his story to an editor, who assigned a reporter on the police beat to call him. Haslam told the reporter about Laak. The story ran just a few paragraphs with the headline: "Canadian Authorities Blasted by Maine Man for Nazi Claim."

"The Canadian cops said there was absolutely no truth to the Alexander Laak story," Haslam told the reporter. "They said it was something cooked up by the Russians. But three days after we played the tape on the air, the man went into his garage and hanged himself. Why would he hang himself if he was innocent?"

The *Winnipeg Free Press* story was picked up by United Press International and ran in the *Portland Press Herald*. It didn't generate much of a reaction in Portland — I mean, who cares about Canada, right?

But someone saw it. And someone cared.

CHAPTER 29

The Harvard Square Theater in Cambridge was a shit hole, basically, an old dump squatting on Church Street, near West Georgia. It wasn't as dingy and dirty as Cambridge's pit — where skateboarders and punks hung out and scared off the tourists — but it was bad enough. A half-century earlier, it had been a wonderful cabaret, a plaque out front said, "A popular place for dancing." It had been shut down during the Great Depression and went through several owners and lots of bankruptcies in the years that followed.

While the Harvard might have been something amazing when Duke Ellington and Tommy Dorsey played there, it was now a shadow of what it used to be. It looked like a good place to be mugged, not see a memorable show.

But on that fateful night, no one much cared — not the hundreds of punks swarming the place, and definitely not the dozen or so punks from Portland, Maine, who had coughed up a fair amount of dough to get tickets.

To us, the Harvard was the perfect place to see the Clash perform one of their first-ever North American shows.

"Pinch me," I said to X, staring up at the Church Street marquee, and the Clash's name. "I can't fucking believe we're here, brother."

And I couldn't. The show brought out punks and wannabe punks from all over the East Coast. Some of the people there looked totally ridiculous — fake punks with Sex Pistols T-shirts and mustaches (which X would later suggest was a punk rock oxymoron) — but most of the others were the real article, real punks. We had never before been surrounded by so many people who were like us. It was profoundly weird, but also totally awesome. For years, we had always been part of a tiny minority, and then — for one night, anyway — we suddenly became part of a majority. It was a weird feeling, but it made for a fucking glorious night.

At the big rock 'n' roll gigs in the '70s — at, say, the Rolling Stones or the Who or Led Zeppelin shows — there was always the smell of dope drifting through the air and lots of mellow, well-behaved long-haired fans sitting in their assigned seats. "Smiling. Singing along. Sharing gourds of wine," I said, grimacing as the Upchucks laughed. "They're enough to make you puke."

At the best punk gigs — including this one — the air was thick with a kind of edgy expectation, not dope smoke. The drugs of choice that night were cheap beer and speed, and lots of both. As a result, there was a thick vein of menace throbbing just below the surface. It had the four of us feeling like something crazy might happen at any moment, in an explosion of sweat and spit. It honestly seemed like someone could reach out in the dark and throttle you. "Which, in a punk way, has a tendency to make you feel more alive," I suggested over fish and chips at Bartley's in Harvard Square. "Gimme danger!" The Upchucks laughed some more.

Everywhere we looked, there were punks — punks in biker jackets, punks with tattoos, punks in chains, punks with safety pins gouging skin that looked abscessed. More punks, in fact, than I, or most of us, had ever seen in one place at one time. Between the occasional moments of uneasiness, it felt thrilling, like a historic night was unfolding. It felt electric. It felt like the ideal night for a show by the Clash, the biggest punk band in the world.

Let me try and explain. The Clash, you see, got us all hooked with their first amazing album in 1977. On it, they hollered about racism, and youth unemployment, and the hippies who hung out at Strolling Bones shows. To us, the Clash *were* the most important punk band. The Sex Pistols were more famous; the Ramones invented the genre. But the Clash actually were, just as their record company declared that year, THE ONLY BAND THAT MATTERS.

As X wrote in *The NCNA*:

> Members of the Clash are the ones who actually read books — and push their fans to read them, too. They write songs that say that politics are important. They demand your attention. They are the first (and the only) band that tries to be the biggest and the

most radical band, all at the same time. Somehow
they make those two opposites work.

When the show was over, hundreds of punks stumbled out into the crisp Boston night. X, me, Patti, and Sister Betty, meanwhile, loitered on the main floor at the Harvard Square Theater. We were exhilarated and exhausted. The band's performance had been incredible, incendiary. It made us feel happier than any of us had been since before Jimmy Cleary's death.

It made us feel part of something.

After the show, we didn't particularly want to leave. X had secured beds for us at the closest youth hostel in Cambridge, but going to sleep right then was out of the question. We were wired, not tired. As we stood there, a sinister-looking older guy stepped up. "Hello, kids," he said in a thick British accent. "Where ya from?"

"Portland," said Patti. "Do you know where that is?"

"Oregon?" he asked.

"No, the Portland in Maine," they said. He shrugged.

"Well, whatever," said the man, who turned out to be named Johnny Green and was the road manager to the Clash. "Where ya stayin'?"

"Well," I said, looking at my watch, "we've missed curfew at the hostel, so we've got nowhere to stay, now." X raised an eyebrow. This was a flat-out lie, but he didn't correct me. Patti and Betty giggled.

"Nowhere to go?" roared Johnny Green. "Then you must come with me, children!"

Johnny led us through a dark corridor to a back room, which was basically nothing more than a narrow, stinky closet deep in the guts of the Harvard. The four of us edged into a room thick with the smell of dope. Off in a corner, a ghetto blaster was playing some dub reggae and people were laughing. Everywhere on the walls there was band graffiti, and a prehistoric and grubby couch was up against a wall. And sitting on and around the couch — looking pink and sweaty and flushed — were the Clash.

"My head is going to explode," I whispered, transfixed.

Green waved in the direction of the band. "There's Mick, there's Paul, there's Topper, there's the gang," he said, indicating soundman Mickey Foote, plus a group of huge Rastafarian guys. "And there's Joe. Get yourself a beer or something and make yourself at home." He ambled off.

In photographs in the *NME* or *Creem*, Strummer had always looked to me like a slightly older version of X, but with short hair. Strummer was pale and intense, with a squared jaw, an off-center nose, and this penetrating gaze. But when he stood up, we saw that he wasn't very tall at all.

Strummer had an easy, affable manner. We tried not to stare at him, but it wasn't easy. He was one of those guys who became the center of every room. He certainly was for us.

Joe fucking Strummer!

When we shook it, Joe Strummer's hand was moist and warm, which made sense — he'd just been playing his heart out on stage, and he was drenched with sweat. He grinned at us, revealing a mouthful of broken, greenish teeth. Strummer's eyes were a bit glassy, a side effect of the massive spliffs that were making their way around the room.

The other members of the Clash didn't seem all that interested in us, but Strummer greeted us like long-lost pals. "Welcome," he said. "Where y'all from?"

We told him, and Strummer paused, frowning. "Portland?" he said. "In Maine? Isn't that where all that shit has been going down?"

Fuck. He knew. *He knew.* I started to respond, but X shook his head: *Let it go.*

So I did. "That was an amazing show, Joe," I said instead, trying to change the subject. "Can I be a typical fan and get your autograph?" I whipped out a notebook I used for sketches I donated to *The NCNA*.

"Typical?" Strummer thundered. "There's nothing typical about my signature, young man!" He scrawled away in my notebook while the Upchucks scrambled to get his autograph, too.

X didn't ask for one, so Strummer squinted at him, then looked at his chest.

Under his black leather jacket, X was wearing his homemade Clash T-shirt, the one on which he had re-created every single detail of the famous logo found on the cover of the first Clash LP, the one we all fell in love with. In 1978, there weren't too many stores to purchase punk rock gear. So we Portland punks made our own stuff: buttons, T-shirts, stickers, and so on. We even narrowed the flared jeans our mothers had bought for us, by hand, so they'd be as skinny and as tight as the trousers the Clash wore.

"Where'd you get that?" Joe Strummer said, jabbing a finger at X's T-shirt.

"I made it," he said, shrugging. "It's not a very good rep —"

"It's bloody great, man," he said, cutting X off. "You did that yourself? That's bloody great. It's great you did it yourself. Keep control of the means of production, ya know?" He laughed — a raw, deep-throated laugh.

Back then and even now, punk frowns on the sort of bullshit hero worship that you see in traditional rock 'n' roll. Punk was against hierarchies, and it was always trying to break down the invisible wall between the performer and the audience. But at that stage in our lives, truth be told, Joe Strummer was a fucking giant to us. He towered above most other mortals, because he was so passionate, and so political, and so incredibly cool.

On those many days when I don't want to be me, I will always try to be Joe Strummer.

Autographs obtained, I snapped some photos of the band on my Polaroid. When it was time for the band to depart for the next night's gig, at the Palladium in New York, Johnny Green led the four of us out a side door and onto Church Street. After exchanging a few more good-byes, the jail-like door clanged shut behind Green. While me and Betty kept busy flipping through the Polaroids, Patti asked X, "Why didn't you want Kurt to tell him about Portland?"

X shrugged. "There's been enough stuff that's sad," he said. "We deserved at least one night that wasn't."

Fucking right.

CHAPTER 30

The next morning, X, the Upchuck sisters, and I checked out of the Cambridge hostel and walked up Stuart Street, in no particular rush to get to the Amtrak station. Along the way, the Upchucks decided to check out some Chinatown gift shops before we boarded the train for the ride back to Portland. X, however, saw something else that caught his eye.

Across the street, a large poster had been taped in a street-level window, with the words "WHITE GUILT" printed across a large stop sign. Beside the stop sign, someone had taped up another sign: a circle superimposed on a cross, with what looked like some Viking symbols, or something, at the center. On the train ride to Boston, X told me he had read an investigative story about the growing European neo-Nazi skinhead movement, in a copy of the *Searchlight*, the British antiracist magazine. They had published a sidebar story about various Far Right symbols, including Viking-style "runes" and what they called "the Celtic cross."

To Celts, apparently, the Celtic cross was basically an ancient Christian symbol found on old tombstones and stuff like that. To neo-Nazis and white supremacists, though, the cross had a totally different meaning: it was Odin's Cross, this swastika-like symbol, which was about the division of the four main racial groups — and the triumph of Christianity over Judaism. The symbol had been banned, X told me, in Germany and Italy for its connections to organized hate groups.

X and I crossed the street to check it out. A sign advertised that it was something called "The European Culture Institute," and another hand-painted sign said that it was open, so we stepped inside. A bell rang. At the receptionist's desk — which was abandoned — there was a typewriter and a phone. Beside the typewriter was a manual giving instructions on how to make a bomb. On some messy shelves, there were books with titles like *High Speed Math*, *Constitutional Law*, and *The Magic Power of Witchcraft*. On one wall, a small poster was stamped with the letters Z.O.G., and a red slash through them. This, X later explained, was the acronym for the Zionist Occupation Government — what the neo-Nazis called elected governments, who they believed were controlled by the forces of "international Jewry."

I'm not making this shit up, by the way. Wish I was. But I'm not.

"Hello?" X said, easing his backpack onto the floor. No one answered.

Four offices opened onto the reception area at the European Culture Institute. Off to one side, X could see a mimeograph room and a small kitchen. In the reception area, there was a lectern thing, a stage, and about fifty chairs.

X walked to another bookshelf, near the reception desk. Hundreds of "British Israel" texts and pamphlets were stacked alongside dust-covered histories of the two world wars by authors like David Irving. The books and pamphlets had titles like *The Real Jews* and *Migrations of Israel*.

X opened a copy of *Migrations* and read: "In truth, there can be no denial of the fact that the Anglo-Saxon, Celtic, Germanic, Scandinavian, and related peoples are indeed the descendants of the ancient Israelites. Down through countless centuries, and across the face of Asia and Europe, our forefathers trekked to the new Promised Land to fulfill the numerous prophecies of scripture. One of these prophecies was that the Jews, or the House of Judah, would be exterminated by God on Judgment Day." X stopped and turned when he heard a sound.

"May I help you?"

X closed the book. In the doorway to the largest office, a short, overweight guy stood watching us. The man was stuffed into a dress shirt, dress pants, and black bowtie. His skin was so pale it was almost translucent. His short, dark hair had been slicked into place, almost like Hitler's, which I suppose was the desired effect.

A Hitler haircut! I mean, who does that?

"Who are you?" the man said, in a nasal voice.

"I'm sorry," X said. "We're from out of town, and we saw the signs and saw that you were open, so ..."

"It's all right," the man said, "visitors are welcome. What brought you here?"

"The signs," X said. I said nothing, not sure where X was going with this.

"Which one?" the man asked.

"The Celtic cross was interesting," X said. "It's an interesting symbol."

"Yes, Odin's Cross," the man said, grinning like it was some big conspiracy. "It's rather important. I take it you know what it means?"

X nodded.

"And you are of Western European heritage, then?" the man asked.

"I guess," X said. "We're from Portland."

"In Maine? Of course. I know many, many people there," the man said, closing the door to his office, but staying where he had been standing. "Many interesting things are going on in Portland, these days."

What a fucking creep.

X nodded, just as a steam clock out on Stuart Street gave this hollow whistle. X looked at his watch. "We have to go soon," he said. He held up the copy of *Migrations of Israel.*

"Are these books and leaflets for sale?"

"The books are, but the pamphlets are free," the man said, waving a hand at the bookshelf, while still maintaining a careful distance. "If you like, we can also put you on our mailing list. You can leave your name and address on the clipboard on the reception desk."

"I'd appreciate that," X said. He scribbled down a false name — "Jamey Jones," a play on a Clash song title — and the post office box of Sound Swap in Portland. "I'd like to buy this book, if I could, and any pamphlets you have on British Israel."

Ten minutes later, we were back out on Stuart Street, where Patti and Betty were waiting for us. X put the pamphlets and the book he had purchased in his backpack. "What's that stuff?" Patti asked him.

"Evil," X said, as we started walking again toward the train station. "But the kind of evil that I think inspired Bauer and his friends."

CHAPTER 31

The Brotherhood — or as its members had apparently taken to calling themselves, the New Order — got together in their barnlike "barracks" on a rundown farm in Potter County, Pennsylvania.

In its rituals, and in its words, the group wanted to be like Adolf Hitler's SS, the informant's report said. At the moment, however, they basically resembled what they really were: a group of unhappy-looking white losers in their thirties and forties, overflowing with anger and hate. There were a couple farmers, a former marine, a teacher, a trucker, and quite a few unemployed guys.

Taking part in the swearing-in ceremony was one of the three out-of-state "brethren," a couple who had met through another whack job group called the National Alliance, and six Aryan Nations members. Most of the men were Identity Christians, that insane "religion" X had told us about. One of them would later become the police informant. An older guy, the leader, stepped forward and made a big show of looking around.

"I am so proud, kinsmen," he said. "I am so proud that you have come together this night. Coming together in this way, as brothers in blood, is step one."

The next step, he explained, was to establish a set of common goals. The third was to find funds for the movement and the fourth was recruitment of new members. "The fifth step," he loudly declared, pausing for effect, "the fifth step is the elimination of enemies of the white race. And the final step — the final solution, you might say — will be the creation of a guerrilla force, of men like you, to bring the battle right into urban areas and wipe away the cities and the Jew filth and the mud-people scum. To wipe away what hasn't been already destroyed by the race riots.

"And then, we can start over, rooted in the land. And then, we can re-animalize the white man. We can return to nature and what is natural, as Elijah prophesized."

Without speaking, the group then got closer together in their circle, standing around one man's six-week-old daughter, who was placed in a blanket on the floor. The only light came from a few candles. The men held hands and repeated their oath, which the leader had apparently written for the occasion: "Let us go forth by ones and by twos, by scores and legions, and as true Aryan men with pure hearts and strong minds, face the enemies of our faith and our race with courage and determination. We hereby invoke the blood covenant and declare that we are in a full state of war and will not lay down our weapons until we have driven the enemy into the sea and reclaimed the land that was promised to our fathers of old, and through our blood and his will, it becomes the land of our children to be."

The baby had not cried. After their ceremony was over, her father carefully picked her up. Receiving a few pats on the back, he took his daughter outside, where his wife was waiting in their idling pickup truck. The men milled about, pleased with themselves.

They were excited, too, and full of questions about the big adventure that lay ahead. The one from Maine, Northman, half-raised his arm, and when he did, quite a few racialist tattoos could be seen. "I've got a question," he said. The men stopped talking to listen to him. They liked this big, plainspoken white man from the North. "How do we convince our white kinsmen to return to what is natural and to nature? It's not going to be easy. Too many of them are addicted to the idiot box and the Jewsmedia and living in big cities."

The Brotherhood's leader spoke. "The cities are tombs," he said. "And they will be graveyards for muds and Jews and race traitors.

"They will be graveyards for the rootless ones."

CHAPTER 32

The Downeaster headed north, clack-clacking over gaps in the rail as it did the milk run through the New Hampshire backcountry. Patti Upchuck rubbed her eyes and squinted at Betty and me, who at that moment were twisted over our seats, deep asleep. I was snoring, she later told me, amused.

Patti looked around her. The railcar was dark, almost totally empty of passengers, but X was not there.

She and I were used to this, of course. Since they had started their quiet, almost-top-secret relationship, she had discovered that X would often disappear for lengthy periods. She figured he was writing essays for *The NCNA*, or lyrics for a song, or reading (and actually enjoying) obscure Russian literature. He would return, always, without saying what he had been doing or where he had been.

She got up, soundlessly, so as not to wake up her sister or me. After a brief stop in the railcar's washroom, she headed toward the observation coach. They called it the Skylite Dome Car.

She found X there, papers and books spread out on his lap, a single light illuminating him. It was really late. There was no one else in the car. He looked up.

"Hey," he said. "Welcome."

"Hey," she said. "Couldn't sleep on the super-comfy seat they'd provided us with, amazingly. Saw you had flown the coop."

"Yeah," he said. "Figured I'd head up here and take in the stars, and catch up on my reading."

"What are you reading?" she asked, settling into the seat beside him, leaning her head on his shoulder. "The stuff you got at that place in Cambridge?"

"Yeah," X said, shaking his head. "It's terrible. Really hateful stuff, but all written as if it's academic or scientific."

"What's the gist?" she asked, warily examining the spine of *Migrations of Israel*.

"The gist of it," he said, "is that Jews are not the true Jews. The true chosen ones are white, Anglo-Saxon people, and that the Jews are imposters. The authors even seem to believe that the Jews are the descendants of Cain, and therefore the devil. They're Satan's children."

"That's insane," she said. "Is it legal to publish this kind of stuff?"

"Yes, unfortunately. First Amendment and all that," X said. "I even picked up another pamphlet, from something called the Aryan Nations, that calls mixed-race marriages 'the ultimate abomination,' and that says that non-whites are 'mud people,' quote unquote."

"That is just so awful," she said. She paused. "So …
why did you get these things, babe?"

"Know your enemy, I guess," he said.

"What do you mean?"

He didn't say anything for a few moments. "I didn't
want to upset you," he said, touching her hand. "But
Kurt and I have been poking around, talking to various people."

"Like?"

"Like a reporter at the *Press Herald*, like some people
with connections to the police," he said. "And there's no
question that whoever killed Jimmy, Mark, and tried to
kill Danny were motivated by hate, but …"

"But?"

"But not just that," he said. "It's not just some skinheads who are racist and anti-Semitic and anti-gay or
just anti-punk. It's more than that."

"What?"

"It seems to be connected to *religion*, somehow."

"Religion?" she said, sitting up and looking directly
at X. "I don't understand."

He looked out the window as New Hampshire
whipped by in the dark. "British Israelism. That's what
it's called. It's this bogus religion that's been around for
a hundred years," he said. "It was like some secret society at the start. But it's gotten popular. And, in the past
few years, some lunatics in California and Idaho and
Washington State have taken this British Israel stuff and
gone off into an even more radical direction."

"How?"

"They don't seem to be content to wait for Jesus to return in the end times," he said. "Not that they think Jesus was Jewish, by the way. In their propaganda, Christ is this militaristic figure who uses violence to kill Jews." He paused. "They want to speed up Armageddon. They don't want to wait for the end times."

"So what has that got to do with some Portland kids who are into punk rock?" she asked, feeling uneasy. "What have we got to do with that?"

"I don't know," he said, "But Marky was found in the same position, with the same wound, as Christ. And Jimmy, as everyone knows, was crucified … It's like someone wants to make us atone for something. And that we are the Antichrist, for real."

"Like Rotten sang on 'Anarchy'?" she asked him.

"Maybe," he said. He looked tired. "I don't know. It's all insane, I know." He tapped the book in his lap. "But these people are real. And I think they're the ones who have taken some kind of interest in us."

CHAPTER 33

X stared at the blank sheet of paper in his typewriter. I stared at X.

He had planned to write a review of the Boston performance by the Clash for *The NCNA* after school, but the assault on Ken Haslam was difficult to put out of our minds. It was blasted across the front of the *Press Herald* his father had left on his bed that morning. The maiming of the retired broadcaster had again left all of us feeling shocked. The neo-Nazi skinheads were getting bolder, and more violent.

X looked up at the walls of his almost spartan room. On one, he had pinned up a poster of Iggy Pop and the Stooges from an early Michigan show, when they were starting out. On the other, above his bed, he had recently placed a framed, enlarged photograph of himself outside a community hall gig we did the year before, featuring me, Danny Hate, and Jimmy Cleary, smiling along with a few of the Social Blemishes. We had thrown our arms around each other's shoulders. It looked like it had come from a different life.

The phone rang. X's mother called out. "It's for you, Christopher," she said.

"Who is it, Mom?"

"No idea," she said. "A boy. He wouldn't give his name."

X picked up the receiver outside his bedroom and signaled me to stand close so I could listen. It was John Chow, one of the two young punks we had met downtown a few weeks before. The boy sounded out of breath and was almost whispering into the receiver. "X, is that you?" he asked.

"Yeah, it's me," X replied.

"It's John ... Chow."

"What's up, John?"

John spoke quickly. In the background, X could hear his brother talking. "I can't talk for long," he said. "Our dad was saying that something is going down with the skinheads. It looks like they're getting ready to charge them with the murders."

"That doesn't make sense," X said. "They didn't do it. They're the scum of the earth, but they didn't do it."

"That's what our dad says, too," John said, whispering now. "He says it's all about politics. It looks like they may take them in to court to be charged today or tomorrow."

X peered at the clock on the wall facing the stairs. It was late in the afternoon, probably too late in the day for anything to happen in court. Besides, if the skinheads were going to be charged, we knew that the police and the DA would want to generate as much hype as possible, as they had done with Bauer and Babic's bail hearing. It was more likely that the skinheads would be charged when the police had attracted the media's interest.

"Got to go, X," said John hurriedly. "Be careful."

X sat on the arm of the living room couch a moment, running his fingers along the scar on his head.

He looked at me. "It doesn't make any sense, " he said. "The skinheads are going to be acquitted. Why risk that?"

I didn't have an answer; I said nothing. X fished a slip of paper out of his wallet. It contained Ron McLeod's phone number. He dialed it.

They skipped the small talk. "So," McLeod said to X, as I again listened in, "I presume you heard? That they're going to charge them tomorrow?"

"Yeah," X said. "Is it true?"

"Yes," McLeod said. "It's true. But it certainly is bizarre."

"Why?" X asked. "What's changed? My friends and I were in Boston for a few days. Did something happen?"

"I don't know," McLeod said. "I'm not sure what caused it. The attack on Ken Haslam certainly got the story going again."

"Is he all right?" X asked.

"Well, he's been blinded in one eye for good," McLeod said. "But he and his wife are with family back in Canada. They didn't feel comfortable staying in their home."

"Can't blame them," X said. "It's sickening, attacking an older man like that. Was that what convinced the cops to charge Bauer and the others, you think?"

"Maybe," McLeod said. "There's been a fair bit of media pressure, as I'm sure you've seen. Our paper's editorial board has written a big piece and demanded that the police and the city devote more resources to solving the murders, among other things. There's also been a lot of discussion about it all on talk radio. Maybe the Haslam attack, plus the media pressure, has gotten to them."

"No offense, but I don't think anybody cares about a newspaper editorial," X said. "It has to be the attack on that old guy."

"You're right, and no offense taken," McLeod said, laughing. "You're probably right: no new leads, no charges for weeks, and then they suddenly decide to charge these skinheads? But unless some incredible new piece of evidence has been found that I haven't heard about, it all seems very odd."

X and McLeod made plans to meet very early the next morning, again at the Dunkin' Donuts. X returned to his room, pulled on his thrift store hunting sweater, and threw on his leather jacket. Reaching the front door, he called up to his mother, telling her we were heading out to my place.

"Let's go for a walk," he said.

Outside, we started in the direction of my place. X tapped my arm and pointed up the street. I saw a dirty late-model sedan, parked further up. Its occupants, plural, seemed to be watching us.

X was looking, too. He spoke.

"They've been following us since we got back from Boston."

CHAPTER 34

"SKINHEADS TO BE CHARGED IN PUNK MURDERS," the front page of the *Daily Sun* screamed the next morning.

> Portland police plan to charge a trio of jailed white supremacist skinheads with the murders of two youths late last year, police sources have confirmed. The three young men, who have been in custody for several weeks on assault charges, will be arraigned in court today for the murders of James Cleary and Mark Upton. An investigation into the near-drowning of a third Portland youth, Danny O'Heran, continues, but sources say that the police believe the incident was an attempted suicide."

A very unhappy-looking Ron McLeod was hunched over a copy of the paper when X and I joined him at Dunkin' Donuts. When he saw us, he threw down the tabloid with obvious disgust.

"What a load of crap," he said, sounding indignant. "Have you guys read this?"

"The suicide suggestion is total bullshit," I said, and asked McLeod why the police were leaking to the *Sun* and not to the *Herald*.

"Because they're pissed off that we've been critical of them editorially," McLeod said. "And I suspect that Murphy and Savoie also don't like the fact I've been talking to you." He paused, frowning. "Hey, don't you have school today or something?"

I shrugged. "When we get there, we'll just tell them that the cops wanted us downtown to question us about the murders. These days, they don't seem to care if we're there or not."

"Well, my editors certainly care that the friggin' *Daily Sun*, of all papers, is beating us on this story. Have you guys got anything you can tell me that would explain why they're suddenly rushing to charge these guys after doing nothing for weeks?"

"That's your department, not ours," I said. "We don't have a clue what the police are thinking. Or if they even think at all."

X looked down at McLeod and said, "There are a couple things."

Here we go.

McLeod leaned forward. "I could sure use something."

"The religious symbolism at the murder scenes, I think it might have something to do with a religion called British Israelism or Identity." X pulled out a couple of the leaflets he'd picked up in Boston and handed them to

McLeod. "And I think we're being followed. Or, at least I'm pretty sure *I'm* being followed, anyway."

"Really? By who?" McLeod asked.

"No idea," X said. "I've spotted a dark brown four-door two or three times since we've been back from Boston. It always stays far enough away that I can't see who's in the car. But it looks like more than one guy."

"How can you tell they're guys?"

"Because they look big. I've seen the car near my folks' place and by the school. Is it the cops?"

"Might be," McLeod said.

"Is it worth ditching school entirely and coming down to see these scumbags charged with the murders?" I asked.

"I wouldn't if I were you," McLeod said. "You'll probably be called as a witness to the assault, Kurt. And you're the victim," he said, turning to X. "For now, you should both just stay away. Besides," McLeod continued, tapping the front page of the paper, "this trial will be one of the best-covered events in recent Portland legal history. You'll probably know every detail about today's little drama by the time you get home this afternoon."

CHAPTER 35

Sharon Martin didn't want to be an Assistant District Attorney. She especially didn't want to be an Assistant District Attorney on this particular day, sitting — as she was — in the stately Portland district courthouse, the media gang waiting behind her, and three skinheads glaring at her from the prisoner's box. Their defense counsel was to her right, shuffling papers and trying to look smart. Maybe they were hoping that their appearance in a big case like this one would lead to a lot more client retainers.

Martin sighed, doodling on the margins of her notepad, where she had prepared some opening remarks. In front of her, on the large District Attorney's table, were great big stacks of police reports and witness statements, a dog-eared copy of Knoll's *Criminal Procedure and Practice*, and one junior DA whose name she had already forgotten. She sighed again, wishing that she was teaching criminal law back in Boston, and not practicing it in a courthouse up in puny Portland.

Martin hadn't been able to get a teaching job because she looked far too young. She was a blonde and really attractive, too. She had finished at the top of her law class — the gold medalist. But her looks sometimes had worked against her, and she ended up in Maine, prosecuting cases in which she had little interest.

She had ended up in Portland because that was where her fiancé wanted to be. Her fiancé — who wasn't particularly handsome and who had been runner-up in Boston University's gold medalist sweepstakes the year they both graduated — had an intense interest in maritime law. The best place to practice that was in Portland, apparently, so they moved here. Sharon was offered lots of articling positions at various fancy firms, but took one instead with the District Attorney. Her parents and her law professors at BU had been horrified, but Sharon figured the DA's office was the straightest route to a teaching position. On that, she was unusually wrong, but she had been wrong about her fiancé, too. Two years after they were called to the state bar, and a year after they married, she caught him in bed with one of the partners at his firm, and that was that. She now lived alone, in a cramped apartment near the water on Portland's northeastern fringes.

Sharon looked up as the crowd, which included Ron McLeod and the Upchucks, continued to watch, and the junior attorney with the forgotten name almost snapped to attention. He asked her if she needed anything. "Some water would be nice," Sharon said, and the young lawyer got busy looking for a pitcher of water and two glasses. There wasn't any in the courtroom.

There wasn't any winning case in Courtroom 200, either. Sharon had been reading the police reports, witness statements, and whatnot over and over, and it was obvious — to her, at least — that proving the skinheads' guilt, beyond a reasonable doubt, was going to be basically impossible. After going through all the evidence Detectives Savoie and Murphy had put together, she had gone to see Portland's District Attorney, a pompous old fart who called himself A. Fripper Archibald — but who the media and the thirty-odd assistant DAs called "A Frigging Asshole." Archibald had listened to her take on the case, and to her conclusion that the skinheads — while obviously total scumbags — couldn't have killed Jimmy Cleary and Mark Upton. He lifted an untrimmed eyebrow and kept his manicured fingers steepled.

"Your task is not to reason why," he wheezed. "Your task is to secure convictions, so that the mayor and the governor's office get off our collective backs. Do you understand me, Ms. Martin?"

Back in her tiny office on Newbury, near the courthouse, Sharon met with Detective Savoie. She had sensed that Savoie, unlike his partner, thought the case against the three skinheads was weak, at best. Sprawled in the chair facing her desk, reeking of cigarette smoke and looking as messy as usual, Savoie expressed sympathy. "You shouldn't be surprised, Martin," he said, after hearing about her conversation with A. Frigging Asshole. "The guy is an asshole, and he's just looking for an appointment somewhere. He knows that isn't going to happen with this punk shit still making headlines."

"But," Sharon said, exasperated, "the case sucks. With a minimum of effort, even the most ineffective duty counsel is going to get them off. They're going to walk, because the evidence just isn't there, Detective."

"Believe me, I know," Savoie said, rubbing his tired, hangdog face with a hand. "But you're getting the same political pressure we are. They want someone to go to jail, and they want it done yesterday. So you've got to do your best."

"It won't be difficult to establish reasonable doubt, as you know," she said. "Whoever killed Cleary and Upton tried to kill O'Heran. It wasn't a suicide attempt. That's obvious. And one of these skinheads was in custody when O'Heran almost died, and the other two were probably on a Greyhound, heading to neo-Nazi heaven in Canada. They couldn't possibly have done it."

"That's why we didn't charge them with the O'Heran thing — which we still don't know for sure was an attempted murder, by the way, because the kid is still in a coma," Savoie said, sounding miserable. "They're only going to be charged with the Cleary and Upton murders." He trailed off. They sat in silence, unhappy.

CHAPTER 36

The judge in Courtroom 200 was Sean O'Sullivan, a former criminal defense lawyer who — through his friendships within the Democratic Party — had been elevated to the bench two years before. His arrival had caused a ton of controversy and was attacked by some angry old white Republicans as "pork-barrel politics at its worst." But O'Sullivan got to work right away and he was both smart and fair. He was liked by both the DAs and the criminal defense bar, which apparently was pretty hard to do.

O'Sullivan had this shock of red hair, graying at the sides, and a big bushy mustache which hid the corners of his mouth. This was helpful for the occasions when he found himself grinning at the antics of the idiots who often stood before him in Courtroom 200. On this day, however, he wasn't smiling much.

Sitting in his paneled chambers, just outside his courtroom, O'Sullivan was really, really unhappy. From the little he knew about *U.S. v. Martin Bauer, Peter*

Wojcik, and Dragomir Babic, the prosecution's case was a total joke. Rumors were all over the courthouse that the police had disclosed — reluctantly — evidence that provided more than a reasonable amount of doubt that Bauer, Wojcik, and Babic had committed the murders of Jimmy Cleary and Mark Upton.

O'Sullivan was super unhappy for another reason, too. From his clerk, he had heard that there was already an overflow crowd in Courtroom 200, most of them media. "There is even a reporter from *Rolling Stone,* Your Honor," his clerk informed him, breathlessly. "*Rolling Stone* magazine!"

The clerk, by the way, blabbed all the time to Ron McLeod. Ron McLeod would then blab to us. Thanks, court clerk!

O'Sullivan shook his head and cursed. The prosecution against Bauer, Wojcik, and Babic — while probably justifiable for lots of other crimes — was not justified for the crimes they'd actually been charged with. All of which confirmed to O'Sullivan that the skinhead trial had the telltale hallmarks of a political show trial. As in, some politicians wanted to stop the bad ink flowing from the Portland punk rock murders. So, the skins were just then talking to Detective Murphy in their cells. Without Savoie.

O'Sullivan dialed his clerk's local. "Are we ready?" he asked. Told that everything was in order, O'Sullivan stood, briefly checked out his reflection in the mirror behind his door, then stepped into the short hallway between his chambers and Courtroom 200.

His clerk preceded him. "All rise!" he said, a bit louder than he usually did. O'Sullivan marched into the courtroom, which was — as he'd been warned — packed to the rafters with reporters clutching notebooks and pens, and dozens of punks glaring at the skinheads. Patti Upchuck was there as a reporter, too, taking notes for *The NCNA*. As he strode toward his elevated oak desk, at the center of the courtroom, O'Sullivan could see that the three skinheads weren't standing.

On either side of them, O'Sullivan saw that the police and their own lawyers were hissing at them to stand up. The skinheads stayed put, however. They were wearing their street clothes, again, with grins on their stupid faces.

I'd like to wipe those grins off your faces, you sociopathic motherfuckers.

O'Sullivan sat down, and the media and everyone else did likewise. At that moment, the three skinheads rose, as one, and started staring at O'Sullivan. Their lawyers looked like they were going to have heart attacks. "Is there a problem, gentlemen?" O'Sullivan said, calm. "As your counsel have no doubt explained to you, standing when the presiding judge enters and leaves is a sign of respect. Do you have a problem with that?"

Bauer curled his lip. "We don't recognize your authority over us," he snarled. "Your laws mean nothing to us." At that, the three skinheads all simultaneously shouted the fourteen words: "We must secure the existence of our people and a future for white children!" They then gave fascist salutes.

That done, they waited, shooting hate-stares at O'Sullivan. The courtroom was pin-drop silent, except for the sound of reporters furiously scribbling away in their notebooks. Eventually, everyone's eyes came to rest on Sean O'Sullivan, to see what he'd do. Under his thick red hair, his scalp was tingling.

He had the power to cite the skinheads for contempt and throw them in jail until they apologized to the court. But he knew that the trio of neo-Nazis preferred being in jail to being on the street — where, he also knew, hundreds of Portland punk rockers wanted to meet up with them in a dark alley somewhere and beat the living shit out of them. Or worse.

The three defense lawyers looked at him, wide-eyed, unsure what he would do. Sharon Martin, knowing him a bit better, had a hunch what he would do. She was right.

"Gentlemen," O'Sullivan said. "I sense that you are looking for a fight. I'm not going to give you one. We have important matters to deal with here, today, so you can remain standing for all I care, while the rest of us comfortably sit, until your legs completely give out. I assure you that, however much you try, you will not be permitted to turn these proceedings into a circus.

"So," O'Sullivan said, "knock yourselves out. You can all stand until the cows come home."

Their protest now a big public relations failure, the three skinheads looked at each other, then slumped down into their seats.

"Very well," O'Sullivan said. He turned to his clerk and nodded. "Proceed."

The clerk read out the indictment against Bauer, Wojcik, and Babic, which said that they, "Martin Otto Bauer, Peter Josef Wojcik, and Dragomir Babic, on or about the 20th and 22nd day of November 1978, in the City of Portland, Maine, murdered Jimmy Cleary and Mark Upton in a manner that was planned and deliberate." The clerk paused for dramatic effect, but none was necessary. He looked at the skinheads. "How do you plead to the charges as read?"

Wojcik and Babic looked at Bauer, who nodded. All three stood again, slowly, and looked at the clerk. With one voice, they shouted their response:

"Guilty!"

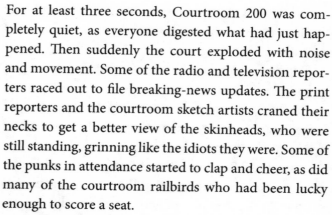

For at least three seconds, Courtroom 200 was completely quiet, as everyone digested what had just happened. Then suddenly the court exploded with noise and movement. Some of the radio and television reporters raced out to file breaking-news updates. The print reporters and the courtroom sketch artists craned their necks to get a better view of the skinheads, who were still standing, grinning like the idiots they were. Some of the punks in attendance started to clap and cheer, as did many of the courtroom railbirds who had been lucky enough to score a seat.

At the front of the courtroom, however, there was shocked silence. Sitting together near the DA's desk were Jimmy Cleary's parents and Mark Upton's mother, and all of them started crying when they heard the plea. Sharon Martin and the three defense counsel stared at the accused, looking stunned. Right behind Sharon, the look on Detective Savoie's face betrayed anger and bewilderment all at the same time. Meanwhile, Detective Murphy had his muscled arms crossed. He didn't look surprised at all. In fact, he was beaming, looking totally vindicated in his belief that the skinheads were guilty.

It made no sense.

Up on the bench, Sean O'Sullivan glared at the three neo-Nazis, his reddish skin getting redder. Forgetting the presence of the gavel he was supposed use on such occasions, O'Sullivan loudly brought down his fist on his desk, slamming it until all present were looking at him. "Quiet!" he hollered. "Quiet! This is a courtroom, not a newsroom! Quiet!"

Order achieved, O'Sullivan took a deep breath. He fixed his glare on the skinheads, who were still amused by it all.

"Do you understand the consequences of your plea of guilty?"

"Yeah," Bauer sneered. "It means we get to spend more time with our Aryan brethren until the revolution begins. We welcome it, Jew boy."

Instantly, O'Sullivan jabbed a finger at the police officers, and courthouse security gathered near the prisoner's box. "Take them out of here, now," he yelled, seething. He jabbed the same finger at Sharon Martin and the three defense counsel. "Ms. Martin, you three: meet me in my chambers immediately." Before anyone had time to react, O'Sullivan stomped out of the courtroom, heading toward his chambers. His clerk scurried after him, yelling "All rise!" over his shoulder as he went.

Martin and the three defense lawyers shuffled into his chambers. "Quite the performance your clients just gave," O'Sullivan said, as he attempted to keep his cool. "Did any of you three know that was going to happen?"

The lawyers, looking alarmed, stammered that they did not.

"I thought so," said O'Sullivan, shifting his gaze on Sharon Martin. "And you, Ms. Martin? Did you have any clue that was coming, today?"

"No, Your Honor," Martin said. "I was as shocked as everyone else."

"Fine," said O'Sullivan, tilting back in his leather-bound swivel chair. "No one knew. I see. Well, here is what is going to happen next."

O'Sullivan continued, measuring his words carefully. "I do not intend to accept their pleas at this time," he said. "They have counsel, they did it in open court, and they claimed to understand the nature of the charges, and the consequences. The pleas are therefore presumptively valid." He paused. "But I will not accept them at this time."

"W-why, Your Honor?" one of the lawyers asked.

"Because, from what I have seen of the evidence to date, I have considerable concern about the validity of their pleas," O'Sullivan said. "*U.S. v. Agdey,* folks. No less than the Supreme Court of the United States compels me to consider whether the plea has been given in circumstances where undue pressure was applied on the accused to plead guilty." O'Sullivan glared at them. "You are familiar with Agdey case, are you not, gentlemen? It was decided some six years ago. And at the nation's highest court, as well. Remember?"

The lawyers all nodded furiously, pretending to remember the case. O'Sullivan turned his attention to Martin. "Ms. Martin, I want to see the lead detectives in this case in my chambers, immediately."

"Yes, Your Honor. They're here. I'll get them right away."

"Good," said O'Sullivan. "Because something stinks here, and I aim to find out what that is."

CHAPTER 37

The court clerk, Ron McLeod's helpful courthouse source, watched as Detective Terry Murphy shifted in his seat in Judge Sean O'Sullivan's chambers, looking extremely uncomfortable. His partner, beside him, was watching him through the corner of his eye, while Sharon Martin was frowning at him, very unhappy. Sean O'Sullivan — who was even angrier than Martin — continued glaring at Murphy over the tops of his reading glasses. The clerk took notes, a summary of which would later be passed along to a grateful Ron McLeod.

"Let me get this straight," O'Sullivan said, as if speaking to a slow learner. "You went and saw the accused alone, without your partner or their legal counsel present? Is that right?"

"That's right," Murphy said, shifting again. "They all said they waived their right to have their counsel present. So I proceeded with further interrogating them about the two murders."

"I see," said O'Sullivan. "And did you not think it was a good idea to have Detective Savoie with you when you met with the three accused, to charge them? Or a DA?"

"I apologize, Your Honor," Murphy said, grim-faced. "I didn't expect them to plead guilty so quickly, so I didn't think it would be a problem. I'm sorry." He paused, looking up at the judge. "But at least the families will have some closure now?" He said it like it was a question.

O'Sullivan glared at Murphy, while Martin shook her head. "Closure, I see. Here's the problem, Detective," O'Sullivan said. "I am not entirely convinced by the legitimacy of the pleas those little bastards entered in my court, this morning. And I am not entirely convinced that they wouldn't have walked, had this case ever gone to trial." He paused, glancing at Sharon Martin. "No offence, Ms. Martin."

"None taken," she said.

"I have an obligation to assess whether the guilty pleas were voluntary, Detective Murphy, and here you were meeting them earlier, all on your own," O'Sullivan said. "That's problem one. Problem two is that, in the event that one or all of these monsters ever decides to withdraw their plea, and appeal, their little private chat with you will almost certainly become a legal issue and a PR nightmare. And that will not be helpful, will it?"

Murphy looked down, apparently wishing that all of this was over. He wondered if Martin was going to tell the Chief of Police.

O'Sullivan leaned back in his chair and addressed Sharon Martin. "In light of this, and in light of the state of the evidence, Ms. Martin, I intend to reflect on whether I should indeed accept the guilty pleas of the accused," he said. "I will entertain arguments from you, and defense counsel, in writing. But I warn you that I am not presently inclined to let the pleas stand."

"I understand, Your Honor," Sharon Martin said, wondering yet again why she ever chose to work as a District Attorney.

"Good," Sean O'Sullivan said, turning his attention to a stack of case law at the corner of his desk. "All of you have a nice day. Even you, Detective Murphy."

CHAPTER 38

"I'm sorry, Christopher," Assistant District Attorney Sharon Martin said, "but I'm not clear why we're meeting."

It was less than a week after the guilty pleas by Bauer, Wojcik, and Babic. The judge still hadn't ruled on whether the pleas would be accepted.

Reluctantly, Martin had agreed to meet with me and X. I stood by the door to her tiny office.

X ignored what she had said. "I'm not here to advocate for some neo-Nazis," he said, without emotion. "If they were all hanged, for any reason, no one would care. But they shouldn't be jailed for murdering our friends. They didn't do it."

"I see," Martin said. "Forgive me for being surprised by that. But you're not a police officer. And the accused have all pleaded guilty."

"That's irrelevant, and you know it," X said. "By accepting their guilty pleas, you ensure the real killer gets away with murder." She blinked, apparently amazed by X's self-confidence. Or arrogance.

X reached into the folds of his jacket and extracted some papers. "Have you heard of the Aryan Nations and Christian Identity?" he asked, placing the wrinkled pamphlets on her desk. "Identity is a phony religion that is taking the extreme Right by storm these days. And the Aryan Nations are its most violent converts."

Sharon Martin picked up the pamphlets and flipped through them, her revulsion obvious. "This stuff is awful," she said. "Where did you get this? This is hate propaganda, by any reasonable definition."

"Boston," X said. "And I agree. It's awful. But it's the philosophy that many of the skinheads, and almost everyone in the Far Right, subscribe to. And it is a factor in each of the murders — maybe even the reason why the murders took place."

"How do you know that?"

"I don't ... not for sure," X replied carefully, "but I'm willing to bet that religious symbols, related to Identity, were found on, or near, Jimmy, Mark, and Danny." He paused, watching her very carefully. "They were, weren't they?"

"I wouldn't tell you even if I knew that to be the case, which I don't," Martin said, looking shocked. "But, even if this Identity Aryan insanity is related to these prosecutions, it is irrelevant to what I am doing. Murder is murder, whether motivated by religion or not."

"I know that," X said. "But if the skinheads didn't do what they've been charged with — and they didn't, I'm

telling you — then this so-called religion is very relevant. Because it means that the killer is still out there,
and it means he believes he still has orders from God to
do it again. And he *will* do it again."

"He? One killer?" she said. "Why do you believe it
was one killer?"

"I didn't before. But I do now," X said, taking back the
pamphlets. "I've been reading up a lot on the Aryan Nations.
They have violent rhetoric, but so far, they haven't actually
been caught killing anyone. They've been very careful, in
fact, not to be caught doing anything too violent."

"Why?"

"Because they have been under continual police sur-
veillance since they moved to rural Pennsylvania, that's
why," he said. "There's an army of FBI agents watching
them. They'd be insane to commit all of these crimes in
the space of a few weeks in just one small city."

"From what you've said, they already sound insane,"
she said. "Why would you think such a group is being
careful?"

"Because," X said, standing up to leave, "to them, we
aren't worth the trouble. The Aryan Nations have bigger plans than a bunch of punk rockers in Portland.
Whoever is doing this might follow their beliefs, but he
isn't following their plan.

"He's out there, operating on his own."

After that, all of us started to see the mystery car every-where — sliding along, all dark and mysterious and shit, always at the edge of our vision. Together or by ourselves, we'd all spotted it, but we were always too far away to identify who was inside.

It was a pain in the ass. If it was the cops, why didn't they just identify themselves?

"It looks like a cop car," I said, out of breath, follow-ing one unsuccessful effort to sprint after the vehicle. "It's gotta be the fuckin' cops."

"Not sure if that's better than the neo-Nazis," X said, leaning against a fence near Holy Cross, also catching his breath.

"Do you remember what Marky said about the car he saw outside Gary's the night that Jimmy was killed?"

"Yeah. Dark brown, or black," X said. "Which is about ninety-nine percent of the cars in any city."

"But it could be the guys who killed Jimmy," I said, as we started walking.

"Could be," X said, shrugging, and we cut down the alleyway that led to my place. "Dunno. Whoever it is, they know that we've spotted them, but they keep com-ing back in the same car. Which says to me that their objective is to spook us."

It was working.

"So, do we tell the cops?"

"They're useless … or at least Savoie is," X said as we reached my place. "The Assistant DA said she'd look into it, but you know they won't."

CHAPTER 39

Luke Macdonald was excited.

"I got them!" he told X and me. "I got the guys that've been following us!" Luke, X, and I had met for an emergency get-together at Sound Swap. Luke had called us early Sunday morning. He'd been out on Saturday afternoon with his dad's super-expensive camera and a big honking lens. He'd staked out an alleyway between my place and X's, he said, and — just as it was getting dark — he caught the stalkers.

"I got maybe half-a-dozen shots before they took off," Luke said. "They probably saw me, but they didn't come after me."

X asked Luke to describe what he saw.

"Dark brown Chevy, dirty, plates covered in mud," Luke said, excited. "And there were definitely two guys in the front. Big."

"Great work, brother," I said, clapping Luke on the shoulder. "Can you get the shots developed fast?"

Luke shook his head. "Not until Monday at school," he said. "I need the PAHS darkroom. I've done it before. It's easy."

It was Sunday, and everything was closed. X and I looked at each other.

"Okay," X said. "Monday it is. Guard that film, Luke."

Luke nodded. "You got it, man," he said. "There's no fucking way anyone's getting this stuff from me."

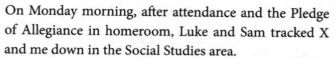

On Monday morning, after attendance and the Pledge of Allegiance in homeroom, Luke and Sam tracked X and me down in the Social Studies area.

We both jumped to our feet when we saw Luke. His face was a total mess. There was a gash across the bridge of his nose and clumps of clotted blood below his nostrils. One eye was just a slit and blackening fast, and there was a nasty purple bruise on his forehead, above the black eye. His T-shirt had been ripped at the neck.

"Jesus, Luke," I said. "What the hell happened?"

"I'm okay, but the bastards tore my Sid shirt," Luke said, frowning, looking down. "And I just got it, too."

"Who did it?" X asked, but we already knew the answer.

"Four skins," Sam said. "They must've seen him and followed him after he took those shots. They jumped him when he was transferring at the Maine Mall. We were supposed to meet up early this morning to develop the photos from yesterday."

Mr. Leduc, one of the Social Studies teachers, walked over and asked us to move our discussion out into the hallway. Then he noticed Luke's face. "You need medical care, Luke," he said, sounding concerned.

"I know, sir, thanks," Luke said. "I've already been in to the office and they've called the police. But the nurse isn't in yet."

Out in the hallway, X put an arm around Luke while Sam and I slumped against a row of lockers.

Everything is just getting worse and worse.

"Are you going to be okay, big guy?" X asked. "They worked you over pretty good."

"Yeah, I'm okay, brother," Luke said. "I'm a lot more worried about what my dad'll say when he hears all of his expensive fucking camera equipment is gone." He winced. "And the fact that all the evidence is gone, too, of course."

"Don't worry about that," X said. "I called the DA last night and gave her a description."

"What'd she say?" Sam asked.

"It wasn't even a Maine car," X said. "The mud covered up most of the plate, but they think it's from Pennsylvania."

"Jesus whipped," I said. "Pennsylvania? Didn't you say that's where that Aryan group is based?"

"The DA didn't want to talk about that. But, yeah," X said. "She told me the plates could have been stolen. But some of those guys seem to be up here now."

"Great, that's just great. But why would these Aryan pricks want to tail us?" Sam asked. "Why not get some of their local guys to do it, or whatever?"

Before X could respond, we were interrupted by an announcement from the PAHS administration, requesting that Luke report "immediately" to the office. Luke shrugged and started walking. Sam, X, and I followed.

The administration's office was in the middle of PAHS, near the school's gymnasium and across from the main entrance. Pushing open the doors to the lobby, we spotted some familiar faces.

"Hello, boys," Detective Savoie said, his flabby old face like a wrinkled shirt. Detective Murphy was standing to one side of him and the school's brainless, anally retentive vice-principal on the other.

"Two homicide detectives show up for the mugging of a high school student on a bus? Impressive," I said, not impressed at all.

Savoie, I fucking hate you, I think to myself. *I'll bet you're a closet Nazi, you fat prick.*

"Yeah, well, guys," Savoie said, irritated. "We want to talk to your friend Luke here, but we also want to talk to all of you. Especially after the DA told us this morning that someone has been following you guys and you didn't bother to call us. Again."

"Slipped my mind, I guess," X said, not hiding his contempt. "Sorry."

Savoie's face went red. He looked like he was going to have a stroke. Murphy put a big hand on X's shoulder. "Chris, if someone is still after you guys, we want to find them," he said. "We just want to help out here. Is there anything you can tell us about what these guys looked like?" He sounded genuinely concerned.

Savoie was still struggling to keep control. "Look, the administration told us you took some pictures. Where are they?"

"Too late," Luke said. "The guys who attacked me took all my dad's camera equipment and film."

"Shit!" Savoie yelled, causing about a dozen students and teachers to stop and watch the scene unfold. "You should have come straight to us!"

Ha! This is getting good. Tension is good.

X, Luke, Sam, and I said nothing. We just stared back at Savoie.

The detective really looked like that stroke was imminent. His partner just looked embarrassed. Recovering his voice, the vice-principal turned to the cops. "If you don't mind, gentlemen, we'd appreciate it if you could continue this discussion elsewhere. Luke needs to be seen by our nurse ... And you'll forgive me for saying that our school has had quite enough drama over the past three months."

CHAPTER 40

The autopsy report said that the volley of .45-caliber bullets slammed into the torso and head of the controversial radio talk show host as he stepped out of his Volkswagen Beetle. It was just past 9:00 p.m. The bullets ricocheted throughout the man's body, shattering into lead fragments — severing his spinal column, ripping apart his heart, and turning his brain into pulp. He fell onto the driveway at his Toronto home.

McLeod got his hands on a copy of the Toronto police report, natch.

The Brotherhood's man, the one who had lent his infant daughter to be used at the initiation ceremony, lowered the silenced MAC-10 machine gun and sprinted to the curb, where a dark sedan was waiting for him. In it, behind the wheel, were three other members of the Brotherhood, one of them the informant, and their leader. The shooter jumped into the vehicle and the Brotherhood screeched away, toward Lake Shore

Boulevard. The shooter gave a broad smile. "Did you see that?" he said. "He didn't make a sound. He just went down like I pulled the fucking rug out from under him." They all laughed.

The Brotherhood had made its second successful assassination, and the four men were happy. The talk show host's crime had been to criticize the Far Right on his CFRB radio program, and to ridicule their plan to wipe away the vestiges of civilization and return to a time where Aryan men were "rooted" in the earth. He'd called them "rural red-necked mouth-breathers and knuckle-dragging hicks," and that is why they decided to kill him.

The Brotherhood's first execution, turns out, had taken place a few days earlier. The victim was an Aryan Nations member who liked to shoot off his mouth in bars. The neo-Nazis thought the man was a security risk, and so a decision was made to eliminate him. McLeod told us the man was lured to a remote wooded spot about two hours away from the Aryan Nations' Pennsylvania compound. As he stepped out of a member's car, a hulking, muscular member of the Brotherhood smashed the back of his skull with a sledgehammer. That didn't kill him, to everyone's surprise. So the big man fired a shot from a Ruger Mini-14 into the man's forehead. That killed him. The job done, the Brotherhood's members — the informant included — then buried the man's body.

The big man — the one with the sledgehammer, and then the Ruger Mini-14 — was Northman.

Northman hadn't been present for the murder of the Toronto talk show host — he had to work — but he wished he had been. The informant later said he celebrated the death of the "talk show Jew," just as he and his kinsmen had been happy about the execution of "the big mouth." The revolution — the revolution to wipe out the muds, and the Jews, and the race traitors — had finally begun. The revolution that would see the return of a simpler, cleaner time. A new Reich, as their leader had said.

Northman stopped his car at the Interstate tollbooth and he grinned up at the pimply faced young attendant. "You again?" the guard said, friendly. "You sure are logging a lot of miles, these days."

"That's for sure," Northman said, extracting a single to pay for the toll. He looked at the video camera, recording the exchange. "I gotta find a new line of work."

"Well, let me know when a spot opens up," the boy said, eager. "I'd give anything to do what you do."

"I'll let you know," Northman said, pocketing his wallet and shifting into drive. "Have a good one."

And with that, Northman started again on the long drive back home, and back to the final confrontation with the one he hated the most, the punk called X.

CHAPTER 41

We stopped seeing the mystery car right around the time Luke took his lost-for-good pictures, and right around the time the threatening notes and symbols began. In our lockers at PAHS, at some of our homes — basically, anywhere we hung out — members of the X Gang, the NCNA, and the Room 531 crowd started to receive cryptic (and often less-than-cryptic) threats. *Die Jew, Heil Hitler, 88, you're a fag,* crap like that. We couldn't figure out who was doing it. But it was totally obvious that the messengers were connected, in some way, with psychopaths in Christian Identity and the Far Right.

Not very fucking subtle, these Nazi bastards.

So, we had another meeting with the DA, Sharon Martin. As before, it took place in her miniature downtown office. But along with me and X, this time, were X's dad and Patti. We had all brought along copies of the hate propaganda and threats we'd received, and some Polaroids of hate graffiti in our neighborhood. X and I stood at the door to Martin's office, while Thomas and Patti sat in the only two available chairs. Thomas placed the hate stuff X had received — along with everything that had been sent to me, Patti, and Sister Betty — on Martin's desk blotter. Beside them, he laid out photos I'd taken of various neo-Nazi and white supremacist symbols — the Celtic cross, the SS double lightning bolts, the swastika — that had recently been left behind at the X Gang's regular haunts. Martin said nothing as she slowly went through the notes and the photos. We watched her.

Finally, she sat back in her chair and shook her head. "I'm very sorry all of you are being subjected to this sort of thing," she said. "Some of these messages are clearly threats. So I reiterate my suggestion that we bring in some officers with experience in this area, so they can investigate and take steps to protect those who need protection."

I spoke first. "Detective Murphy is a good guy, but the rest of them have been totally useless," I said. "The murder investigations have been a complete farce."

"There is an excellent detective on the force that I think would be helpful. He has a lot of experience dealing with cases like this. I'll ask if we can get him involved." Martin was talking about the Chow brothers' dad, turns out.

Suddenly there was a knock at the door. X and I moved so it could open all the way. A junior lawyer from the DA's office stuck his head in.

"Um," he said, looking around at the visitors in Martin's cramped office.

"What is it?" Martin said, irritated.

"Judge O'Sullivan has sent word over that he's going to rule on the guilty pleas," the junior said. "He wants you over in Courtroom 200 in one hour sharp."

A few minutes earlier, in his chambers — and as the indiscreet court reporter and the dazed defense lawyers looked on — O'Sullivan fixed a menacing gaze on Martin and asked her if she, as an officer of the court, believed there was "a factual basis" for the pleas that Bauer, Wojcik, and Babic had made. After nearly a minute of total silence, Martin finally said, her head lowered, "No, Your Honor. As an officer of the court, I do not now believe there is a factual basis for the pleas as entered in court."

O'Sullivan looked at her, feeling satisfied but unhappy all at once. He was satisfied because Martin, who he obviously thought was a highly ethical attorney, had told him what he knew she knew was the truth. But he was pissed off; one, because she hadn't stood up to her boss and refused to prosecute the skinheads, and, two, because he knew his ruling would set off a colossal media and political shit storm. And he and Martin would be at the center of it.

"Gentlemen," he said, his contempt obvious, as the clerk captured his every word. "Lest you think that you have pulled off some sort of a historic legal coup, let me tell you why I am going to be refusing your clients' guilty pleas, and why I am very reluctantly putting them back on the street in a few minutes' time. It is not because any of you are good at your jobs.

"In your written submissions to me on this matter, not one of you — not one — indicated that you had carefully canvassed the implications of a guilty plea with any one of your clients. You didn't do that, even though you are required to do that.

"And, as you should be aware, that would be tantamount to a fraud on the court. And a fraud on the court represents a miscarriage of justice. And a miscarriage of justice would serve to bring the administration of justice into disrepute. And I will be damned, by God, if justice is brought into disrepute on my watch, in my court. Even with clients as clearly despicable as yours."

"That is what I intend to rule. Now, all of you head into Courtroom 200 before I change my mind."

They did, quickly.

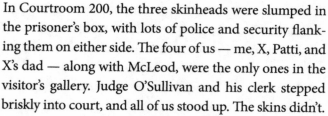

In Courtroom 200, the three skinheads were slumped in the prisoner's box, with lots of police and security flanking them on either side. The four of us — me, X, Patti, and X's dad — along with McLeod, were the only ones in the visitor's gallery. Judge O'Sullivan and his clerk stepped briskly into court, and all of us stood up. The skins didn't.

From the bench, over the top of his reading glasses, O'Sullivan peered at the accused with open disdain. "I won't ask you to stand, gentlemen, because I know you do not have any respect for this court," he said. "I would say that the feeling is decidedly mutual, but I think you know that already."

O'Sullivan looked down at the papers in front of him and continued: "I have received the submissions of counsel. As is well established, the court is always under a duty to inquire as to the validity of guilty pleas entered before it. The court is not bound to always accept guilty pleas, particularly in cases where the charges are very serious. The charges here, murder, are the most serious. In cases like these, there cannot be a superficial acceptance of responsibility. The accused must be competent, their plea must be free and voluntary, and there must be a factual basis for the plea they have made." There was a long pause before he continued. "I also note that the accused must not be *coerced* into making the guilty plea."

Oh, no. Here goes.

At this, O'Sullivan stopped and looked up at the skinheads. For the first time, the sneers had slipped off the pale, sociopathic faces of Bauer, Wojcik, and Babic. For the first time, they seemed really, really uncomfortable about something. They seemed afraid, even.

I looked around. Like O'Sullivan, like Martin, X wasn't surprised, at all. He had his arms crossed and his expression seemed to be saying *Knew it.*

O'Sullivan squinted down at his notes. He quickly mentioned a few relevant cases, and then he glared at the prisoner's box. "This court considers that accepting the guilty pleas would represent a miscarriage of justice, and would bring the administration of justice into disrepute. As such, gentlemen, your plea is struck from the record, and you are, for now, free to go, pending the assault matter that is within the jurisdiction of district court. Good day."

And with that, O'Sullivan brought down his gavel, stood up, and swept out the courtroom, his clerk hustling after him.

CHAPTER 42

North American punk rockers between the years 1977 and 1979 didn't know much about organizing protests. In those days, we were way more busy trying to avoid getting the shit kicked out of us. And getting together in one place often led to beatings.

Britain's Rock Against Racism gigs and rallies inspired North American punks, however. Tens of thousands of Brit punks showed up to those. Those rallies reminded us that there was, as X said, punk strength in punk numbers. And the decision of Maine's judicial system to put Martin Bauer, Peter Wojcik, and Dragomir Babic back on the street gave us a really good reason to come together in great numbers.

Three neo-Nazi skinheads who had *admitted* they were guilty of murder had been set free. Even though X, me, and the Upchucks believed the skins were probably blameless in the murders of our friends, the overwhelming majority of Portland punks felt otherwise.

Same with the public. All over town, all over the state, the three skinheads were considered guilty as charged, throw away the key.

There was real, honest-to-god outrage, then, when they were let go. Local labor unions, feminists, and environmental groups — along with student leaders from the University of Maine and a half-dozen area high schools — were super pissed off, too, and they wanted everyone to know it.

So, at noon on the Friday following the judge's decision, about three hundred people assembled outside the main doors of the district courthouse on Federal Street, and plenty of others gathered in Lincoln Park, directly across the street. In the crowd were X's parents, as well as various siblings and relatives of Jimmy Cleary, Mark Upton, and Danny O'Heran. It was a sunny kind of a day, not too cold, and none of us had bothered to obtain a permit, on purpose. The Portland police, as a result, were out in full force. A half-dozen of them had donned riot gear.

They look fucking ridiculous. Morons.

X and I silently observed the stupid cops as labor organizers tested their bullhorns on the courthouse steps. In all, there were about two dozen officers there, but no sign of either Murphy or Savoie.

Two men stood near the line of cops, both with short, cropped hair and wearing long coats. We pegged them as detectives right away. When they saw us, they walked straight over. The first one, who had black hair and an easy manner about him, extended his hand. "Hello, boys," he said, smiling. "My name is Richard

Chow. I'm a detective with Portland PD. This is my colleague, Detective Steve Wright. We've been assigned to investigate the threats some of you have been receiving. I believe Sharon Martin may have told you about us."

I shook Detective Chow's hand, then Wright's. X, reluctantly, did likewise.

When Detective Chow spoke again, it was to X: "I think you might know my sons. They like the same music you do."

X nodded. "We've met them," he said. "They're smart guys. You must be proud of them."

"Yes, I am," the detective said, smiling and pulling his glove back on. "Their mother and I are also interested in keeping them safe and sound. So we have a personal interest, you might say, in ensuring that these crimes get solved and ensuring the bad guys get put away."

"Us, too," I said.

"Good," Detective Chow said, waving a gloved hand in the direction of the gathering crowd of protesters. "I understand you boys helped to organize this rally or protest or whatever it is?"

"Protest," I said. "We want to protest the way in which the justice system has botched solving the murders of our friends. And other stuff, too."

"I understand," Chow said. "You have that right, although it would have been better if you'd obtained a permit. But I suspect you did that on purpose, maybe to provoke a confrontation?" He smiled.

"We don't like asking for permission," X said, his voice even.

"So I've heard," Chow said, still smiling. "In any event, you have my word that we won't intervene if people remain peaceful. We would only ask that you stay off Federal Street and keep open a path for pedestrians. And that you get a permit for your next protest. All right?"

"Okay," I said.

"Good, good," Chow said. "So, have a nice protest, and Steve and I look forward to meeting with you to discuss the unpleasant material you have been receiving. Good day."

With that, the two detectives walked off and started talking to some of the uniformed officers.

At that moment, the Upchuck sisters appeared with Mike the bouncer. He was wearing biker boots, a biker jacket, and his FTW T-shirt, and looking completely out of place. "Look what we found," Sister Betty said, an arm hooked through Mike's. "Our friend here wants to protest, too."

We exchanged handshakes with Mike. "Really?" I asked. "What do you want to protest?"

"Everything in general," Mike said. "But cops in particular."

"Then you've come to the right place," I said. "We generally hate everything, and we hate cops in particular."

"Sign me up," Mike said, as the first of the sort-of spontaneous speeches began. The protestors started moving toward the courthouse steps, applauding the first speaker. X looked around. There were probably more than four hundred protestors now, and about three dozen police. For law-and-order Portland, which had never been big on protests of any type, that many rabble-rousers showing up on a cold winter morning was a huge deal. So, there were three TV news crews shooting video for the local CBS and NBC affiliates and what looked like about a dozen print and radio reporters, too, watching everything carefully. Ron McLeod was one of them.

Around the courthouse, in the windows of the dull old office towers that housed myriad State of Maine public servants, people were looking down at the motley crew of punks, unionists, students, and average citizens. Some of the protestors were carrying signs. "NO JUSTICE, NO PEACE," some read. "SMASH RACISM AND FASCISM," declared a few others. One sign was attracting a lot of cameras: "COPS AND KLAN, HAND IN HAND." Leah Yeomanson, the drummer with the Punk Rock Virgins, was carrying it. Cops were glaring at her.

"Leah's sign sure is edgy," X said, looking amused.

"I dig it," I said.

As a bearded, burly local labor leader started to speak, attacking the outcome of the skinhead prosecutions, another labor guy approached X. He introduced himself as Jim Muretich, with the American Labor Congress. "We were wondering if you could say a few words, Chris," Muretich said. "A lot of the people here are your friends."

"It's X," he said, "and I'm not much of a public speaker. What do you want me to say?"

"Sorry … *X*," Muretich said, smiling. "Say what you want. Say why you and your friends are here."

I nudged him. "C'mon man, do it. You'll do good." Mike and Sister Betty nodded. Patti leaned closer. "You should do this, babe," she said. "It's important."

X looked at Patti and me for a moment, then nodded. "Okay, I'll say something."

Three union leaders, three student leaders, and one antiracism activist spoke, yelling well-intentioned stuff about the rise of organized racism and how unjust the U.S. justice system was, *blah blah blah*.

When it was X's turn, he jogged up the steps and took the megaphone from Muretich. Dozens of punks started to shout: "X! X! X! X! X!"

When the shouting died down, he held the megaphone up. "Hi, guys," he said, as the punks shouted greetings back at him. "My name is X. And, as God is my witness, I say to the bastard who killed my friends, and who is probably listening to us right now …" He paused, looking toward the street. Detective Chow was furiously shaking his head back and forth, clearly unhappy.

"I swear that we are going to find you, and we are going to *end you*."

Oh, boy. Here we go.

CHAPTER 43

The reopening of Gary's wasn't a super big deal. No hoopla, mainly because the owners didn't ever want to spend any money they didn't have to. The signing of the Hot Nasties to Stiff Records, however, was a big, big deal for all of us.

It was fucking huge. *Stiff Records!*

Stiff was a British independent label. Without it, punk rock wouldn't have attracted so much attention at the start — or, possibly, even existed. Formed in 1976, Stiff wasn't affiliated with the great big multinationals who insisted on dropping coma-inducing corporate crap on the uncritical masses. "If it ain't Stiff, it ain't worth a fuck," was Stiff's unofficial slogan, which the media always reprinted with asterisks, which fooled no one. Stiff was indisputably punk.

To us punks in the hinterland, in remote places like Portland, Maine, Stiff's slogan was also the truth. If it wasn't on Stiff, it usually wasn't worth listening to.

Elvis Costello, Nick Lowe, the Damned, Wreckless Eric, Ian Dury, Madness, Devo, and many other punk or new wave acts signed to Stiff in the early days. The signing of Akron, Ohio's Devo was, for North American punks, an important event, even though Devo's music could be occasionally irritating ("Kiss for college kids," Robert Christgau hilariously wrote in *Creem*). It was important because it meant that Stiff — and the very few other labels like it — were prepared to sign punk and new wave bands who weren't British. North American bands, even.

Like, say, the Hot Nasties!

The label had first heard about the Nasties in the pages of the *New Musical Express* in November, when no less than Charles Shaar Murray had written that positive one-paragraph review of the band. After that, however, the Nasties had only appeared in sensational media reports about the Portland punk rock murders, or when Jimmy Cleary was referenced as the band's deceased lead singer. So Stiff's guys sent away for *The Invasion of the Tribbles* EP — and after giving it a spin, they wanted to sign them.

Stiff's Jake Riviera and the Nasties' Sam Shiller shared a couple of late-night phone calls about the band's future. At first, Sam had said that the band couldn't go on without its lead singer and cofounder. Riviera, a legend who had managed pub rockers Dr. Feelgood, among others, encouraged the band to stick together and keep at it. "We want to remix and rerelease the Nasties' extended play over here," Riviera said over the phone. "If it does well, we would look at some more singles and maybe an album. A tour would be a good idea, too."

But to do a tour and more recording, the Nasties needed a new lead singer. Initially, Sam, Eddie, and Luke considered everyone from X to the Modern Minds' Moe Berg. But, after apparently little debate, they settled on the only punk they apparently felt could do it right.

Me.

I knew every Nasties chord and lyric, true. I had seen the band at every single show they had ever played, true. And, while the Social Blemishes' style was more chaotic and noisy than the Hot Nasties tight pop-punk stuff, they felt I was a good enough singer and rhythm guitarist to fit in. I was the logical choice, they told me.

But I wasn't so sure. It was a big step, filling Jimmy's shoes. So me, Sam, Eddie, Luke, X, and the Upchucks met for a historic punk rock summit in the basement at Sound Swap. "How could I ever replace Jimmy?" I asked, shaking my head. "It's fucking impossible. It can't be done. It's insane."

"Brother, we're not asking you to *be* Jimmy," Sam said. "Nobody could ever replace Jimmy. We want you to be you."

"Our sound was never going to be the same after losing Jimmy," Luke said, sitting on the wooden stairs down to the basement, cradling the brand-new Fender Bullet bass he bought after Stiff came calling. "We knew if we stayed together, everything would have to change. We can't go back to what we were."

I was still unsure. I looked at X and the Upchucks. "What do you guys think?"

"Kurt, after Danny got put in the hospital, you weren't even going to keep the Blemishes going," Sister Betty said, while Patti nodded her head. "This makes sense. I mean, fuck, it's Stiff Records."

X, with his arms folded and sitting on Sound Swap's stairs, looked at me. "Chances like this don't come along very often, brother," he said, his voice low. "You know what Jimmy would have said."

I wish Jimmy was here. I fucking miss him so, so much.

After ten seconds ticked by, I raised my hands in surrender. "All right," I said, "I will be a Hot Nasty. Or at least I'll try."

And so the Kurt Blank–led Hot Nasties made their debut on the puny stage at Gary's, the week that the bar reopened to local punks. The place was packed to the walls, well over the legal limit. Hearing the band's songs again made for an emotional night. Sister Betty wept openly, while her older sister covertly wiped away mascara streaks on her cheeks. X, sitting with them at one of the tavern's miniscule round tables just off the dance floor, asked if either Upchuck needed some Kleenex. "Doesn't this make you even a little emotional, X?" Betty said, wiping her eyes.

"Sure," he said. "But not sad. It's good."

The reconstituted Hot Nasties continued to play. Midway through our rendition of "The Secret of Immortality," when Sister Betty was again bawling, X felt a tap on his shoulder. He looked up: it was Mike the bouncer, signaling for him to follow. X followed Mike to the front of the bar.

Mike pushed open the door that led to Gary's puny lobby entry. Waiting there, looking uncomfortable, were the two Chow brothers.

"We couldn't let any more people in," Mike said, "but they said they were here only to talk to you, anyway."

"Thanks, Mike," X said, as Mike disappeared back into the bar.

X glanced in the direction of Frank, another bouncer, who was immersed in that morning's *Sun*. "Hey, guys," X said to the Chow brothers. "It should be okay to talk here."

"How do the Nasties sound?" Peter asked, sounding wistful.

"They sound pretty good," X said. "It's a bit bittersweet, though. Different."

John nudged his brother. "So, we had some information we wanted to give you," Peter whispered, glancing nervously in the direction of Frank, who remained totally disinterested. "You have to be careful what you do with it."

"Of course," X said. "What's up?"

John spoke for the first time. "Have you ever heard of a town called Exeter?"

CHAPTER 44

X was in the passenger seat, me in the back. Mike drove.

I fidgeted with my camera and tried to make conversation. "I thought bikers drove, you know, motorcycles, not family trucksters."

"Family trucksters?" Mike asked, eyeing me in the rear-view.

"Station wagons," X said, surveying the landscape slipping by on Interstate 95. "That's what our parents drive. So Kurt calls them family trucksters."

"Oh," Mike said, chuckling. "Got it. Family trucksters. Well, it works for us today. I didn't want to attract too much attention, and I don't think we did."

That's actually kind of debatable, Mike.

The trip to Exeter, New Hampshire, had started early on Saturday morning and had been pretty uneventful, but we definitely hadn't gone unnoticed. The town itself was like dozens of other small New England towns: a couple hockey rinks and football fields, a couple liquor stores, a couple grocery stores, a couple gun shops, one government office, one post office, one hairdresser, and several garages and churches. And the locals, all of them on super-high alert for any newcomers.

In Exeter, in recent weeks, there had been plenty of newcomers, and it seemed the locals didn't much like it. There had been pickup trucks with muddied plates from places like Pennsylvania and Maine and Canada, all heading straight through town and out toward "that acreage." There had been some big, foul-mouthed boys with shaved heads piling into the liquor stores and buying up as much cheap beer as they could. There had been the sound of gunshots — too many of them, out of season — echoing from the outskirts of town. And on one occasion, there had been a bespectacled reporter from the *Portland Press Herald* poking around, asking lots of pointed questions about the family who lived out on that acreage.

They didn't like it, not any of it. Before the trouble-makers arrived, Exeter had been a nice town, a quiet place, where older folks came to retire and the younger ones worked at shipbuilding or in the lumber mills. It was a conservative place, politically, but certainly no place for extremists.

For the trip to Exeter, Mike, X, and I abandoned our leather jackets and pulled on broken-in jean jackets instead. I tucked my spiky, bleached-blond hair under an old trucker's cap and X took out his earrings. We took our lead from Mike.

It was kind of weird, this big old biker helping out a bunch of much younger punk rockers. We didn't ask him why. But X's hunch was that he liked the fact that we didn't like cops, and he was angry that there had been a murder of a punk kid on his watch. Made sense.

Anyway, our first stop was the post office, where some old-timers had gathered for their regular Saturday morning exchange of gossip. As X and I hung back, Mike approached a couple of them. He told the elderly Exeter men that he was in the market for a couple of used generators and was looking for an acreage outside town where he'd heard they were for sale.

"Oh yeah," one of the old-timers said, clearly unconvinced. "That place. I'd get my generators somewhere else, if I were you."

It was the same story at a tavern, at a hockey rink, and in the parking lot outside one of the liquor stores. Nobody wanted to talk about "that place" — or at least nobody wanted to talk about it to a trio of strangers. Finally, outside a small school, the Living Faith Bible School, Mike found a man chopping away at ice at the edge of the walkway to the front doors. The man paused in his work and identified himself as Chester Stanwick, the pastor and principal. "Oh, yes," Stanwick said. "I know the place. I know the family quite well, in fact."

The family who lived on the acreage numbered five, Stanwick told us — "two young children, the mother, the mother-in-law, and *him*."

Him, it seemed, was an angry, troubled man, according to the pastor.

Stanwick knew what Identity was, and he knew what the pseudo-crazy religion did to its true believers. A year before, he explained, the couple had enrolled their two daughters in the Living Faith Bible School. All had been fine for a while, he said. "Then, one day, one of the girls showed up with a book — or, it was more of a pamphlet, actually— something called *The Hoax of the Twentieth Century*. She was showing the book to other students and talking to them about it," Stanwick said. "When we found out what she was doing, we asked her to take the book home."

The book was hate propaganda, banned in many countries. It tried to make the case that the Holocaust was a massive lie.

"The day after we sent the girl home with it, the father barged into my office, where I was meeting with a church elder. He yelled a few curses at me, and then he lunged across my desk and tried to take a shot at me. I saw it coming, so I was on my way in the opposite direction," Stanwick said, laughing. "He hit me in the chest, but it didn't hurt much. The church elder and I persuaded him to calm down and agree to a meeting with the church leadership, to arbitrate the dispute."

At the meeting, Stanwick and other church members explained that they did not want their school associated with hate propaganda or Holocaust denial. The girls' father was not impressed. He announced that they planned to immediately withdraw the girls from the school. "And we haven't seen them since," Stanwick said. He paused, carefully looking us over. "I don't know who you fellows are, but I'm pretty sure you're not just here to pick up a couple used generators.

You should be very careful if you're heading out there. He's armed to the teeth."

Great. Terrific.

After bidding the pastor farewell, we headed west out of Exeter in the direction of the acreage. A half-mile before where Chester Stanwick had said it was located, Mike spotted a state police cruiser parked directly behind a muddy, unmarked sedan. "Cops," he said. "They may be here for the crazy fucker who lives there, but they may be here because someone tipped them off that the three of us were in town. I don't think we need to be carded by the cops today, do you boys?"

"Nope," we agreed, so Mike swung the station wagon around, back in the direction of the Interstate and Portland.

We rode back mostly in silence. Two hours later, we were back in the city. As Mike pulled up to the curb outside X's, Patti and Betty Upchuck came rushing out of the house.

Uh-oh.

"What's wrong?" X asked as he stepped out of the car.

"It's two of the skinheads," Patti said, looking a bit freaked out. "Wojcik and Babic. It's all over the news."

CHAPTER 45

The severed heads of Peter Wojcik and Dragomir Babic had been found in their shared second-floor East Portland apartment, placed neatly on the countertop in their puny kitchen. The gruesome details became public a few days later because the killer, or killers, had taken well-lit Polaroids of the grisly scene and mailed them to the police reporter at the *Sun* and to Ron McLeod at the *Press Herald*. Neither paper published the photographs, of course, but — under a big, bold warning that "details contained in this news report may upset some readers" — they both printed detailed descriptions of what the photos showed. The disclaimer, of course, ensured that everyone read the details.

Reporters are con men.

Bit by bit, the rest of the details leaked out. A neighbor on the first floor had called the landlord and then the police when blood seeped through his bedroom ceiling. The responding officers found the bodies of Wojcik and

Babic on a sheetless bed. Their tongues had been hacked out and tossed in a corner. On the wall above the bed, the number *88* had been smeared, a foot high, in their blood.

Subtle.

McLeod later told us that the police report said the apartment had contained little furniture, but two sawed-off shotguns were leaning against the wall in the bedroom. Stacked in the corners of the main room were hundreds of pamphlets and books generated by the Aryan Nations and the White Aryan Resistance. Some were the same as the ones that had been left for members of the X Gang and other Portland punks. On a wall in the bedroom was a large poster of Hitler. And in the living room, they had tacked up a swastika flag that looked old enough to have actually come from the Second World War.

Detectives Murphy and Savoie hadn't been assigned to the case. Judge O'Sullivan's very unpopular decision to toss out the skinheads' guilty pleas and set them free had caused a lot of heartburn for Portland's mayor, and for the Chief of Police. Chow and Wright had been assigned to the double murder, a fact that probably pissed off Murphy and Savoie big-time.

"Big, big mess," Ron McLeod told us later on, over the phone. "Big mess."

No shit, Sherlock.

CHAPTER 46

X sat at his Selectric in his bedroom, the page blank-staring at him. He looked at his notes again and flipped through the photographs I had taken. Both me and Patti had advised him against what he was about to write. But he started typing anyway.

"A CONSPIRACY OF HATE AND MURDER," he wrote, as a placeholder headline. He could change it later, but it would do for now. It fit.

What he was writing, he knew, might get him sued. It would make some angry people even angrier. It would make him more of a target than he already was. But, with so many now dead, and with so many hurt, and with no end in sight, he told us he felt he didn't have much choice. He *had* to become the target. Patti and I didn't like that strategy one bit, but he wouldn't listen. I sat on his bed, strumming the Fender Patti had given him at Christmas, watching.

Fuck, he is so stubborn.

In the quiet of his bedroom, the sound of the type-writer keys seemed to be almost as loud as Eddie's snare drum. As he finished a page and pulled it out, he'd hand it to me.

> There is a cancer in the city's corridors of power. It is a cancer that is spreading, one that has already resulted in four murders, one attempted murder, and a system that is as corrupt as it is incompetent.
>
> The cancer is a toxic mix of neo-Nazism, white supremacy, and a hate group that literally seeks to wipe away everything that is modern and urban, and start all over again in a primitive, Far Right nirvana that will only accept so-called "Aryans." And the organization that is supposed to be preventing this? The organization that is, instead, indifferent to this spreading cancer — or, perhaps, even secretly assisting it?

He paused for a moment, and then kept going.

> The Portland police department and high-level sources have told the NCNA that Portland cops are suspected of possibly being complicit in the very murders they have been charged with solving.

The column went on from there, adding previously unknown stuff about the murders of Jimmy Cleary and Mark Upton — and stating clearly that the same people had tried to kill Danny O'Heran, and that it wasn't a suicide attempt. It talked about why the three skinheads — two dead, and one missing — couldn't have done any of the killings. And it linked the Aryan Nations' wave of murder and crime to the Portland punk rock murders.

The piece ran some 1,500 words and would be broken up by my photos and line drawings. There was a detailed rendering I did of the Aryan Nations' hooked cross, a photo of the New Hampshire sheriff's cruiser at the remote acreage outside Exeter, and a shot of the protest outside the Portland courthouse.

Along with all of that, at X's request, I had carefully — and very reluctantly — done up three official-looking India ink drawings of the scenes where Jimmy, Mark, and Danny had been found. Below Jimmy, the cutline was "Crucifixion." Below Mark, it was "Martyrdom." And, below Danny, it was "Baptism." In this part, X wrote:

> All of the killings (or attempted killings) of our friends were ritualistic and were the result of the killers' insane, sick, twisted mind. And all the murders and attacks are connected to the killers' counterfeit religion, which calls itself Christian Identity.

Laying out that edition of *The NCNA* was done late one afternoon in the Industrial Arts area in PAHS's basement. Members of the paper's staff, along with some Room 531 regulars, had kept watch to make sure that no teacher or member of the administration could see what we were doing. It was printed off on the presses at *The Casco Bay*, a kooky libertarian weekly that didn't give a shit what *The*

NCNA had to say, as long as we could pay. Which, after the success of the last Gary's gig, X and I could.

We distributed *The NCNA* just outside the parking lots at PAHS and PHS, as usual, but with one key difference: X had suggested he, Patti, and I keep all the copies in the trunk of my car, and that I make certain to keep the engine running. Just as PAHS's vice-principal came charging out the school's front doors, a copy of *The NCNA* clutched in one hand, me and Patti understood why. "Time to split," X said, and we did. "Things are about to get interesting."

By the time the three of us pulled up at X's house a few hours later, almost every copy of *The NCNA* had been passed out. His mother was waiting for us, really, really pissed off. "We've had repeated calls from that reporter at the *Press Herald*, Detective Savoie, Detective Chow, and a libel lawyer representing the Portland Police Association, X," she said, flipping through the message slips. "Do you know what you're doing?"

Yeah, he's declaring war on the cops, Mrs. X. That's what he's doing.

We all watched as X collected the few remaining copies of *The NCNA* from the back of my car. "I do," he said, seeming unfazed by his mother's concerns. "I'm trying to provoke a reaction."

And, holy shit, did he ever.

Mrs. X frowned when she saw the headline emblazoned across the front page. "NEO-NAZIS, MURDER, AND THE PORTLAND COPS WITH BLOOD ON THEIR HANDS," it read.

"Dear God," she said.

CHAPTER 47

The benefit was for Rock Against Racism, the U.K.-based outfit that — like everyone else, pretty much — had heard about the murders and near-murders in Portland, Maine, and was greatly alarmed by the rumblings about violent hate groups. By 1979, RAR had become the best-known anti-hate movement around. The fact that RAR was supporting some Portland punks was super important. It made a statement.

For the show, Gary's dirty walls were covered with shiny, black and pink RAR banners and posters sent to Sister Betty and me by antiracist organizers in London. The cover charge was five bucks — pretty high, I guess, but everyone knew it was for a good cause. Anyone who attended got an RAR badge and a shot at winning one of the banners.

The local scene, bit by bit, was coming back. The Nasties' record deal, the smell of spring in the air, the arrival of some exciting new acts (like the Golden Portlanders, and the Sandwiches) — plus the bloody end to two of the three

neo-Nazi skins and the total disappearance of the third —
had all combined to lessen some of the unease local
punks had been feeling for months. So, when the RAR
benefit was announced, hundreds of local kids wanted to
attend. The show featured the Punk Rock Virgins as the
headliner and the Mild Chaps as the opening act. The gig
was billed as a "Punk Chicks and Chaps Night" by Sister
Betty and me, mainly because we had organized most of
it. X, meanwhile, had been suspended from school for the
sin of publishing the cop-hating edition of *The NCNA*.
He had refused to reveal to PAHS's administration the
names of anyone else who had been involved in putting
it together, and so they sent him home for a few days,
meaning he had plenty of time to help us out.

Nobody had sued him, because truth is a defense.

And everyone knew he was right.

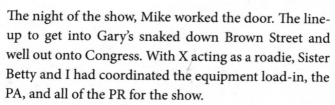

The night of the show, Mike worked the door. The lineup to get into Gary's snaked down Brown Street and
well out onto Congress. With X acting as a roadie, Sister
Betty and I had coordinated the equipment load-in, the
PA, and all of the PR for the show.

Inside, X and Patti and those of us in the new Hot
Nasties stood up near the stage during the Mild Chaps
set. We'd gone to Matthew's for chicken and chips, and
by the time we returned to Gary's, there was nowhere
left to sit. The place was packed. It was totally amazing.

Betty was really excited. During lulls in the action, the two of us gave interviews about the importance of opposing organized racism to WBLM, 1310 AM, and even a terrified-looking *Daily Sun* reporter.

Midway through the Mild Chaps set, Koby, the Gary's waitress, approached Sam and Sister Betty. "Hey, honey, there's a reporter out front who wants to talk to you about all of this stuff," she croaked into Betty's ear, balancing a tray full of empty draft glasses. "Mike said he wants to film you outside or something."

"Okay, thanks, Koby," Betty said, then turned to Sam. "Wanna come? You'll be famous, like me!"

Laughing, they walked over to X and Patti. "I have to talk to another reporter out front, okay? Be right back," Betty said.

"Okay," Patti said. "Don't be long. We're on soon."

Outside Gary's, the lineup to get in was getting shorter. Only about a half-dozen people remained outside. Mike was checking the clearly fake ID of a group of clearly underage girls when Sister Betty and Sam stepped through the main doors. "I'm here for my cameo," Betty said, arms wide. Mike looked at her, frowning.

"What?" he said.

"Never mind. Koby said there was a reporter out here who wanted to talk to us."

"Oh, yeah," Mike said, returning to the fake ID. He pointed a finger west, toward Free Street. "Frank said they're in their van around the corner in the lot, getting set up. Cable station or something."

"Okay, sweetie, thanks," she said, patting Mike on the arm.

CHAPTER 48

"There's no van there," X said, returning to Gary's Brown Street entrance. He had searched the parking lot at the side of the tavern, the alleyway at the back, and all along Brown and beyond. Betty and Sam were gone. Vanished.

No. NO NO NO NO NO.

Patti, her voice quavering, turned to Mike. "Who told you there was a reporter outside? Did you see any reporter?"

"No, I was checking IDs," Mike said, his expression dark. "The door guy, Frank, told me they were looking to speak to one of the organizers. I'll ask him."

Gary's entrance was deserted, save for a hooker sitting on a chair getting warm. Frank was watching *Kojak* on a tiny black-and-white TV high atop a shelf in the corner. "Hey, Mike," Frank said, as we approached the desk. "What's up?"

"That guy who said he wanted to interview one of the kids, did he show you any ID or anything?"

"Nope," Frank said. "Just said he wanted to interview the organizers, is all. Why?"

"He's not there, and neither are our friends," X said, squeezing Patti's hand. She was leaning forward and looked like she might faint. I took her arm.

"What did this guy look like, Frank?" Mike asked. "Do you remember anything?"

"Sure," Frank said. "Shaved head, air-force style jacket. Big guy."

"Oh God," Patti said, the blood draining from her face. She grasped X's arm. "They've got Betty."

Christ. Who would want to hurt Sister Betty?

I felt sick. Mike reached for the battered payphone and dialed the operator. "Yeah," he said into the receiver. "We've got some trouble at Gary's on Brown. We've got a couple kids missing, looks suspicious." He paused and looked at X, who was helping Patti to the only other chair in Gary's tiny lobby. "Anything else?"

"Yeah," X said. "Tell them to let Detectives Chow and Wright know."

Mike did so, and hung up. "They say they'll be here soon," he said, wringing his big hands. Patti was weeping.

The hooker, who until this point had said nothing, asked, "What's up, Mike? Someone in trouble?"

"Don't know, Suzie. Hope not."

Suzie extended a skinny arm around Patti Upchuck. "Well, if it helps any, the big guy with the shaved head wasn't alone. He was with another guy." She pointed to the entrance at the side of Gary's. "There were two of them."

"What did the other guy look like?"

"Bigger than the one with the shaved head, but pretty normal looking," Suzie said, squinting her heavily made-up eyes as she tried to remember. "One of those lumberjack checked jackets, hair wasn't too short. Jeans, boots. I couldn't see much of his face, because he was standing sideways. But he had some tattoos on his arm."

"What did the tattoos look like?" I asked her.

"I couldn't see much," Suzie said. "There was one on his wrist, I think. Looked like a knife through a cross or something."

"It's them," X said, barely audible.

"Why you so sure?" Mike asked, puzzled.

"It's a neo-Nazi symbol," he said. "It's kind of the new swastika."

"Great. Fucking terrific," Mike said, clenching his fists. He turned on Frank. "Christ on a crutch, Frank, how did these guys fool you into thinking they were reporters, for fuck sakes? Were you asleep or something?"

"Sorry, Mike, sorry," Frank said, raising his hands in protest. "Since the punk rock stuff started up around here, everyone has looked a little strange, right?"

Shaking his head, Mike turned back to Suzie. "Did you see which way they went? Did you hear them say anything to each other?"

Suzie shrugged. "Nothing," she said. "They headed off toward the lot on the Free Street side. But the way the guy at the door was, you could see that he was in charge. The one with the shaved head looked sort of scared of him."

"Okay, thanks, Suzie," Mike said. "You're going to have to stay here until the cops arrive, okay? They'll probably want to ask you some questions."

"Oh, Jesus, Mike, do I have to? I don't need no hassles."

"Yeah," Mike said, firmly. "You have to. These are good kids and they could be in big trouble. And you and Frank are the only people who can give a description of the two guys who may have grabbed them."

On the chair beside Suzie, Patti started sobbing again, while a single siren could be heard outside, getting closer. Mike turned to X and me. "Go back in the bar, tell everyone we need people to start looking for them," he said. "Maybe Betty and Sam are around here somewhere, maybe they're okay. When you get back, meet me up in my room." X ran into the bar, and Mike turned back to Suzie. "Look after her for a minute, would you, Suz?" he said, gesturing to Patti.

"Of course, Mike." She put an arm around Patti. "It's okay, honey."

It wasn't.

CHAPTER 49

While Patti was on the phone to her mom, and while the entire Portland punk scene was out looking for Sister Betty and Sam, X and I dashed up to Mike's room.

We found our biker friend standing by his bed, along with two other big guys — Mike's unaffiliated biker pals from the gig at Coyle Street. Mike jerked a thumb at them. "This is Pete and Marty. Kurt and X. You've all met before," Mike said, looking at us. "You got people out looking for Betty and Sam?"

I nodded. "We rounded up about a hundred of them. Cops just arrived, too. Just two uniform guys. No detectives." I paused. "Why are we up here, Mike? Shouldn't we be out looking for them?"

"We're not gonna find them around here, kid," Mike said. "They're long gone. And I've had it with this bullshit."

"So?"

"So," Mike said, stepping back from his bed to reveal a half-dozen rifles, two handguns, knives, brass knuckles, and some big chains. "So, we're gonna get them back, and Pete and Marty are gonna help."

"Where have they gone?" I asked, bewildered. "When are we leaving?"

Mike glanced at X. "We think they may have taken them to that acreage in Exeter," Mike said. "Or so say X's sources. We've got to get up there fast."

He paused and pointed a big finger at me. "You need to stay here, Kurt," he said. "You need to look after Patti and keep doing the search." I looked at X, but he didn't say anything.

Fuck that, Mike. I'm not staying here.

━━━━━━━

Downstairs at Gary's, meanwhile, no big police search was underway at all.

X and I had raced back downstairs. Patti was off the phone, and she was having no success persuading the two Portland police officers that anything was wrong. That was all the dispatcher had sent to Gary's: two uniformed cops. No Detective Chow, and no one else either.

This is insane.

The cops, one male and one female, stood in the lobby, police-issue notepads and pens in their hands, but neither was actually taking notes. They looked like they couldn't give two shits about our friends. Every minute or so, their police radios beeped and screeched, and — listening to it — it was pretty obvious that no massive search was underway for Sam Shiller or Betty Kowalchuk.

Patti was alternating between terror and rage, clenching her fists at her sides. "I've given you their descriptions!" she said. "Why the hell aren't you calling them in, or whatever it is you do with that information?"

The male officer looked at her. "Calm down, Miss," he said, not bothering to disguise his dislike. "We know our jobs. We'll pass along their descriptions when we know that the two young people are, in fact, missing." He paused and looked down at his notes. "Betty Kowalchuk and Dan Schuler."

"Sam. Shiller. Not Dan Schuler," I said, angry. "Why the hell aren't there more officers here?"

The male and female officers exchanged a knowing look. "Let's just say we received some information," the male officer finally said. "We've been advised to first determine if there has, in fact, even been an abduction. Teenagers take off on their friends all the time."

Jesus Christ! They don't even believe Betty and Sam are gone!

X whipped around and stared at the officer, his uneven pupils flashing black. "*In fact*?" he hissed, repeating the words the officer had used to sound authoritative or whatever. "*In fact*, they have been. *In fact*, one of them was about to go on stage in front of two hundred people. She wouldn't have just taken off. *In fact*."

The female officer shrugged. "Teenagers take off all the time," she said, loudly chewing her gum. "How are you so sure they didn't go off together somewhere?"

"We're sure," Patti said. "I know my sister. She would never do that."

"Particularly," X said, seething with rage, "since there have been multiple attacks on our friends, and particularly since the Portland cops haven't done anything about it."

He watched the officers, to see if they were listening. They seemed to be, maybe, for the first time. "That's why she wouldn't have taken off," I said, "because it's totally fucking dangerous."

The two uniformed cops started to look a bit uncertain and a lot uncomfortable. The female officer spoke up, reluctantly. "Well, we received a call that there was some big benefit happening here tonight, from someone who would know, and that there might be some mischief calls to get publicity. That's why it's just the two of us right now."

What?

X stared at the officers. "Someone who would know?" he repeated. At that moment, at that instant, I could see that X *knew*. He knew.

He turned to me and Patti.

"This is a waste of time," he said, putting an arm around Patti. "Mike's waiting for me. I'm going with him to look for them, okay? I might be gone for a while." He looked at me. "Brother, are we good?"

"Yeah," I said, still pretty unhappy about what had transpired up in Mike's room. "We're good."

But before Patti or I could say anything else, X was speeding toward the stairs, and up to Mike's room.

CHAPTER 50

This is what they told me.

Northman's gutted trailer had been divided into two sections: the side where the door was, containing two cots, a portable fridge, a tiny washroom, a long wooden box containing a dozen Ruger Mini-14s he brought from Potter County, and two rectangular tin boxes containing thousands of rounds of Remington .223 ammunition.

The other side was smaller. All around, it had been framed with two-by-fours, then padded with layers of sound insulation. Across the ceiling, a single six-by-six beam had been bolted, diagonally. Hanging from the beam were two lengths of heavy chain, set about six feet apart. There was no light, apart from a portable lantern on the floor by the small padded door.

Martin Bauer shoved Sam and Betty through the door, which more or less separated the two sections of the trailer. For whatever reason, Bauer had taken the burlap bag off Betty's head. With the bag still on his head, Sam slammed into a two-by-four and started to bleed. "Get in there, kike and dyke," he said. "Up against the wall."

Betty had started to cry again. "It's okay, Betty," Sam said. "It'll be okay."

"No, it fucking won't be," Bauer sneered, snapping the handcuffs onto Sam's wrists until they bit into his skin. He pushed Sam over to the chain dangling from the ceiling, ran it between his wrists, and pulled, hard. Bauer snapped a padlock onto the chain, so that Sam's arms were pulled upwards.

Bauer moved over to Betty and repeated the procedure. By now, she was wailing. "Don't touch me, you bastard!" she screamed.

"Don't touch her, you fucking prick!" Sam yelled, still unable to see anything. Without hesitating, Bauer kicked him in the stomach.

"I'll fucking do to her what I want, Jew boy," Bauer said, as Sam gasped for air. "I'll …"

"You'll do nothing to her," Northman said, his voice flat, familiar. His face still covered by a bandana, he had apparently returned from parking the van on the abandoned logging road, the one they had used to enter the isolated corner of the High Aryan Warrior Priest's property without being seen. "We don't soil ourselves on that, understand? They're bait, that's all."

"Yes, kinsman," Bauer said, looking cowed. "Yes, sir."

"Good," Northman said, checking the chains that bound Sam and Betty. "Let's get the gear out of the van."

Northman stepped out. Bauer ripped the bag off Sam's head. Sam squinted and blinked, frantically scanning the walls of the soundproofed room.

"Look around as much as you want, kike," Bauer said, heading to the padded door, not looking back. "You're never ever getting out of here, you race-mixing pieces of shit."

Betty didn't want to, but she started to sob again. Bauer stepped out, pulling the door shut behind him.

An hour later, Mike was pushing the station wagon hard. In the back seat, Pete and Marty were looking out the windows, the soft-sided hockey bag full of guns between them. In the front passenger's seat, X was carefully holding one of the handguns, a blued .22 caliber Walther semi-automatic.

A half-mile or so behind them, an AMC Gremlin discreetly followed.

CHAPTER 51

Detective Chow rarely got mad, but he was mad now. Standing in the lobby at Gary's — as Patti Upchuck, Luke Macdonald, Leah Yeomanson, Frank the bouncer, and Suzie the hooker looked on from about ten feet away — Chow was grilling the two uniformed officers. He pulled back his sleeve and looked at his watch.

"These two young people have now been missing for almost four hours," he said, seething. "At any point, tonight, did it occur to either of you that they were indeed missing? And that you should therefore call in for help, particularly since some friends of these young people have been killed and assaulted? Did it?"

The two uniformed cops looked very unhappy. They scanned the lobby floor, silent. Detective Chow shook his head. "That's all for now. Go join the other officers in the search, please." It wasn't a request. The two officers quickly scurried away. The punks were impressed.

This Chow guy is all right. For a cop.

Detective Wright, Chow's partner, stepped through the front door, notebook in hand. "No closed-circuit cameras or anything in this neighborhood, of course," he said to Chow, voice lowered. "But three hookers further down Congress said they saw a couple of big guys loitering near a van. Said it had no markings on it indicating it was a news organization."

"Descriptions?" Chow asked.

"Shaved head, bomber jacket on one," Wright said, scanning his notes. "That would be Bauer, I expect. The other guy had hair, maybe facial hair. White. Not too old, physically big. That's it."

"All right," Chow said. "That's something. Any luck with Murphy or Savoie?"

"Reached Savoie, he said his partner's been out with the flu going around," Wright said. "Said the same thing you did."

"Exeter?"

"Yep," Wright said. "Want me to call the FBI detachment up in Portsmouth?"

"Yes, please," Chow said. "They should exercise great caution. These people will be armed to the teeth, and we may need to start finding a judge to give us a warrant."

CHAPTER 52

Betty said the first blow was a punch, directly to Sam Shiller's face. There was a cracking sound. Martin Bauer had hit him hard, fist tightly clenched, and it broke Sam's nose. Blood gushed over Sam's mouth, chin, and his homemade Wire T-shirt. Betty started to scream.

Bauer didn't hit him again. He paused, staring intently at Sam's face, as if admiring a work of art. "There," he said. "Jew juice everywhere. That should do it. Looks nasty."

Sam spat out blood while gasping for breath. His knees had buckled after he was hit, and he twisted on the chain that held him. Betty, meanwhile, screamed ferociously. "You bastard! You fucking bastard!"

"Shut up, bitch," Bauer said, almost bored. He brought up his arm and slapped her across her face, hard. "You're next." Betty had stopped screaming, but she was heaving sobs, wide-eyed with fear.

Bauer called out: "He's ready." Almost immediately, Northman entered the tiny room. He was so big, he had to bend over as he stepped into the soundproofed room. He was still wearing the bandana across his face. When he stood up, he seemed to fill the room.

Northman fiddled with a Polaroid camera, totally uninterested in the presence of Sam or Betty, who stared at him. When he was satisfied that the camera would work, he looked up at Sam for a long time, his blue eyes unblinking. After a minute or so, he silently handed the camera to Bauer and reached into the pocket of his lumber jacket. He extracted a box cutter.

Betty immediately started to sob again, but Northman had already slashed Sam's forehead. The cut wasn't deep. But more blood flowed down over Sam's face and dripped off his chin onto the floor. Northman watched for a few seconds, then stepped over to Betty and grabbed the spiked hair at the back of her head. She was screaming and twisting, in a frenzy.

Slowly, Northman pulled the box cutter's blade through her scalp, near her forehead. As with Sam, blood immediately started pouring down her face. Northman then reached up and pulled down the collar of Betty's hand-made X-Ray Spex T-shirt, ripping it. He stepped back and looked at her, his head cocked slightly to one side.

Satisfied, Northman turned to Bauer, who had been standing by the door, smirking. He took back the camera. "Get the light, hold it like I told you," he said. Bauer rushed to get the light.

Bauer stood a few feet to one side of Sam, the portable light at arm's length and pointed upward. The light's glare cast dark shadows over Sam's bloody face, and made him look a lot worse. "Good," Northman said. "Don't move." He started taking Polaroids from different angles, silent. The only sounds that could be heard were Betty's weeping, Sam's gasping for air, and the clicking of the camera.

After taking a half-dozen shots of Sam's face, Northman turned to Betty. Bauer hustled over and positioned the light at Betty's side. The effect was similar: she looked like she was a bloodied corpse. Northman started taking pictures again.

That done, Bauer moved to Northman's side and positioned the light over the dozen or so Polaroid snapshots, as Northman flipped through them. Northman nodded while the images of Sam and Betty came into focus. They were shocking.

"Good," Northman said, gathering up the Polaroids. He glared at Bauer above the bandana. "I'll be back in a few hours. Don't do anything to either of them, her especially. Understand?"

Bauer nodded. Northman was taking the photos — wrapped in a sheet of Aryan Nations letterhead — to the *Portsmouth Herald*, the newspaper that served the Exeter area. Someone at the *Herald* would call the police, of course, but they would also share the photographs with other media, including Portland media. They would have the desired effect.

"That little bastard X will be here before you know it," Northman said, bending slightly to exit the tiny room. "Be ready."

CHAPTER 53

The swing gate to the acreage had been left unlocked and slightly ajar. None of us knew it at the time, but this was an unusual, and probably unprecedented, event. Someone was expecting visitors.

I'd pulled over by the side of the road, way before the gate, and was squinting in the dark. I thought I could make out what looked like Mike and X near the gate. The police cruiser that had been idling there on our previous visit was gone. There weren't any headlights, either, coming from east or west. There was a full moon, and it was super quiet.

Through the trees, a faint glow could be seen, coming from what looked like a rundown shack. Someone was home. I squinted. Mike seemed to be tapping X on the shoulder and saying something. X was nodding. I couldn't hear anything they were saying.

I watched as Pete and Marty pulled out guns from the hockey bag in the back seat, and Mike popped the hood.

Pete handed someone a sawed-off shotgun, and then they all looked at X for a bit longer. Mike said something again, and X nodded again. X seemed to be holding something.

The three bikers then turned and slipped through the gate onto the property. They had not gone a dozen steps when they stopped. Off in the distance, to the south, a very faint sound could be heard — an engine, or a motor. Through the trees and the bush, it sounded like it was far away.

I started moving closer, on foot, my dad's hunting rifle (the one he'd forgotten to take when he moved out) strapped to my back. I kept to the trees that lined the road.

When the sound faded, the three big men continued moving forward. Their speed and stealth surprised me. I wondered if they had done this sort of thing before, and concluded they probably had. Within seconds, they were out of sight, swallowed up by the dark brush. I stopped again, watching as X peered into the shadows. He then went and sat in Mike's station wagon and quietly pulled the door shut.

I edged closer. I was pretty sure X hadn't seen me. No one had seen me.

What the fuck am I doing?

Inside the gates, I could sort of almost make out Mike, Pete, and Marty. They'd stopped some thirty feet from the house, where they were crouched behind a cord of wood. Around them were some children's bicycles, a broken trampoline, and a couple old generators scattered throughout the muddy clearing. Up by the back door, there was a doghouse, but fortunately, no dog.

A bluish light seeped through the biggest window, and I could faintly hear voices. Someone was inside, apparently, watching TV. I watched as Mike tapped Pete on the arm and Pete nodded. Pete remained there, staring at the house, while Mike and Marty moved further into the property. The pastor in Exeter had told us that two children lived in the tumbledown house, so it seemed pretty unlikely that Sam and Betty were being held there.

Mike and Marty backed away and crept down a dirt trail that went past a portable sawmill and off toward the south. They were heading toward the engine noise they had heard earlier.

After a couple minutes, I couldn't see them anymore. Even with the full moon, it was too dark. So I slowly crept closer.

He and Marty had stepped into another clearing. Behind them, the shack was no longer visible. In front of them, they could see the whitish outline of a trailer. Mike extinguished his tiny flashlight. As their eyes adjusted to the dark, they saw that the trailer was old and rusted; it looked like it had been there a long time. Its wheels were gone, and it had been propped up, more or less level, with rough lumber that looked like it had come from the portable sawmill.

There were windows at one end, but they had been boarded up. At the opposite end of the trailer, tattered curtains could be seen in another window next to a door with a large padlock hanging from it. Outside the door, there were two old folding patio chairs and the remnants of a campfire. A few feet away sat two rusting propane tanks.

A pale light was coming through the window of the trailer.

"Don't fucking move!"

Mike and Marty remained still.

"Don't turn around. Drop them. I've got a thirty-thirty pointed right at you, you fuckers," the man hissed.

After a few long seconds, they knelt, slightly, to place the sawed-off shotguns on the ground. They raised their hands.

"You fat cunts make a lot of noise," the man said, his voice still low. "Could hear you a mile off."

Mike turned around. Martin Bauer stepped out from behind the rear hitch of an ancient broken-down pick-up. Despite his size, despite the Winchester .30-30 in his hands, Mike could tell Bauer was nervous. His hands were shaking.

"I didn't say turn around, motherfucker!" Bauer yelled, loud enough for Pete to hear him. I watched as the big biker started moving toward them, sawed-off shotgun already cocked.

"Just you here, boy?" Mike said, loudly. "Where's your boss? He scared, too?"

Bauer moved out from behind the pickup. "I've got the gun, motherfucker," he yelled. "I'm not scared of fuck all."

"Right," Mike said, calculating. His .45 was still tucked into the back of his jeans, and Bauer probably hadn't seen it in the gloom. But he wouldn't be able to get to the gun before the skinhead had fired off at least a couple rounds from the Winchester. He kept Bauer talking.

"Right," he loudly repeated, moving his hands down slightly.

"Keep your fucking hands where they are!" Bauer yelled, now standing out in the open, but still beside the ancient pickup truck. He sounded afraid. "Put 'em back up!"

Mike did.

Mike, guessing that Pete was close, again raised his voice. "Just you and that old thirty-thirty, boy? That's all your boss left you?" he said, derisively, loudly.

"Shut up! Shut up!" Bauer yelled, his voice panicky. "I'll shoot you where you stand, old man!"

"No, you won't," Mike said, just as Pete fired off a barrel above their heads. Almost immediately, Mike and Marty tumbled to the ground, and rolled behind a tarp covering some lumber and insulation. Mike reached around for his .45.

Bauer scrambled back behind the pickup truck — but he was still able to fire in Pete's direction. He shot twice, and hit the biker once, just below his right knee. Pete dropped to the ground, hard, cursing.

Before Mike could return fire, Bauer was already bounding away, running full-tilt toward the logging road. He had cut through the brush and was gone. At the same time, from inside the trailer, a muffled female voice could barely be heard.

"Go help Pete and I'll get the kids," Mike said to Marty. "Watch for the skinhead coming back or anyone coming from the house."

A hundred feet to the west, a shit-scared Martin Bauer was crashing through the woods like a wounded deer, circling around toward the front gate. He probably figured he could steal the High Aryan Warrior Priest's truck and get out of there. He was a believer, but he hadn't signed on to do a gun battle with three armed bikers all on his own. Let Northman deal with them.

He got to the fence at the north side of the acreage and peered back into the woods. The bikers were tending to their wounded friend, and working to free the Jew and the punk slut, he knew. He relaxed, slightly: he would have enough time to get away. He'd hitch south, maybe to Boston, then Texas. Disappear for a few months.

Then he saw X, sitting in Mike's car. X had heard the shots, but he still hadn't seen Bauer. He was looking in the wrong direction.

Bauer moved soundlessly over the fence. He slowly started to bring the .30-30 into position.

CHAPTER 54

Before Bauer could shoot, a single shot rang out, and he grunted, then slammed into the still-frozen ground. He was still. He was dead.

X jumped out of the station wagon, the .22 in his hand, and looked at Bauer. He heard a sound and whirled around.

"Hey, brother," I said, still holding my dad's hunting rifle. "It's me."

———

Inside the dark trailer, Mike held his little flashlight in one hand and the .45 in the other. He could now hear Betty screaming for help from the other side of the small padded door. Pressed up against the plywood wall, the .45 ready, Marty yelled, "Betty, is anyone else in there?"

"No," she yelled back. "Just me and Sam. I think he's unconscious. Mike, is that you?"

"It's me, kid," Mike said, squeezing through the doorway.

"Thank God," she said, crying. "Mike, please check on Sam, okay? Bauer hit him really hard."

Mike peered at Sam's face, which was bloody and swollen. He touched Sam's neck with two big fingers. "He's breathing. Unconscious, but alive. Bastard worked him over pretty good." Mike pointed the flashlight up at the beam where they'd been chained. "Where'd they put the keys, Betty?"

"I don't know," she said. "Are you sure they're gone?"

"For now," Mike said, scanning the floor and walls. "Let's get you guys out of here before they decide to come back."

On one of the cots in the next room, beside a portable lamp, Mike found a ring of keys. After a few seconds fumbling for the right ones, he managed to free her. He noticed that her shirt had been torn, her breasts partly visible, and her jeans were hanging open. She caught his look and zipped up her jacket and pants, her hands trembling. "I'm okay," she said. "He was going to, but he didn't have time. Stopped when he heard you guys outside. Let's get Sam and get out of here."

While Mike held Sam upright, Betty removed the padlock and chain that held him to the crossbeam. Sam groaned, his eyes swollen shut. "Let's go, buddy," Mike said, easing Sam through the doorway. Once outside, he carefully lifted Sam over his shoulder. The guitarist wasn't heavy.

Mike called out to Pete and Marty. "Guys! Let's go."

Through the gloom, they could see Marty kneeling on the ground beside Pete. Around Pete's upper leg, Marty had tightly tied his bandana. Mike started to speak to them, and then a shot was heard. It seemed to come from the direction of the road. Mike and Betty stopped in their tracks.

They waited, completely silent. Then Marty spoke, pointing toward the path. "We got company," he said.

Sam still on his shoulder, the .45 in his hand, Mike swung around. There, in the gloom, he could see two little girls, no more than ten or twelve. They were in pajamas and staring wide-eyed at the scene before them: a skinny, disheveled leather-jacketed teenage girl with blood all over her face; two big men on the ground, one who had been bleeding from his leg; and another big man, holding a gun, and with a bleeding, beat-up boy slung over his shoulder. The boy wasn't moving, but he was groaning a little.

Betty took charge. "Hello, girls. It's okay," she said gently, moving forward, her arms wide. "Where's your mom and dad?"

The oldest girl spoke. "They're out drinking in town," she said matter-of-factly. "They'll be back later. Grandma's at bingo."

"Are you okay?" Betty asked them, crouching down as she got closer. "Did you see what happened?"

"No," the older girl said. "But we're okay."

"Good," Mike said. He turned to Betty. "Stay with them up by the house. We'll get these two to the car. I'll be back for you."

Mike continued toward the main road as quickly as he could, Sam still slung over his shoulder. Marty came up the rear, steadying a cursing Pete has he hobbled along the path.

Once she had led the sisters back to the house, Betty crouched down beside them. She asked their names. Greta and Lena, the sisters said.

"Do your folks go out like this often?" Betty asked them. "Leave you alone?"

"Sometimes," said Greta, the older sister. "But Northman told them they should. He gave them and Grandma money to go out, and he got us McDonald's and he told us to stay inside and watch TV. But when we heard the guns, we got scared."

"Who is Northman?" Betty asked. "Is he the man who owns the trailer?"

"No," Greta said. "Our dad just lets him use it."

"Is Northman his real name?"

Before they could answer, Mike came racing down the drive. He looked shaken. "We've got to go, right now," he said, taking Betty's hand. "Right now, Betty."

"What about the girls?" Betty said. "We can't just leave them."

"We have to," Mike said. "They'll be fine." He looked at the two girls, who were clearly scared of the big biker. "Girls, when we're gone, I want you to call the police and tell them to get here fast. Can you do that?"

"Yes," Greta said. "We can."

"Good," Mike said, yanking Betty toward the road. "Let's go."

They started running toward the station wagon. There, in the gloom, Betty saw that Sam and Pete had been propped up in the back of the station wagon, and X and Marty were standing around the car, waiting. And then she saw me, standing there too, and she started crying.

The two girls waited a minute, then ran into their house, locking the door behind them. Everything was silent again.

Kneeling in the woods near the portable sawmill, Northman also watched Mike's station wagon disappear from view. He turned and headed back into the woods.

CHAPTER 55

The mood in the barnlike barracks — located at the edge of the Aryan Nations compound in Potter County — was serious. The Brotherhood, the informant confirmed in the police report, was in a dark mood.

The assassination of the Jewish Toronto talk show host, the elimination of the big-mouth, the bank robberies, the bombings of synagogues and the porn shops: all had been bloody, but all had been part of the plan. First step, create the Brotherhood. Second step, identify the common goal: to create chaos. Third step, get the funds the movement would need to keep going. Fourth step, recruit new members.

Fifth step? The fifth step was the elimination of the enemies of the Aryan people: the Jews, the race traitors, the media, the politicians, the muds, the degenerates — like the fags, and the dykes, and the perverts. And, of course, the degenerate punks.

By doing that, the Brotherhood believed, a race war would start, and society would break down. The Aryan guerrilla force — led by the Brotherhood, naturally — would take the battle into urban areas. In the aftermath of it all, a new society would replace what had been there before. One that would be Identity, occupied by Aryan kinsmen, and based in the countryside. The Volk, back to being rooted in the land. Making it great again.

To do all of that, even with a group as hardcore as the Brotherhood, was always going to be difficult.

To do it with a wild serial killer in their ranks was impossible.

Because there was no doubt, now, that Northman had become much more interested in murdering punk rockers than he was in building a new Aryan homeland. "He has become selfish," the leader said, as the other members of the Brotherhood sat in a rough circle, quietly nodding their heads. "He is prepared to risk all that we have done, all that we hope to achieve, because he has a fixation on a bunch of godless punks."

He continued: "I don't give a shit about these punks. They're vermin, and they don't deserve to live. But, until we reach the fifth step, they also don't deserve the attention that Northman has given them. It jeopardizes everything." Pause. "Northman has become a liability. Enough is enough."

Some of the men raised their hands. Where was Northman now? Had he fled? What should be done about him? Is the situation beyond repair?

"I'm afraid it is, kinsmen," the leader said. "It has gone too far. There is no question that Northman was always a source of strength, and a tremendous source of confidential government information. But he has become a liability."

All knew what this meant. There was a long silence, and then three members of the Brotherhood stepped forward. There was the schoolteacher from Boise, the truck driver from Metaline Falls, and the former marine from Billings. "We'll go," said the schoolteacher. "We'll deal with it."

"Good," the leader said. "And I believe it will need three of us to do it right, brothers. Northman is a very capable warrior. He will not go quietly."

All nodded, and started discussing their plan.

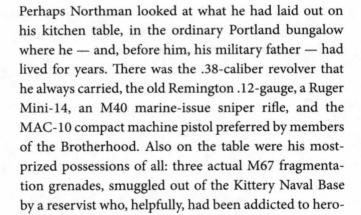

Perhaps Northman looked at what he had laid out on his kitchen table, in the ordinary Portland bungalow where he — and, before him, his military father — had lived for years. There was the .38-caliber revolver that he always carried, the old Remington .12-gauge, a Ruger Mini-14, an M40 marine-issue sniper rifle, and the MAC-10 compact machine pistol preferred by members of the Brotherhood. Also on the table were his most-prized possessions of all: three actual M67 fragmentation grenades, smuggled out of the Kittery Naval Base by a reservist who, helpfully, had been addicted to heroin and was in need of quick cash.

Northman took it all in. If the end was near, he planned to take as many race traitors with him as he could.

X would be among them.

CHAPTER 56

Mike closed the back hatch to the wagon and then he looked closely at me and X. "Does anyone else know what's over there?" he whispered, jerking his head toward where Martin Bauer's body was hidden by brush, some fifty feet away. "Did Pete or Marty see? Anyone?"

We shook our heads.

"Good. Let's keep it that way. You tell no one else what happened, you got it? No one. Ever," Mike said, extending a big hand. "Now, give me the gun."

I gave him my dad's old hunting rifle. Mike looked at it, then looked at me, evaluating. He put a hand on my shoulder. "It's all right," he said, as X watched us. "Everyone did the right thing. He was going to kill you guys, just like he tried to kill Pete. You never had a gun, you never saw the skinhead, got it?"

I nodded. "Good," Mike said. "Now let's get the fuck out of here before the cops come, or before any of these other Nazi pricks show up."

He jumped behind the wheel of the station wagon, cranked the wheel, and sped away. X looked at me for a moment and said nothing. Before I knew what was happening, he pulled me close and hugged me.

"Thank you," he said. "Now, let's go." We ran to my car.

The station wagon sped toward Portsmouth and its regional hospital, with me and X not far behind in my Gremlin. It was the only health center in the area, and Sam and Betty obviously needed medical attention. Betty had been in the front beside Mike. He'd had his arm around her.

Portsmouth Regional Hospital, we knew, would be a problem. X and I rode in silence. I looked at my hands on the steering wheel. They weren't shaking or anything.

I just killed a guy and I'm totally fine. Not what I would've expected.

Twenty minutes later, Mike swung the station wagon into the parking lot, a few steps from the hospital's emergency entrance. We pulled up behind him.

It was around 3:00 a.m., and no one was around. Mike and Marty jumped out to help us extract Sam from the back part of the wagon. He was conscious, sort of, but he was in no shape to walk on his own. X and I each took an arm. Betty followed, bent over. We must have been quite a sight.

"I'll find you when you get back to Portland," Mike said, watching us hobble toward the hospital emergency entrance.

"Okay," I said. "Mike, Marty, thanks. Take care of Pete."

"We will," Mike said. "Be fucking careful yourselves."

CHAPTER 57

Detective Chow looked at X, and X looked at Detective Chow. Neither of them said anything. There was a long, long silence. We were sitting on metal chairs in the waiting room in the emergency department at the Portsmouth Regional Hospital, and nobody else was there. Detective Wright was in another part of the hospital, taking a statement from Betty. Sam, meanwhile, was upstairs getting X-rayed, while about a half-dozen uniformed police officers and a couple of FBI agents were in the hallways outside their rooms. Sam's and Betty's parents had been told that their kids were alive, and they were presumably in their cars speeding toward Portsmouth.

For the time being, the only actual journalist present was a kid from the *Portsmouth Herald*. He had helpfully brought along copies of some gory Polaroids of Sam and Betty, which the man who went by the name Northman had dropped off at the newspaper's unstaffed reception desk a few hours before.

We had watched as Detective Chow thanked the young reporter for the envelope containing the photographs, snatched them out of his hands, and walked away. The kid was flustered, but seemed hopeful the gift of the Polaroids might result in an exclusive later on.

Back in the waiting area, Detective Chow was waiting for X and me to say something. He had just told us that the Exeter sheriff had sent two squad cars to the acreage outside town — "finally," Chow added, with apparent irritation about the local cops' priorities.

They had found a body, he said.

"It appears to be Martin Bauer," he told us, his eyes unblinking. "He had been shot somewhat recently. When you went to that property to rescue your friends, did you happen to see him?"

"No," X said.

I shook my head, but I could feel my guts churning.

"Would you boys be more comfortable speaking to me with a lawyer present?" he said, smiling slightly. "Perhaps your father, Christopher? I understand he's a lawyer."

"He is," X said, "but no, I don't need a lawyer. Why would I?"

Chow smiled again, more broadly this time. He looked at me.

The silence returned. All that we could hear were the sounds of the hospital: the distant murmur of the nurses' station, the mechanical hum of the pop machine, the pinging of some medical equipment.

"Did you two drive up to Exeter on your own?" Chow asked.

We both nodded.

"I see," Chow said. "The two of you come here, alone, to rescue your friends from a murderous gang of armed thugs? Is that right?"

We said nothing, and waited.

"I'll be frank with you," Chow said, his smile disappearing. He looked around the empty waiting area. "There's no one here, so no one will hear what I am about to say to you. No one ever will, either."

We remained silent.

"I believe we both know that you were not alone tonight," Detective Chow said. "I also believe that, if I were to ask to test your gloves …"

"I don't wear gloves," X said.

"Then, if I were to test your hands," Chow said, looking at me, "I might find the residue of something. Gunpowder, perhaps."

Uh-oh.

Chow kept looking at me. I was immobile, dreading what was coming next. But I was wrong about what was coming next.

Detective Chow suddenly stood up and extended his hand. X slowly stood up to take it, looking as bewildered as X ever could. He turned to me and shook my hand, too.

"I don't intend to ask you boys about any of those things right now," he said, smiling that smile again. "This entire matter has gone on long enough. It is time to end it, don't you agree?"

"Yes, sir," I said, silently exhaling. "We agree."

As we stood in the corner of the waiting room, a bit unsure what to do, an older nurse approached. She looked at a message slip. "Is your name X, young man?" she asked, frowning at the odd name.

X nodded.

"There's an urgent call for you from a family member," she said. "Follow me."

Who the fuck knew we were here?

Detective Chow nodded that it was okay to go, so X and I followed the nurse down the hallway to a pay phone near the nurses' station. I watched as my friend picked up the receiver.

"Hello?"

The voice on the line was familiar. "Hello, Chris. It's time we met, wouldn't you say?"

"We already have, you bastard," X said. "Where?"

No hesitation. "Where it all began," the man said.

CHAPTER 58

X and I followed the Kowalchuks — Patti, Betty, and their terrified parents — back to Portland in the Gremlin. Apart from some bruises and scrapes and the cut that Northman had inflicted on her scalp — which had required more than a few stitches — Betty seemed fine. To everyone's relief, she hadn't been raped by Martin Bauer, either.

Thank God.

Back in Portland, near the center of town, we made our move. The Kowalchuks drove through a yellow light, heading toward South Portland. We abruptly stopped and, when they were a block or two away, we turned back toward Free Street. The Kowalchuks' car disappeared. I pulled over on Middle Street.

"You sure about this, brother?" I asked, for the hundredth time. But X was already out of the car.

Fucking hell.

I got out, too, and we jogged over to the cafeteria in Post Office Plaza to meet Peter and John Chow. They were where X had told them to be, in a secluded spot far from an entrance. Peter handed X a backpack, which seemed to be pretty heavy.

"Be careful, X," John said.

"I will, guys," he said, as we headed toward the exit. "I'll have it all back to you tomorrow. Thanks."

Half an hour later, X and I finally arrived at Gary's. It was late on a Sunday night, and no one was around except Frank the bouncer. He was watching *The Rockford Files*. When he saw X, Frank slid two keys across the counter.

"Is he here yet?" X asked, collecting the keys.

"No," Frank said, sounding bored. "Mike told me to give you these."

"Thanks," X said. He pointed in the direction of the bar. "Anyone in there?"

"Just some guys delivering kegs," Frank said, returning his attention to the TV screen. "They may have left by now."

"Okay, thanks," X said. He headed up to Mike's room, still carrying the bag the Chow boys had given him.

I followed.

CHAPTER 59

When X came back downstairs, alone, Frank was nowhere to be seen. He crossed the lobby and reached for the door to Gary's bar. It was unlocked, as Frank had said it would be.

Inside, only a few lights were on: along the bar and up near the stage. All of the chairs had been placed on the tabletops, casting long shadows, like a thousand black fingers. Near the back exit, the kegs that had been delivered were stacked, more or less neatly, against the wall.

"Hello?" he called out.

"Back here," said the familiar voice. "Near the stage."

X walked along the bar slowly and rounded the corner. There, slouched at a table with two chairs, under a single light, sat the man they called Northman.

He waved X toward the empty seat.

"Hello, Chris."

X slid into the chair and looked at the man, his uneven eyes black. "Detective Murphy," he said. "I didn't see the desk guy on my way in."

"Frank?" Murphy smiled, placing his .38-caliber police revolver on the table. "Frank's dead."

X stayed still, saying nothing.

"I have to say, Chris, you surprised me a few times in the past weeks," Murphy continued, his fingers drumming on the .38. "How long have you known?"

X gestured toward Murphy's wrist, at the tattoo. "Kurt and I saw part of it the first night we met you here," he said. "The Aryan Nations symbol on your arm, the crowned sword going through the *N*. I didn't know what it was then, but I found out later." He paused. "And when I heard someone had told the cops to go slow when Sam and Betty were kidnapped, I knew — only a cop would have that authority."

Murphy looked down at his arm, surprised, and laughed. "Wow! I'm impressed," he said. "But if you suspected for that long, why didn't you do something?"

X shrugged. "You're a cop, I'm just a punk," he said. "Nobody would have believed me."

"That's true," Murphy said. He grinned at X, obviously enjoying himself. "So, aren't you going to ask me why?"

X shrugged. "I know why," he said. "You're a racist bastard. You hate everyone who isn't like you."

Murphy laughed and wagged a finger. "That's too simplistic," he said, smiling. "You're smarter than that."

"Why kill Marky and try to kill Danny, then? What did they do to you?"

Murphy shrugged. "The little faggot? Because he saw me, obviously. He was a loose end," Murphy said. "And the other boy? That was just to keep things hopping. I would've finished it, too, if I hadn't've been interrupted by some tourists. But did you appreciate my little scriptural flourishes? The crown of thorns, the wound in the side, the baptism in the water? Your friends were in serious need of religion, I thought."

"And the meat on Marky's groin?"

Murphy shrugged. "He was circumcised," he said. "Thought he was a Jew, so I left behind some bacon to make a bit of a statement. I thought it was funny."

"The skinheads," X said, after a pause. "They did what you told them to. They even pleaded guilty to cover up for you. Why kill them?"

Murphy toyed with the safety on the .38. "They're not very bright, those boys," he said. "They drink too much, talk too much. More loose ends. They would have talked, eventually." He squinted at X. "Even the one your friend killed. Thank you, by the way."

X said nothing. Murphy laughed. "Guess you'll have to edit that part out of the tape you've got under your big sweater, there, eh?"

"I'm not taping anything," X said.

"Whatever. Doesn't matter," Murphy said. "You'll be dead soon enough. Any other questions?"

"Two," X said, stalling for time. "Why Jimmy? And why do all this in the first place?"

"Fair questions." He scanned Gary's filthy ceiling. "Jimmy Cleary was never supposed to happen. I was after you, right from the start. You were the leader of this whole thing. I saw your *NCNA* crap and figured you'd be the perfect one to take out. A perfect symbol of the urban rot and sickness. But Jimmy was the one who came out the back way that night. It was cold. I got tired of waiting." He laughed. "After that, I kept going. It kind of blossomed from there. I was enjoying myself."

X briefly closed his eyes, but said nothing.

"And why do it?" Murphy said. "That's simple, too. We are the Volk, the true Aryan people, God's chosen ones. We want to wipe all of it out — the cities, the industrialization, the technology, the modernity — and go back to the earth. We are the real environmentalists, you might say. We want to wipe all that away, and become rooted once more to the earth. The SS tried, but they failed, obviously. They wanted that, too."

X stared at him. "But what do we have to do with any of that?"

"Because," Murphy said darkly, leaning forward, looming over X. "Because you punks are the literal embodiment of everything that is dirty. You hate God, you hate order, you hate authority, you hate morality, you hate anything that is decent. You are city vermin, and I decided that the revolution needed to start with the extermination of you and your friends." He stopped, glaring. "And you, in particular."

X glared back. "It didn't work for the Nazis, and it won't work for you," he said. "Someone will stop you."

"Really?" Murphy said, smiling again, leaning back in his chair and waving his arms around. "Nobody has yet. Certainly not you. So, do we have a deal?"

"I'm here, aren't I?" X said. "You get me, and all this stops."

Murphy smiled. He cocked his head to one side. "But why trust me, Chris? After you're dead, I could just start all over again, right?"

"Sure," X said. "But to make sure that doesn't happen, I made a call before I came downstairs."

"To that zipperhead Chow?" Murphy laughed again. He was still enjoying himself. "Sorry, but I'm not too worried about that idiot. The skins are all dead, and nobody around here has ever seen Northman's face. After I deal with you, there's no one left, Chris."

"I didn't call Chow," X said, his voice flat. "I called Potter County."

The smile disappeared from Murphy's face and he sat bolt upright. "You're a fucking liar!" he snapped.

X shook his head. "It's the truth," he said. "I called your Aryan pastor, and he put me on to the one he called the leader. I told him everything we knew about you. I would imagine the FBI was listening in the whole time, too."

Murphy stared at X.

"I wouldn't be surprised if they have some guys on their way here now to take care of you, Detective Murphy," X said.

"You little bastard!"

Murphy picked up the .38 and shot X point blank in the chest.

CHAPTER 60

The .38 blew X off the chair he was sitting on, and spun him to the left, six feet away. His body slammed into the filthy, cracked dance floor at Gary's, and he did not move again. There was a plate-sized stain of blood spreading on his old hunting sweater. Northman studied him for a moment, then took aim at X's forehead. As he did so, the Brotherhood's hit squad burst through the doors at the back of the tavern.

They had been in the lobby, trying to determine how long Frank had been dead, and who had killed him, when they heard a loud voice — Northman's voice — coming from the bar. Then they heard the gunshot.

Northman jumped to the wall facing the Gary's stage, and carefully peeked around the corner, in the direction of the main entrance. The teacher and the truck driver, he could see, were hovering behind the end of the bar, both carrying handguns — they looked like the stolen SIG Sauer P220s. The marine, meanwhile, was crouched behind a table, near Gary's entrance. He appeared to be holding a MAC-10 with a suppressor attached. When he saw Northman's face, the marine fired off a rapid burst. He didn't even come close.

Flattened against the wall, Northman made a calculation. All three members of the Brotherhood's hit squad were relatively close together, and he had seen no one else. If he threw one of his M67 fragmentation grenades, he would probably kill all three. If he was going to make it to the alleyway door, he needed to be sure that they were all dead, or out of commission. If they weren't, Murphy wouldn't make it to the alleyway, where his white panel van had been parked. But the sound of the exploding grenade would attract every cop in Maine, and he might not get far.

So he waited. He remained silent, and completely still, while the three brethren made the next move.

He didn't have to wait long. The teacher had started to make his way along the far wall. He was hidden by the bar, which ran virtually the entire length of Gary's, and was pretty dark. Murphy heard the teacher's boots scuffing across the old tile floor. When he was opposite Murphy's position, the marine and the truck driver started to fire off some rounds, to give him cover. But Murphy, expecting this, was ready.

The teacher rose up from behind the bar, the SIG Sauer P220 pointed in his direction, but Murphy fired first. The .38 caught the teacher directly in the forehead, and blew brain matter and blood all over the Budweiser mirror directly behind him. He was killed instantly, and crashed to the floor.

"See that? You're next, kinsmen, unless you get out of here, now," Murphy called out. "I don't want to kill my Aryan brothers. But I will if I have to."

Murphy could hear the marine and the truck driver whispering, but he could not make out what they were saying. He glanced at the alleyway door. He knew that he would not get five paces before one of the two remaining shooters took him out. He had to improve his odds before the police arrived. They wouldn't be long, now.

He reached into his bomber jacket and took out one of the M67 grenades. This would give him all the cover he would need. It would blow to bits everything within a twenty-foot radius and make a huge sound, but he now had no choice.

Murphy carefully placed the .38 on a table to his right, then extracted the pin on the top of the grenade. He moved forward, and kept squeezing the spoon lever with his left hand, which kept the grenade from detonating. He then waited, listening.

When the whispering stopped, he knew the truck driver and the marine were on the move. Murphy stepped out, for a moment, to throw the grenade. As he did so, the marine — who had gotten much closer to Gary's stage area — fired at him. One of the 9mm slugs struck Murphy in the arm, shattering his elbow. He screamed and cursed.

The M67 went only half the distance Murphy had intended. It caused an enormous BANG, sending debris and dust everywhere. Fragments from the grenade ripped into the truck driver's back and blew him into a row of chairs that been stacked near the bar. He was dead.

Dust was falling onto everything, like filthy snow, and they could hear the sound of beer seeping out of kegs onto the dirty floor. Murphy remained still, waiting.

The marine, who had ducked behind a table when he saw the grenade, was for a moment stunned, but otherwise alive. His ears were ringing. In his hands, he still clutched the MAC-10.

Murphy was on the floor, cradling his left elbow in his right hand. Blood was seeping out between his fingers, and he knew his arm was now useless. Unless the marine was dead, he would have to shoot his way out. He reached back to retrieve the .38, but it was gone.

He heard the familiar voice.

That voice.

Murphy spun around to see X — pale, breathing heavily, and leaning against the wall. X was holding the .38 and he was not at all dead.

"X is the hidden factor," he said to Murphy, raising the .38. "Today, it's a bulletproof vest, borrowed from the Chows."

BANG.

And, with that, he shot Murphy once, directly in the center of his chest. Northman crashed backward, dead, without saying another word.

A moment later, the marine reached the corner and saw Murphy's inert form. The marine also saw the punk boy on the dirty floor, clutching at his chest, and holding a .38. The marine lifted the MAC-10 to kill him.

Before he could fire, another shot rang out, and the marine dropped his arm. He looked bewildered.

He then slammed to the ground, beside Murphy.

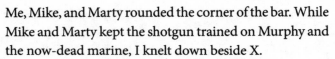

Me, Mike, and Marty rounded the corner of the bar. While Mike and Marty kept the shotgun trained on Murphy and the now-dead marine, I knelt down beside X.

"Are you okay, brother? Were you shot?"

X managed a small grin, pointing at his bloody chest. "Yeah, but I'm wearing the vest," he said. "It feels like I've got a couple more broken ribs. But I'm not dead."

Mike reached down and removed the .38 from X's hand. Sirens, a ton of them, were wailing in the distance. "Hold on," Mike said. He wiped the .38 on his "FUCK THE WORLD" T-shirt, then placed it near Murphy and the dead Marine.

Mike looked closely at X. "You never had a gun, you never even held a fucking gun, got it? You haven't seen Kurt since the hospital, and you don't know where he is," he said. "Murphy told you to meet him here. From the cops' perspective, all these pieces of shits killed each other, end of story. I ran downstairs when I heard all the shooting, and I found you alive, got it?"

"Yes," X said, wincing in pain. "Nobody will believe any of it, but I got it."

Mike looked up at Marty and me. "You two better get the fuck out of here, now," he said. He handed Marty his .45. "Take my car. It's in front of this bastard's van. I'll find you later. Go."

Marty didn't need to be told twice. The sirens were getting closer. His shotgun in one hand, Mike's .45 in the other, Marty bolted out the door to the alleyway. I hesitated, looking at him. X spoke: "Go, brother. I'll be fine."

I sprinted out just behind Marty, past the same spot where our friend Jimmy Cleary had died months before.

As me and Marty took off, and the sirens closed in.

CHAPTER 61

Sharon Martin and detectives Chow, Wright, and Savoie sat at the boardroom table in the boxy stone headquarters of the Portland Police Department and looked at X and the rest of us.

X's dad was with us — plus Patti and Betty Upchuck, me, and Sam Shiller. Sam still had bandages across the bridge of his nose, following some surgery to repair the damage Martin Bauer had done to the bone and cartilage in his face. X, meanwhile, was still wearing bandages across his chest, visible under his beloved Clash T-shirt. Sister Betty was fine, but the long cut on her scalp could still be seen against her pale skin.

We remained expressionless as Sharon Martin spoke. "The police service and the Attorney General have announced that there will be a formal inquiry into whether there are others like Terry Murphy within the ranks," she said. "I will be part of that inquiry. Apart from that, I can tell all of you that there will be no other prosecutions in these cases. We will be working with the government of Canada to facilitate the extradition of the surviving members of the neo-Nazi group that calls itself the Brotherhood. But it is our belief that Murphy was solely responsible for the murders of Jimmy Cleary, Mark Upton, the employee of the bar, and the three skinheads. He was also almost certainly responsible for the attempted murder of Danny O'Heran and Ken Haslam, although he was likely assisted by the skinheads in both of those cases. Finally, the FBI has informed us that Murphy has been linked to the execution of a former member of the Brotherhood some weeks ago in Idaho." She paused. "He may go down as one of the most prolific murderers in the history of the State of Maine."

Detective Chow leaned forward, slightly, also scrutinizing X's expressionless face. "We are unclear why Murphy chose to kill Martin Bauer at the time and place that he did, however. It is puzzling. But we are closing the book on that aspect, and thought we should tell you that." He looked at all of us.

He knows.

X said nothing, his arms crossed.

Detective Savoie addressed us next, his tobacco-stained fingers tapping the top of the conference table for emphasis. "The shootout involving the Brotherhood members and Te —" He almost said Terry, but corrected himself. "— Murphy. That was quite a mess for our forensic guys. And they still can't figure out how or why that one shooter, an ex-marine as it turns out, could get his hands on Murphy's .38 and kill him with it, when he already had a perfectly good, working MAC-10 sub-machine pistol in his possession. Or where the shotgun is that apparently killed the marine, or where the rifle is that killed Mark Bauer." Savoie glared at X. "We haven't yet figured those things out."

X and I knew the truth, of course, but we remained silent. At this point, X's father and the Upchuck sisters were also looking at X, and they seemed concerned. X ignored them and kept his uneven gaze on Detective Savoie.

"Is that a question?" X said, watching the detectives.

"I'd say there are still plenty of questions!" Savoie barked, his face flushing red.

"Like how an experienced detective can have a neo-Nazi killing machine as a partner for years, and somehow not ever notice anything?" X said. "A question like that?"

Ouch.

Savoie looked like he was about to lunge across the table and strangle X. Before he could, Detective Chow put a hand on his shoulder, and Savoie remained where he was, simmering with rage. I suppressed the urge to laugh.

"Anyway," Martin said, glaring at Savoie, who was still grumbling. "There will be discussion and speculation about these cases for many years to come, I'm sure. But, for our purposes, these files are closed. Our task now is to deal with the extradition, and to ensure that the inquiry into the issue of bias in the ranks of the Portland police is done right." She looked at the detectives to her right and left. "And, unless there is anything further, I think that wraps it up for today. Thank you for coming in, all of you."

Sharon Martin started shaking the hands on the other side of the conference table. The detectives all did likewise, Detective Savoie with some obvious reluctance. Again, I stifled a laugh.

As we prepared to leave, Detective Chow spoke. "Forgive me, Christopher, but I must ask: What does the X stand for?"

We all stopped and watched. X almost grinned — *almost* — but said nothing.

Detective Chow gave his big smile, nodding. "All right, then," he said, laughing a bit. "My sons asked me to ask you. By the way, what do you plan to do next? I understand you're graduating."

X shrugged. "I'm taking a year off to travel with Kurt's band. Then maybe study journalism somewhere," he said, face blank. "And then maybe someone will write the story of everything that happened — more or less."

So, I did.

ACKNOWLEDGEMENTS

Thanks to various bandmates throughout the (many) years: Ras Pierre Schenk, Rockin' Al, Bjorn von Flapjack III, Steve Deceive, Snipe, Davey Snot — and, of course, the Blems, the Nasties, and Shit from Hell. Also, our merch girl, Emma.

Thanks in particular to Shannon Whibbs, who spotted the book for the good folks at Dundurn; Allison Hirst, my ever-patient Dundurn editor; and, most of all, to Emily Lawrence, who was my editorial guide and advisor throughout. Emily, you rock.

And thanks, as always, to Lisa, who puts up with the punk who won't ever grow up. You carry my heart.

Blood Brothers
Colleen Nelson

Fifteen-year-old Jakub Kaminsky is the son of Polish immigrants, a good Catholic boy, and a graffiti artist. While his father sleeps, Jakub and his best friend, Lincoln, sneak out with spray paint to make their mark as Morf and Skar.

When Jakub gets a scholarship to an elite private school, he knows it's his chance for a better life. But it means leaving Lincoln and the neighbourhood he calls home.

While Jakub's future is looking bright, Lincoln's gets shady as he is lured into his brother's gang. Jakub watches helplessly as Lincoln gets pulled deeper into the violent world of the Red Bloodz. The Red Bloodz find out Jakub knows more than he should about a murder and want him silenced — for good. Lincoln has to either save his friend, or embrace life as one of the Red Bloodz.

The Merit Birds
Kelley Powell

Eighteen-year-old Cam Scott is angry. He's angry about his absent dad, he's angry about being angry, and he's angry that he has had to give up his Ottawa basketball team to follow his mom to her new job in Vientiane, Laos. However, Cam's anger begins to melt under the Southeast Asian sun as he finds friendship with his neighbour, Somchai, and gradually falls in love with Nok, who teaches him about building merit, or karma, by doing good deeds, such as purchasing caged "merit birds."

Tragedy strikes and Cam finds himself falsely accused of a crime. His freedom depends on a person he's never met. A person who knows that the only way to restore his merit is to confess. *The Merit Birds* blends action, suspense, and humour in a far-off land where things seem so different, yet deep down are so much the same.

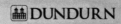